Also by Helen Peters:

The Secret Hen House Theatre

"As a child I loved *The Swish of the Curtain*, and *The Secret Hen House Theatre* is another engaging book about threatened amateur dramatics" *Julia Donaldson*

"Full of action, with a happy ending" *Michael Morpurgo*

"Hannah and Lottie's adventure is full of happiness and sorrow. It's like a new world. It was so gripping and unputdownable it seemed to be stuck in my hands" *Esther Burridge, aged 11*

"The sort of story you want to melt into. The trials and charms of farm life create a world where characters start to feel like friends" from *The Independent's 50 Best Summer Reads*

"There's something timeless about Helen Peters' accomplished and hugely engaging debut … Drawn with humour and affection, Hannah's world is utterly convincing" *The Guardian*

"In the best tradition of Noel Streatfeild and Pamela Brown, Peters captures the very special thrill of devising and producing a show … It feels refreshing to read such an honest to goodness adventure story" *Books for Keeps*

"Where farms meet theatre, the feathers are sure to fly in this fabulous debut novel" *Daily Mirror*

The ❀ Farm Beneath the Water

Helen Peters

nosy crow

First published in the UK in 2015 by Nosy Crow Ltd
The Crow's Nest, 10a Lant Street
London, SE1 1QR, UK

www.nosycrow.com

ISBN: 978 0 85763 261 6

Nosy Crow and associated logos are trademarks and/or registered
trademarks of Nosy Crow Ltd

Text copyright © Helen Peters, 2015

The right of Helen Peters to be identified as the author of this work has
been asserted.

A CIP catalogue record for this book is available from the
British Library.

Printed and bound in the UK by Clays Ltd, St. Ives Plc
Typeset by Tiger Media Ltd, Bishops Stortford, Hertfordshire

Papers used by Nosy Crow are made from wood grown in
sustainable forests

All of the characters and events appearing in this work are fictitious.
Any resemblance to real persons, living or dead, is purely coincidental.

3 5 7 9 10 8 6 4

For Oliver

H. P.

Chapter One

The Audition

"I'll walk from here," said Martha, as the ancient, mud-encrusted car turned from Elm Lane on to the main village road. "I don't want anyone associating me with this bunch of freaks. Dad, stop the car!"

"Don't be ridiculous," said Dad. "You can get out at the bus stop as usual."

Martha glared at him. She pulled a mirror from her school bag and began to make tiny adjustments to her carefully arranged hair.

Hunched in the back seat in a fog of misery, Hannah didn't see how she could possibly get out of the car. How could she walk into school looking like this?

All Lottie's beautiful work, ruined. Lottie would kill her.

And imagine what Miranda would say. She was horrible enough about Hannah's ordinary school clothes. Oh, she was going to love this so much.

"How's that pig, Joanne?" asked Dad. "Is she all right?"

Martha turned accusingly to her father, her face screwed up in disgust.

"As if it wasn't bad enough already, turning up at school in this heap of scrap, you go and add a pig to the mix."

Dad ignored her. Next to Hannah, eight-year-old Jo leaned over the tiny, trembling piglet lying in her lap. Her curly golden hair brushed against its pink skin. "Don't worry, little one," she murmured in its ear. "The vet will make you all better."

"And as for you," Martha said to Hannah, wincing as though Hannah's appearance caused her actual physical pain, "going to an audition dressed like a demented scarecrow. What were you *thinking*?"

"I'm supposed to be a walking advertisement," mumbled Hannah.

Martha snorted. "A walking embarrassment, more like."

Hannah said nothing. It was true. She *was* a walking embarrassment.

It had seemed like such a good plan at the time. Hannah was desperate to play the part of Juliet in her house production of *Romeo and Juliet* and her best friend, Lottie, was desperate to make the costumes. So Lottie had made a costume for Hannah to wear at her audition this morning.

"It will help you get into character," Lottie had said, "and Miss Summers will see I can sew and then maybe she'll trust me to make all the costumes. You'll be a kind of walking advertisement."

The long white medieval nightdress that Lottie had made was beautiful. Until Hannah had brushed past a heap of old tractor tyres on her way to the car.

And there had been such a panic to get to school early for the auditions that she had completely forgotten to change into her shoes after helping Dad to unload the new calves.

So here she was, fifteen minutes late, curled up in a ball of despair in the back seat, wearing muddy green wellington boots and a white nightdress streaked with black tyre marks and tractor oil.

"Anyone would think," said Martha, "that you *enjoyed* shaming yourself in front of the whole school."

"It's not the whole school," muttered Hannah. "It's only Key Stage 3. And it's only Woolf House."

"Thank goodness for that. At least I won't have to watch."

Thank goodness for that, echoed Hannah silently. It was bad enough that Martha had just joined her school in Year 7, but at least she had been put in a different house.

"You realise you haven't got a hope, don't you?" said Martha. "I don't know why you're even bothering."

Dad pulled in at the bus stop outside the school gates. Hannah scrambled over seven-year-old Sam and tugged at the grimy door handle. The door stayed firmly shut. But the piglet wriggled out of Jo's arms and jumped into the front seat, right on to Martha's lap.

"Aarrgghh, get it off me!" screamed Martha, flailing her arms about. "Ugh, it's disgusting! Get it OFF!"

She yanked the passenger door open. And the terrified piglet leaped from the car and bolted through the school gates into the playground.

Hannah stared in disbelief. This couldn't be happening.

Martha froze, open-mouthed in horror. Then, like a sprinter off the blocks, she shot out of the car and pelted towards the school building. Her skirt was rolled up so high that it was almost invisible beneath her blazer.

"Where did it go?" demanded Dad, springing out of the car and scanning the playground, where groups of students were giggling, shrieking and leaping out of the way. As the pig scuttled into view across the tarmac, Dad raced after it, an extraordinary sight among the sea of navy uniforms in his torn trousers, holey jacket and mud-covered boots.

Using all her strength, Hannah finally shoved her door open and almost fell on to the pavement. Righting herself, she scurried towards the school, head down, boiling with embarrassment, while Jo and Sam hurtled through the laughing, screeching crowds in pursuit of the piglet.

Keeping her head down, praying that no one would see her and connect her with the pig, Hannah suddenly smacked full-on into somebody's chest.

"Whoa," said the somebody. "Steady on, Roberts."

Hannah's blood froze.

Jack Adamson. Of course. Somehow, he was always there for her most humiliating moments.

"Gotta hand it to you, Roberts, you sure know

how to make an entrance," said Jack, staring at the nightdress and wellies. "Is that what all the best pig farmers are wearing these days?"

Hannah felt her cheeks burning. "I've got to go," she mumbled.

"Aw, cheer up. Want a mint?"

He took a half-eaten pack of sweets from his pocket and held them out to her.

"No, thanks," said Hannah, avoiding the gaze of his deep brown eyes. She dodged around him and ran towards the doors.

"You'll probably set a trend with that combo," he called. "By the end of the week, the whole school will be wearing it."

Hannah burst through the doors and raced towards the hall. And there was Lottie, immaculate as usual, not one dark hair out of place, hurrying up the corridor towards her.

Lottie gaped as she saw Hannah.

"My costume! What have you done?"

"I'm so sorry. I'm so, so sorry."

"I can't believe you've—" began Lottie, and then her eyes met Hannah's. The full awfulness of Hannah's morning must have shown in her face, because Lottie stopped in mid-sentence. When she spoke again, her tone was completely different.

"Oh, well, never mind. Come on, you might just make it."

"Has Miranda auditioned yet?"

"She's on now. That's why I came to look for you." She pulled Hannah down the corridor. "Why didn't you just change into your uniform?"

"No time. It's in my bag."

"And what's with the wellies?"

"Tell you later. It's been a nightmare morning."

They skidded to a halt in the foyer outside the hall and pushed the double doors open.

Miranda Hathaway, her long glossy auburn hair tumbling around her shoulders, stood centre-stage, pointing into the audience with a trembling finger. Hannah put a hand to her own straw-coloured hair. Had she even brushed it this morning?

Suddenly, Miranda let out a scream so piercing it made Hannah jump.

"O look, methinks I see my cousin's ghost
Seeking out Romeo that did spit his body
Upon a rapier's point – stay, Tybalt, stay!
Romeo! Romeo! Romeo! I drink to thee."

Miranda raised a small blue bottle to her lips and staggered across the stage, collapsing on a chair.

Scattered applause broke out from the other students in the hall. Standing at the back, Hannah clapped politely.

"Typical Miranda, totally over the top," muttered Lottie. "You'll be miles better."

Miranda stood up, flicked her hair over her shoulders and gave a little bow. Miss Summers, the new drama teacher, smiled at her.

"Thank you very much, Miranda. That was fantastic." She consulted a sheet of paper. "Right, that's everybody except Hannah." She looked at the hall clock.

"Oh, I don't think she's coming," said Miranda. "I think she's changed her mind."

Lottie gasped. "The cow!"

"I'm here, Miss Summers," called Hannah, running to the front of the hall.

Everyone turned round. Miranda looked distinctly annoyed. Then she caught sight of Hannah and her eyes lit up as she took in the costume.

"Oh, good," said Miss Summers. "Just in time."

"*Love* the outfit, Hannah," murmured Miranda, as Hannah walked past her. "Where *did* you get those boots?"

Hannah forced herself to block out the snorts of laughter from the front row. She kicked her wellies off at the foot of the stage and ran up the steps.

Miss Summers looked slightly taken aback at the oil-streaked nightdress, but she gave her a warm smile.

"OK, Hannah, we've only got a couple of minutes before the bell, so just do the first speech, would you? The balcony scene."

Standing alone centre-stage, her eyes on the scruffy wooden floor, hearing the sniggers from the students in the auditorium, Hannah felt sick. Her palms were damp with sweat. All she wanted was to run away.

No, she told herself. You know the lines. You've practised and practised. This is your chance – your one chance – to show you're worthy of the part.

You can do it.

She made herself look up. And her eyes lit on Miranda, right in the middle of the front row. Miranda whispered something to Poppy, all black fringe and eyeliner, sitting next to her. Poppy cackled.

She's trying to put me off, thought Hannah. Well, I won't let her.

She shifted her gaze and gathered her thoughts. She wasn't Hannah Roberts, a twelve-year-old girl standing on the school stage. She was Juliet Capulet, a thirteen-year-old girl who had just fallen madly in love with Romeo Montague. And she was alone on her bedroom balcony, thinking aloud.

As she raised her head to begin, Hannah saw, through the French windows that ran along the side of the hall, some kind of scuffle taking place outside on the patio.

She pulled her attention away and focused on a point high on the far wall, imagining the starry night sky of Verona on a warm summer's evening. She thought of Romeo and, for some reason, he had Jack Adamson's face.

"Oh, Romeo, Romeo, wherefore art thou Romeo? Deny thy father and refuse thy name."

In the audience, she saw Jack's friend Jonah nudge his mate Ben and point towards the patio. Great. They were bored already.

With as much energy and passion as she could put into the words, she continued.

"Or if thou wilt not, be but sworn my love,
And I'll no longer be a Capulet."

More people were looking out of the windows now. Nobody was paying any attention to her. Was she really that bad, or was it just that she was the last person to audition?

"'Tis but thy name that is my enemy.
Thou art thyself, though not a Montague."

People were nudging each other, pointing outside and giggling. What was going on?

Focus, Hannah, focus, she told herself.

"What's Montague? It is not hand, nor foot, nor
    any other part
Belonging to a man. O be some other name."

What was that noise outside the hall doors? Running and shouting and ... oh, no, please, no ... yes, it was, it definitely was ... *squealing*.

Oh, help, she thought. It can't be, can it? Surely not. Please, no.

"What's in a name?" she continued desperately, as if saying the words might make everything else disappear. Don't let them come in here, she prayed. Don't let them come in here.

Through the doorway at the back of the hall skittered the little pink piglet, followed by Jo and Sam. Heads shot round. People gasped and shrieked. Miranda leaped on to a chair, screaming, her hands clasped to her chest, as if she thought the tiny creature was about to maul her to death.

Hannah continued to recite her speech, as though it were a charm that might protect her from the madness all around.

"That which we call a rose
By any other name would smell as sweet."

Jonah and Ben joined in the chase, along with Lexie and Amber from Hannah's class. Miss Summers cast frantic looks around the room, as though somebody might appear who could tell her how to handle the situation. Lottie stared at Hannah, her expression a mix of pity, admiration and horror.

Trapped in this nightmare, Hannah continued on her course. What else could she do? She was on stage to make her audition speech and she would make her audition speech.

"So Romeo would, were he not Romeo called,
Retain that dear perfection which he owes
Without that title."

Everyone seemed to be chasing the pig now. And the piglet weaved between them on its tiny trotters, changing direction, running between their legs, scooting out of their grasp when they lunged at it, evading them all as skilfully as a world-class midfielder wrong-footing every defender on the pitch.

"Romeo, doff thy name,
And for thy name which is no part of thee,
Take all myself."

Up the steps and on to the stage skittered the piglet. Hannah dived and seized it with both hands. As she scooped it up, it lifted its tail and produced a stream of warm, pungent yellow urine that soaked into Hannah's white, oil-streaked dress and spread into a puddle on the stage all around her.

The hall erupted into hysterical laughter. Hannah stood frozen to the spot, unable to move or think.

Up the steps and on to the stage ran Jo and Sam. Jo made a grab for the pig, skidded on the wet patch and fell at Hannah's feet. Sam tripped over Jo and landed on top of her. The piglet bolted down the steps stage left and back into the mass of students. Jonah and Ben set off after it, knocking over chairs and crashing into Lexie and Amber, who were chasing it from the opposite direction. Poppy barricaded herself into a corner with two of the upturned chairs, screaming and clutching at her hair.

At that moment, Dad burst through the patio doors, his eyes searching wildly for the runaway pig.

Suddenly, an authoritative voice boomed across the hall, cutting through the chaos.

"What on *earth* is going on in here?"

Hannah looked up from the writing bodies on

the floor, over the hysterical crowd beyond.

At the far end of the hall, standing in the doorway in a pristine grey suit, with a murderous look on his face, stood Mr Collins, the Head Teacher.

Chapter Two

❀ ❀

A Visitor

"What did he say?" asked Lottie, as Hannah emerged from the Head's office at the end of the day.

Hannah made a face, but she waited until they were outside before she spoke.

"Honestly, the way he talked it was like I'd done it deliberately. Can you imagine?" She put on a mock-thoughtful voice. "'Hmm, what I would really like to do today is cause absolute maximum public embarrassment to myself by having a piglet wee all over me in the school hall.' *Why* would he think I'd do that?"

"So what did he say?"

"Oh, he just banged on and on about threats to health and safety and school security and stuff."

"Security! Did he think the piglet was carrying a bomb?"

"Dad told him it had nothing to do with me, but I'm sure he blames me for the whole thing. He hates me anyway, after what happened in the dining hall last term."

"The worst thing," said Lottie, "is that now Miranda will get exactly what she wanted. Just like she always does."

"Yes, and I'll be standing in the back row of the party scenes," said Hannah. "If I'm lucky." She kicked a stone along the pavement. "I was so looking forward to the play, too. I mean, I knew I probably wouldn't get the main part, but I never thought my audition would be ruined by a pig."

"It's so unfair," said Lottie. "You would definitely have been better than Miranda if that hadn't happened."

"I just hope you still get to do the costumes. I mean, it's hardly your fault my dress ended up in the state it did, is it?"

When they reached Lottie's house, the front gate was open. Lottie's mum, Vanessa, in immaculate jeans and a perfectly ironed white linen shirt, knelt in front of a flowerbed, pulling out minuscule weeds.

"You're home early," said Lottie.

Vanessa straightened up and smiled. "My meeting was cancelled, it's a beautiful day and I thought I'd bunk off and see my darling daughter." She hugged Lottie and winked at Hannah as Lottie squirmed away. "How are you, Hannah?"

"Don't ask," said Lottie. "It's been a bad day."

"Oh, dear, I'm sorry. Are you coming in?"

Hannah hesitated for a second. She would have loved to go in, but Lottie and her mum didn't get much time together.

"Oh, thanks, but I'd better go."

"All right," said Vanessa. "Well, give my love to everybody."

As Hannah walked away up Elm Lane, she could hear Vanessa saying, "Now, darling, I've bought loads of treats, so come inside and tell me all about your dreadful day."

Hannah dragged her boots along the ground. Imagine having somebody at home, she thought, who asked about your day and was interested in what you had to say.

At the top of Elm Lane, Hannah crossed the road on to the track that led to Clayhill Farm. She passed the disintegrating wooden gate that sagged permanently open and tried to push Miranda's smug face out of her mind. Taking a deep breath, she filled her lungs with the crisp fresh air that rose from the fields of her home.

The high arch of sky above the farm was a perfect pale blue. The farm was still in its summer clothes, with lush grass in the meadows and green leaves on the trees. It was only if you studied the leaves close up that the odd fleck of brown or gold was visible: a tiny reminder that autumn was on its way.

As she approached the farmyard, Jo and Sam came racing up the track towards her, followed by Jo's cocker spaniel puppy, Rags, wagging her feathery tail. Their school finished earlier than the community college and they had already changed into jeans and T-shirts.

"We saw you from the window," said Jo. "There's a surprise in the house. Come and see."

Sam grabbed Hannah's arm. Hannah pulled it

away. "You're covered in mud. What have you been doing?"

In her soil-coated hand, Jo held a blue notebook with *Bean Arkealogicle Society* written on the cover. She and Sam were the sole members of the Society of Bean, a secret club whose activities seemed mainly to consist of calling each other bean names and drawing cartoons of various bean characters for their monthly magazine.

"We were excavating," Jo said. "We found a Roman coin. Do you want to see it?"

Two years ago, an exploratory dig by the local archaeological society had revealed medieval pottery in South Meadow. The Beans had been fascinated by the dig, and since Sam had been given a metal detector for his birthday, they had spent a lot of time searching for treasure. Now Sam produced a muddy scrap of metal from his pocket.

Hannah glanced at it. "Looks like a squashed bit of tin to me."

"Who knows?" said Jo. "It might be a Roman coin. We need to give it a professional clean and analyse it scientifically."

"Come and see our surprise," said Sam, pulling Hannah into the yard.

In her knee-high wellington boots, Hannah trudged through the muddy puddles and the chicken dung. Pigs snuffled and grunted in their sties behind the yard. The cockerel perched on the stable door threw back his head and gave an ear-splitting call.

An unfamiliar red hatchback was parked outside the cow stalls. Was someone visiting?

At the edge of the yard, Jasper, Jo's enormous pet sheep, munched a clump of grass. His duck friend, Lucy, was nestled into his broad woolly back. Jasper looked up as the children approached and, with Lucy swaying gently on his back, he followed Jo to the garden gate, where he busied himself with another clump of grass while Jo put Rags in her kennel.

Hannah dumped her school bag on the rusty chest freezer in the scullery, then kicked off her wellies and added them to the heap already cluttering the concrete floor.

"Now, you have to be really quiet," whispered Jo. "Follow us and don't say a word."

"What is this surprise, anyway?"

Jo gave her a stern look. "Don't be so impatient."

She opened the kitchen door and they crept across the tiles. Hannah heard a murmur of voices from the dining room. She started to ask Jo who was in the house, but Jo put a finger to her lips and pointed to the keyhole.

Hannah bent down and peeped through. Her mouth fell open.

Dad was sitting at the dining table with his back to her. He wore his best jacket, which was exactly the same as his everyday one except it didn't have holes at the elbows and all the buttons were still attached. The change of jacket was unusual enough. But that wasn't what made Hannah freeze at the keyhole, speechless with amazement.

Sitting at the other side of the table was a fairly young, very pretty woman with long dark wavy hair. She wore jeans and a pink cardigan and she was leaning towards Dad, talking animatedly. As Hannah watched, open-mouthed, the woman laid her hand on Dad's arm.

Who was she? And what was she doing, touching Dad like that?

The woman said something and Dad threw back his head and laughed. Hannah's insides twisted.

Jo reached for the doorknob. Hannah hardly had time to straighten up and adjust her face before Jo threw the door open.

Dad stopped laughing abruptly and turned round. The woman looked up and smiled at the children. A cup of tea stood on the table in front of her. Hannah stared at it. Surely Dad hadn't made it? Dad had never made a cup of tea in his life. He never even opened a kitchen cupboard. How had he found the teabags?

Had *she* made the tea? Had *she* been poking about in their cupboards?

"Oh, hello," said Dad. "Er, Sophie, these are my children." He gestured to them. "Jo, Sam, Hannah. Er, this is Sophie."

"Lovely to meet you," said Sophie.

"Hello," said Hannah coldly.

"Can we have a milkshake?" Sam asked Hannah.

"Yes, come on, I'll make it."

As Hannah closed the door, Sophie said something she couldn't quite catch and Dad laughed again.

Rage stabbed at Hannah.

"Did you like the surprise?" asked Jo.

Hannah opened a cupboard door and fished out the milkshake powder.

"We're spying on her," said Sam. "Who do you think she is?"

"I don't know," said Hannah. "Maybe she wants to keep a horse here."

The Beans seemed satisfied with this explanation. But, Hannah thought, as she went to fetch the milk from the larder, if this Sophie person wanted to keep her horse at the farm, Dad would be showing her the stables. He never invited people into the house.

Martha burst into the hall from the dining room just as Hannah emerged from the larder. She followed Hannah back to the kitchen.

"Have you seen that woman? Has Dad gone and joined a dating agency or something?"

"Shh, he'll hear."

"What's a dating agency?" asked Sam.

"I just walked in," said Martha, "and he was saying, 'They recommended you very highly,' and she said, 'Well, I'm delighted to have been asked. I'm very excited about it.'"

Hannah felt as though someone was tying her stomach into knots.

"Are they going to get married?" asked Jo, her eyes huge. "Are we going to get a stepmother?"

"No way will she marry him," said Martha. "She's really pretty. And young."

"How was your day, Martha?" asked Hannah, to

change the subject.

Martha gave her a withering look. "Great, thanks. Really good. I just love it when my entire family turns up at school with the sole aim of totally shaming me."

"Are they really going to get married?" asked Jo.

"No," said Hannah.

"She looked nice," said Sam.

Hannah handed the Beans their milkshakes. "There you go. Take those upstairs."

"Yum, thanks." They took the drinks and left.

Without looking at each other, Hannah and Martha both edged closer to the dining-room door.

"Another cup of tea?" Dad was saying.

"No, thanks, that was perfect."

"Do you want to come and see the loft now?"

The *loft*?

"Oh, yes, please," said Sophie. "Then I can think about where to put my stuff."

Martha gasped, her face a picture of outrage.

Why on earth, thought Hannah, would this woman be putting her stuff in their loft? The loft was where Mum had stored all their baby things, and her own things from before she got married. Why would Dad let a strange woman anywhere near their loft?

Chairs scraped across the tiles. The door into the hall opened. Something licked Hannah's hand and she spun round.

"Jasper! You know you're not allowed in the kitchen. Come on."

"Ugh!" shrieked Martha. "Get that disgusting

thing out of here!"

Hannah gave him a shove, but Jasper was like a solid wall.

"Ugh, it's dribbling on the floor!" screeched Martha.

"Well, you help, then."

"Are you mad? No way am I touching that."

Hannah gave up. "There's no point trying to push him. The only way to move him is with food." She looked around the kitchen. "Pass me a couple of those apples."

"Get them yourself."

With a murderous look at her sister, Hannah crossed the kitchen and took two apples from the basket of windfalls that Sam had brought in from the orchard yesterday. They weren't really ripe yet, but Jasper wouldn't mind.

She held an apple out in front of her.

"Come on, Jasper. Good boy, come on."

Jasper craned his neck towards the apple and Hannah moved slowly backwards, through the kitchen and scullery and out of the back door.

The shiny red hatchback squatted smugly in the yard. *Their* yard. With the back window left casually open. As though she *belonged* here. What a cheek.

Martha followed Hannah into the scullery and took her school bag from its place on the freezer.

"Guess that's her car, then," she said.

"Guess so," said Hannah. She led Jasper into the yard and fed him the apple.

Martha stepped gingerly across the yard, dodging

21

the chicken dung and giving Jasper a wide berth. She peered through the open car window.

"She's got food from that posh place in Massingham. Snob."

Suddenly her eyes widened. Then they narrowed thoughtfully. She turned and looked at Jasper. Chunks of saliva-coated apple fell from his mouth and dropped to the ground. Martha shuddered. But then she seemed to brace herself.

"Give me that other apple," she said to Hannah.

"Why?" asked Hannah, handing it to Martha.

"Come on, Jasper," said Martha, holding out the apple. "Come over here."

"What are you ... *oh*," said Hannah, suddenly understanding.

Martha gave her a warning look. "If you say one word..."

Hannah widened her eyes in mock innocence. "One word about what?"

Their eyes met briefly. Then Hannah turned and walked indoors. As she shut the scullery door behind her, she heard Martha say, in an encouraging tone quite unlike her usual voice, "Here, Jasper. Here, boy. Good boy. That's right, come on. Lots of yummy treats here."

* * *

Two minutes later, sitting at the desk in her bedroom, her history book open in front of her, Hannah heard footsteps descending the loft ladder. Then Sophie's voice. "This is so exciting. It looks absolutely *ideal*."

Hannah felt sick. This woman wasn't really going to move her things into their house, was she?

No. That would be crazy. They'd only just met.

Unless … unless they hadn't only just met.

Maybe they'd known each other for ages. Maybe Dad just hadn't bothered to introduce her to his family.

"Is that all you'd like to see?" asked Dad. "You don't want to look around a bit more?"

"No, that's fine, thanks. It'll be perfect."

"Well, I'm very grateful. This could be exactly what we need."

Fury rose inside Hannah. What did he think they needed that she could possibly provide?

"Well, I can't promise anything," said Sophie, "but it all looks good. I'll come and…"

But her words were drowned out by the blare of an alarm.

"That sounds like my car," said Sophie.

Hannah's stomach lurched. She heard Martha's bedroom door open and Dad stride in. Martha's was the only bedroom that overlooked the farmyard.

"That blasted sheep!" shouted Dad.

He ran out of Martha's room and down the back stairs, Sophie following him.

With what she hoped was the face of a mildly curious onlooker, Hannah walked to the doorway of Martha's room. Jo and Sam had their heads out of the window, laughing. Martha stood behind them, trying to look as though she wasn't interested.

"He is *so* clever," said Jo. "He can sense food from *miles* away."

Hannah moved to the window and looked out into the yard. Jasper had his head through the open back window of Sophie's car and was gobbling the contents of the shopping bag.

As they watched, Dad hurtled into the yard, grabbed Jasper round the neck and yanked him away from the car. Jasper held firm for as long as he could and, when he was eventually dragged away, he had half a paper bag hanging out of his mouth.

"You bad sheep!" growled Dad.

Sophie was laughing and pressing buttons on her key ring. The alarm stopped.

"I'm so sorry," said Dad. "It's my daughter's sheep. Complete pest."

"Hey!" yelled Jo, leaning so far out of the window that Hannah grabbed the back of her shirt in case she toppled. "Don't be rude about Jasper. He understands, you know!"

Dad ignored her, but Sophie smiled up at the window and waved. "It's no problem at all," she said to Dad. "My fault for leaving the car window open. I thought it would be crime-free up here. I hadn't reckoned on the animals."

"Nothing valuable in there, I hope?"

"No, no, just a few groceries. I'm impressed with his appetite, though. A loaf of bread, a bunch of bananas, half a dozen eggs and a box of chocolate brownies."

"That's nothing for Jasper," said Jo proudly to her

siblings. "To him, that's just a little snack."

"I'm very sorry," said Dad. "Let me reimburse you."

But Sophie waved his offer away. She was petting Jasper's huge woolly head. "Honestly, it's no problem at all. He's a lovely sheep. It was a pleasure to feed him." She reached over and touched Dad's arm. "It was great to see the farm and the house. Thanks so much for inviting me. I'll give you a ring."

She got into the car and started the engine.

Martha, her face twisted with fury, pushed past the others and pulled the window shut.

"Get out of my room, losers."

"She seems quite nice, doesn't she, French Bean?" said Sam, as he and Jo ambled on to the landing. "For a Russian spy."

"Hmm," said Jo thoughtfully. Hannah noticed that they now carried yellow notebooks with "Bean Spy Club" written on the front. "They always pretend to be nice, Broad Bean. That's what spies do. But you can never trust them. Not for a second."

"We wrote down every word she said," Sam told Hannah. "And it was very suspicious."

Hannah said nothing. It *was* very suspicious. She only wished she could believe that Sophie was a Russian spy. That would be so much less disturbing than what she feared.

Chapter Three

The Cast List

As the car drew up at the bus stop on Monday morning, Hannah spotted Lottie walking through the school gates. She ran to catch up with her.

"Oh, hi," said Lottie, as Hannah tapped her on the shoulder. "Are you nervous?"

"There's nothing to be nervous about. I haven't got a hope."

"You never know. I mean, you did get to say some of your lines. She might have been able to tell how good you are. Anything's possible."

"No, it'll definitely be Miranda. Bet you a million pounds."

And yet Hannah still felt butterflies in her stomach as they approached the school building. Even though she knew she had no chance of getting the part, a tiny flicker of hope still burned inside her.

It was ridiculous, of course, but Lottie was right. Anything was possible.

They walked up the wide front steps and through the glass doors into the foyer, its shiny wooden floor pockmarked by the forbidden heels of bygone decades.

Beyond the glass-fronted trophy cabinet and the wooden boards bearing the gold-lettered names of previous Head Boys and Girls, four house notice boards hung on the pale-blue walls. Each house was named after a famous writer who had lived in Sussex and each had a different house colour. Conan Doyle's board was green, Milne's was yellow, Kipling's was red and Woolf's was blue.

Groups of people milled around the foyer but, judging by the low-key atmosphere, the cast lists hadn't gone up yet. Hannah and Lottie walked over to the Woolf House board. It was bare except for the tatty picture of Virginia Woolf that had been there forever and a team sheet for an upcoming football match.

"Hey, Roberts," said a voice behind Hannah.

It was Jack, messy-haired and muddy-kneed, wearing the school's red football strip.

"If you're hoping to get into the team," he said, "you're going to have to start coming to training."

"Oh, ha ha."

"Or was it the cast list you wanted? Fingers crossed your piglet gets the part, eh? I've got high hopes for it after that audition. It'll have to work on its bladder control, obviously, but it'll look great in the costume. You know, with me as Romeo. I've never had a pig as a sidekick."

"Yes, you have," said Lottie. "You hung around with Danny Carr all last year."

Jack tutted and shook his head sadly. "That's not very nice."

"No, it's not," said Hannah. "How *could* you compare that sweet little piglet with Danny Carr?"

Lottie ignored them both. "Anyway," she said to Jack, "you didn't even audition."

"A man of my talent doesn't need to audition. I'm far too busy for that sort of thing."

Lottie gave a scornful laugh. "Sure you are."

"What? I am. Do you know how many channels there are on my telly? It's a full-time job."

Jonah and Ben, both in muddy football strip, bowled up the corridor, jostling each other, Ben's messy blond hair and freckled pink cheeks contrasting with Jonah's straight dark hair and tanned olive skin. Since Danny Carr had left at the end of the summer term, Jack had started hanging out a lot more with these two. Ben was Lottie's next-door neighbour, so (as Lottie's mum never tired of reminding them loudly in public) they had known each other since they were in nappies.

Jack fell to his knees and clasped Ben's hand.

"Oh, Romeo, Romeo, wherefore art thou Romeo?" he said in a squeaky falsetto.

Ben pushed him over.

"That's not very romantic," said Jack, "for someone playing the hot male lead in the house play."

Ben looked startled for a moment. He stared at the notice board. Then he shoved Jack in the shoulder again.

"The list's not even up, you prune."

Jack looked down the corridor. "It will be in a second."

The others followed his gaze. Miss Summers was walking towards the foyer, holding several sheets of A4 paper and a box of drawing pins.

Other people had seen her, too. Crowds started to form around the notice boards. Miss Summers smiled. "OK, everybody, stand back."

She walked to the Conan Doyle board. Typical, thought Hannah. Always alphabetical order.

By the time the first three cast lists were up, the foyer was packed with people, swooping, chattering and screeching like a flock of starlings. Miss Summers manoeuvred her way out of the Milne crowd and walked towards the Woolf House board with her final sheet of paper.

You haven't got a chance, Hannah told herself. You haven't got a chance. But still the butterflies fluttered in her stomach. You never know, a voice inside her said. You never know.

"Out of the way, everyone, please," said Miss Summers, as people inched back to let her through.

Once the last drawing pin was in and Miss Summers had left the throng, the crowd surged forward. Lottie gripped Hannah's arm and dragged her through the mass of bodies until they were close enough to see the typed sheet of paper on the board.

Peering through the gap between two heads, Hannah zoomed in on the word "Juliet". Next to it was a name.

Miranda Hathaway.

A big stone settled in Hannah's stomach.

So that was that.

Well, of course. She had known it all along, hadn't she? Why had she even allowed herself to hope?

Lottie groaned. "How totally predictable." She put her arm round Hannah and squeezed her shoulder. "I'm so sorry, Han. I really hoped she might – you know – overlook the piglet incident. That's *so* unfair."

People shoved and jostled behind them. "Let's get out of here," said Hannah.

"Just a minute."

Lottie ran her finger down the sheet.

Down and down and down.

Right to the very bottom of the list.

There was a pause before she said, "So you're a Capulet lady. Same as me."

A Capulet lady. Miming at the back of the party scene. Just as she had thought.

They pushed back through the crowd to the other side of the foyer, outside the Head's office.

"I'm so sorry, Hannah," said Lottie again. "That is *so* unfair."

Hannah's insides felt very tight, but she shrugged. "Not really. Not everyone can get the main part, can they? I mean, you're a Capulet lady, too."

"But I only *wanted* a non-speaking part. You wanted a proper acting part. And you should have got it. You're a miles better actress than Miranda. Can you imagine how unbearable she's going to be for the next two months? And she doesn't even deserve it. If only that piglet hadn't got out..."

Hannah heaved a big sigh. "I don't want to talk about it."

"No. Sorry."

There was a chorus of squeals from the notice board. Hannah looked round.

She immediately wished she hadn't. A group of girls was jumping up and down, hugging the glossy-haired person at their centre. Miranda.

Miranda caught Hannah's eye. She extracted herself from the group and, flicking her auburn mane over her shoulders, put on the expression that Hannah hated even more than her smug one – the head-on-one-side fake-sympathetic one.

"I'm *so* sorry you didn't get the part, Hannah," she cooed, as if speaking to a toddler. For a terrible moment, Hannah thought Miranda was actually going to pat her on the head.

Hannah smiled brightly. "Oh, that's OK. I'm quite busy this term, anyway."

Miranda nodded, a concerned frown on her face. "Aw, it's sweet that you're putting a brave face on it. But you must have known you wouldn't get it. I mean, Juliet has to be beautiful, doesn't she?"

"Miranda!" said Priya, who was standing nearby. "Don't be so rude."

Miranda turned to her, eyes wide with what seemed to be genuine surprise. "I wasn't being rude. I was just telling the truth. And Hannah doesn't mind, do you, Hannah?"

Before Hannah could form a reply, Poppy swooped

down and enveloped Miranda in a hug.

"Yay for you, Mims! Juliet!"

"Aw, thanks, Pops."

Linking arms with Poppy, Miranda sashayed away down the corridor as though a red carpet were being rolled out in front of her by uniformed footmen. Hannah was filled with an overwhelming desire to punch her.

"Told you," said Jack's voice.

Hannah looked round. But Jack wasn't talking to her. The crowd around the notice board had thinned out and Jack was standing in front of the cast list with Jonah and Ben.

Jack clapped Ben on the back. "You'll be a beautiful Romeo. It almost makes me cry just thinking about it."

"I didn't even notice who'd got the other parts," said Lottie to Hannah. They joined the boys at the notice board.

Jonah pulled a face. "Miranda Hathaway as Juliet? Rather you than me, mate. You'd have been better off with Hannah."

"I was rooting for the pig myself," said Jack, "but Roberts would have been my second choice."

"So Priya's the prince," said Lottie. "And Katy Jones is Lady Capulet."

"Who's Katy Jones?" asked Hannah.

"In Year 9. You know, really tall, with long dark hair. Goes around with Marie."

"Who's Marie?"

"She's playing Juliet's nurse. Quite small, with

fuzzy blonde hair. *Really* blonde."

"Oh, yes, I know who you mean." Hannah looked at the board again. "So you're Tybalt," she said to Jonah.

"I have totally got the best part," said Jonah.

Ben grinned at him. "But I get to kill you, remember?"

"Hmm. We might have to change that bit of the script."

Miss Summers, who had been talking to a group of Kipling students, turned and smiled at them.

"Good morning, miss," Jack said, with suspicious politeness. "Could I have a word about this cast list?"

Miss Summers looked wary. "You can have a word. But the list is final and I'm not going to discuss any casting decisions."

"No, of course not, miss," said Jack. "I'm just a bit concerned, that's all."

"Concerned?"

"Yes. About how the casting blatantly contravenes equal opportunities legislation."

Hannah stared at Jack.

Miss Summers raised her eyebrows. "I beg your pardon?"

"I mean, this is meant to be a school, isn't it? An educational establishment where all pupils are given equal opportunities. People with incontinent pigs and people without."

Hannah's cheeks burned. Would people never stop going on about that pig?

But Jack continued. "Just because a piglet happened to relieve itself on Roberts in the audition – which I agree was unfortunate – she's been totally victimised. She doesn't even get a speaking part. I call that blatant anti-piggist discrimination."

Miss Summers looked as though she was trying not to smile. Suddenly Hannah felt angry. It *was* unfair that the pig had messed up her audition. There was nothing remotely amusing about it.

The bell rang for registration.

"Off you go, all of you," said Miss Summers. "And thank you for pointing that out to me, Jack. I'll check the anti-discrimination laws."

Oh, ha ha, thought Hannah. Hilarious.

Miss Summers walked off up the corridor. Hannah turned to Jack.

"Will you *ever* stop going on about that pig?"

"Hey, what are you getting at me for? I was sticking up for you. You wait. She'll check those anti-piggist laws and then she'll have to sack Miranda and make you Juliet."

Hannah rolled her eyes. "Let's go, Lottie."

But Lottie had drifted back to the notice board.

"I dunno, mate," Jonah said to Jack. "It might all backfire. I reckon she'll make the pig Juliet."

Hannah's frustrations boiled over. She wheeled around and glared at the boys.

"WILL YOU JUST SHUT UP ABOUT THAT BLASTED PIG!"

The door of the Head's office opened. Mr Collins appeared in the doorway. When he saw Hannah, his eyebrows shot up.

There was a long pause during which he kept his eyebrows raised and his eyes locked on Hannah.

"Sorry, sir," Hannah muttered eventually.

Mr Collins raised his eyebrows even further. Then he turned round, walked back into his office and shut the door behind him.

Hannah turned on Jonah and Jack.

"Oh, thanks very much, you two. Thanks a whole bunch."

"What?" said Jack, with his most wide-eyed, innocent look. "It wasn't *us* screaming abuse in the corridor."

"Look," said Lottie, pointing to the small print at the bottom of the cast list. "There's a meeting for the whole cast tomorrow lunchtime, plus anyone who wants to be involved backstage."

"That's great," said Hannah, trying to feel properly excited for her friend. "You'll get to be costume designer for the whole show."

"If she lets me."

"Of course she'll let you. You're brilliant."

"So do we all have to go to this meeting tomorrow?" asked Jonah, as they wandered up the corridor to their form rooms.

"Yes, you do," said Miss Summers, passing them in the opposite direction, carrying a pile of exercise books. "I want everyone involved with the house plays to be there." She glanced at Hannah. "I've got some important announcements to make."

Chapter Four

The
Tea Party

"Do you want to come to mine for tea?" asked Hannah, as they walked home.

"Depends," said Lottie. "Not if it's overcooked beans on burnt toast again."

"Actually, it's shepherd's pie."

"Did you make it?"

"No, Granny did."

"Oh. In that case, yes please."

"Sometimes," said Hannah, "I don't know why I'm even friends with you. Do you need to ask your mum?"

"No, she won't be home for hours. I was only going to stick something in the microwave."

Lottie's mum worked in London and she was always too exhausted to cook when she got home. Lottie ate better food when she stayed with her dad, but that was only every other weekend and the occasional week night. Her parents had been divorced for years.

"You were lucky not to get detention," said Lottie, as they crossed the road at the top of Elm Lane.

"I was lucky not to get suspended. Seeing how

much he hates me."

On the left of the farm track, the fields stretched away to the soft curves of the South Downs, hazy blue in the afternoon light. On the right-hand side North Meadow sloped down to a wide stream. Along the far bank of the stream grew a thick hedge of blackthorn, hawthorn, hazel and willow. Beyond the hedge, a patchwork of smaller fields rose to meet the ancient oak woods that marked the northern border of the farm. Ruby rosehips and deep-red hawthorn berries studded the hedgerows like jewels.

A pair of buzzards circled in the sky above North Meadow, looping and crossing each other in a complex dance. The air was alive with birdsong.

The girls left their bags on the freezer and walked into the kitchen. A buzz of conversation was coming from somewhere in the house. Hannah turned to Lottie, frowning.

"There's people here."

Lottie listened. "Sounds like quite a few people."

"They must be in the sitting room."

Hannah walked into the hall. Who could it be? The sitting room was never used except at Christmas.

The back door rattled open and slammed shut again with a force that could only mean Martha. Hannah heard the thud as Martha's school bag was thrown down on the freezer. She must have been just behind them walking home, but she would never in a million years have been seen dead actually walking with them.

Martha came into the hall. She gave Hannah a contemptuous look.

"I said you didn't stand a chance, didn't I? I don't know why you bothered."

"Did you get a part in *The Tempest*?" asked Lottie.

"Of course. I'm a water spirit."

"Well, Hannah got a part in *Romeo and Juliet*, too. A non-speaking part, same as you."

"I'm only a spirit because Year 7s weren't allowed the big parts. I'll get the main part next year, you'll see."

She started up the stairs. Then she stopped, frowning.

"Who's in the sitting room?"

Hannah shrugged. "You tell me."

Martha marched to the door and flung it open. She stared in for a few seconds. Then she pulled the door shut and swung round to face Hannah and Lottie. She looked as though she was about to throw up.

"I *said* he'd joined a dating agency, didn't I? Have a look in there. He's gone and invited every tragic loser on uglybride.com to our house, and he's giving them tea and cake."

"What are you talking about?" asked Lottie.

"He had that woman round the other day and now he's got a crowd of them here. He must have realised he had no chance with anyone young or good-looking. This lot's ancient. Take a look."

She opened the door again. "Ugh. Disgusting."

"Martha," called Dad, "if you're hanging around in the doorway, make yourself useful, will you, and fill up this teapot."

"No *way*," said Martha. "They're not my mum."

She turned on her heel and stormed up the stairs. They heard her bedroom door open and then slam shut.

Dad appeared in the doorway, holding a teapot. He was wearing his best jacket again. He frowned at Martha's bedroom door. "What was that about?"

"I'll make the tea, Dad," said Hannah, taking the teapot from his hand. "Come on, Lottie."

"Why are we making tea for them?" asked Lottie, as Hannah pulled her towards the kitchen.

"I need to know what's going on in there."

"You don't really think he's joined a dating agency, do you?"

"No. But what *are* they doing? It's so weird. He has never, ever invited people round for tea before. Ever."

"Except that woman the other day."

"Exactly. And now this. We have to find out what's going on. If we go round pouring tea, we can listen to what they're saying."

When Hannah walked into the sitting room with the teapot, the scene before her was even more bizarre than she had imagined.

Somebody – not Dad, surely? – had laid the little round table in the middle of the room with a white, floor-length linen tablecloth, perfectly ironed. In the centre of the table was a three-tier china cake stand which Hannah had never seen before, filled with cupcakes and biscuits and slices of buttered fruit loaf. Hannah's mouth watered at the sight of them. It was almost enough to distract her from the even more extraordinary sight of her dad sitting in an armchair in his best jacket, holding a saucer and drinking tea from one of her mother's antique cups and chatting animatedly with a group of strange middle-aged women.

As Hannah stood there, transfixed, another woman burst into the room like a tornado of enthusiasm. She had a cloud of fuzzy brown hair and wide brown eyes. She wore a long loose dress that looked as though she had made it herself from an old pair of curtains.

"It's amazing!" she exclaimed. "Incredible! These fields are an absolute treasure trove! You've got sneezewort, devil's-bit scabious, dyer's greenweed, creeping willow, carnation sedge – so many rare species. These meadows can't have been ploughed in hundreds of years."

Who was she? Had she come here to find a husband with a farm full of exciting botanical specimens?

"They haven't," said Dad. "There's a hundred and forty acres of permanent pasture here, full of rare flora and fauna."

The fuzzy-haired woman made appreciative murmurs.

Another woman shunted her chair across to join the conversation. Was there going to be a fight over Dad? Hannah couldn't imagine that this lady was husband-hunting. She looked very nice, but she must be at least seventy.

"It's an incredibly important site," she said.

"It's a completely unique environment," said an intense-looking woman with a severe dark bob. "It's absolutely vital that it's preserved."

"They're clever," murmured Lottie to Hannah as she glided past with the cake stand. "Saying all the things your dad likes to hear."

"And the rare breeds," chipped in a woman with a kind, round face and windblown hair. "Large Black and Middle White pigs, Southdown sheep, all sorts of rare poultry…"

"Ooh, great tactic," whispered Lottie. "Praising his animals. That's the winner." She set the cake stand down on the table.

"And we're just starting a herd of Sussex cattle," said Dad. "Took delivery of the first calves last week."

Another woman, wearing a yellow shirt and an earnest expression, leaned across. "And don't forget that it might well be an important site archaeologically. There's strong evidence that there was a medieval hunting lodge here."

"Mmm," murmured Lottie, busying herself with folding napkins. "Not such a good move. He'll go for the one who likes his pigs."

Another woman came over to join the group around Dad. She was small and wiry, with cropped chestnut hair and brown-rimmed glasses.

"The really important argument, I think, from a geological perspective," she said, "is that it's a totally unsuitable site. It's an extremely shallow valley – if, indeed, it can even really be called a valley – and that would mean—"

"Hannah," cut in Dad, "could you clear some of these plates away?"

" – huge earthworks all round the perimeter," continued the woman, "which would not only be unsightly, but—"

"Hannah!" snapped Dad. "Can you take these plates to the kitchen, please?"

Hannah raised her eyebrows. "OK, OK."

He handed his cup and saucer to Lottie. "Thank you, Lottie."

"Cheek!" muttered Lottie, as they went into the hall. "If he wants waitresses, he should pay wages."

"He was trying to get rid of us," said Hannah.

"What do you mean?"

"That woman was saying something he didn't want us hearing."

"Why, what was she saying? Hey, don't look at me like that. I just drifted off a bit at that point."

"Fat lot of use you are. I'm not totally sure either, but something about earthworks. Whatever that means. And it being a totally unsuitable site."

"Unsuitable for what?"

"I don't know. But he didn't want us listening, I'm sure he didn't."

"Let's go in again. Clear some more plates. And I promise I won't drift off this time."

They walked back into the sitting room. But before Hannah had time to tune into the conversation, the civilised atmosphere was torn apart by a piercing scream.

Hannah wheeled around. A ginger guinea pig had emerged from under the tea table in the centre of the room. And before Hannah could take this in, a hand shot out from under the tablecloth and grabbed at the guinea pig.

It missed. The guinea pig scuttled across the room. Jo's curly head burst from the white linen and knocked the edge of the table. In terrifying slow motion, the table crashed spectacularly on to the carpet. People shrieked and jumped out of the way as tea flew out of cups, saucers shattered, sugar scattered across the sofa, the cake stand smashed on to the floor and scones rolled in all directions. And, before anybody could get a grip on the situation, the Beans scrambled from under the tablecloth, scooped up the guinea pig from where it had frozen in terror under the china cabinet, and fled from the room.

There was a horrified silence. The guests stared, wide-eyed, at the devastation. Eventually, Hannah said, in a small, strained voice that did not sound like her own, "Shall I get the hoover?"

"No!" barked Dad. "Don't get the blasted hoover! Just leave everything alone, will you?"

* * *

The visitors left quite quickly after that. And Lottie decided she would find something to eat at home, after all.

Dad ordered Hannah to track down the Beans. She found them in the first place she looked: the empty pigsty that was the headquarters of the Great and Mighty Society of Bean. Their faces were taut and pale and they followed her to the kitchen in terrified silence.

"What on earth did you think you were playing at?" shouted Dad.

The Beans said nothing.

"Well?"

Sam cracked first.

"We were spying," he muttered, squirming under Dad's glare.

"What?"

"They've got a spy club," Hannah explained.

"A spy club? I thought you had a pea club or something."

"*Bean* Club," said Jo. "The Great and Mighty Society of Bean."

Dad made an impatient noise. "The point is, what in Heaven's name were you doing hiding under the table in the sitting room with a guinea pig when I had important visitors in the house?"

"We wanted to find out," said Jo.

"Find out what?"

"Who they were. You don't tell us anything, so we had to spy."

Dad gave an exasperated sigh. "They're just people who are interested in the farm, that's all."

"Why are they interested in the farm?"

Good question, thought Hannah.

Their father looked very tired suddenly. "No particular reason. Now, which one of you lot has hidden the superglue?"

* * *

As she passed through the hall on her way to bed, Hannah noticed that the sitting-room light was on. The door was ajar. She slipped through it to turn the light off.

She froze with her hand on the switch. There, in the middle of the floor on his hands and knees, was her father. At first she thought he was picking up crumbs, and she wondered why he wasn't using the vacuum cleaner.

Then she realised what he was doing.

He was moving very slowly across the carpet, picking up tiny pieces of Mum's precious tea set with his right hand and transferring them to his left, which already cradled a handful of fine china shards.

So that was why he had wanted the superglue.

Hannah understood completely. Whenever anything of her mother's got broken, Hannah felt like another little part of Mum had slipped from her grasp forever.

She hovered for a while, not sure whether he would want to be disturbed. Then she said, "Can I help?"

He lifted his head. There were dark shadows under his eyes.

He didn't speak for a minute. Then he said, "The pieces are so small."

"The light's too dim," said Hannah. "I'll get a torch."

She fetched the torch from the scullery and shone it on the carpet. But Dad's huge rough hands still struggled to pick up the fragments.

"Here," she said. "You hold the light and I'll pick up the pieces."

They worked in silence. The carpet was rough and scratchy and the threads clung to the shards of china, making tiny tearing sounds as Hannah extracted them. She placed each one gently into Dad's hardened, work-calloused palm.

"I think that's all," she said at last. "Shall I have a go at mending them?"

Dad leaned his hand on the arm of the sofa and stood up slowly. He met Hannah's eyes and gave her a small smile.

"Go on, then."

She opened her palm and he tipped the broken china into it. "You'll probably make a better job of it than I would."

"Hopefully, when it's done," she said, "the cracks won't show too badly."

"Just do your best," he said. "That's all you can do."

He turned to leave the room, but then he turned back, as though he'd suddenly remembered something.

"How did those try-outs go? For the school play? Did you get the part you wanted?"

"Er, no, not exactly. I mean, I am in it, but just a tiny part."

"Oh, that's a shame. Well, never mind, eh? More fool them. Right, better go and check those calves."

Chapter Five

An
Announcement

"Oh, I don't think people with non-speaking parts need to bother coming to the meeting," said Miranda, as Hannah and Lottie approached the hall doors on Tuesday lunchtime.

"Miss Summers said everyone should come," said Hannah.

Miranda shrugged. "You'll be wasting your time. But suit yourselves." She strutted into the hall.

"We will," said Lottie sweetly, "but thanks for giving us permission."

In the hall, dozens of people already sat on the floor in little groups. Hannah and Lottie scanned the room for friendly faces.

"Hey, Roberts, hey, Pudding Face."

Jack was ambling in with Ben and Jonah. Lottie scowled. "What are you doing here, loser?"

Jack pressed his hand to his heart. "Aw, you are *so* sweet."

"He's going to do sound and special effects," said Ben.

"Special effects? It's *Romeo and Juliet*, not James Bond."

"Well, it might need livening up a bit. Anyway, I haven't made any decisions yet. I'm not sure I'll have the time. And I keep strict working hours. Every third Wednesday, 3–5pm, leap years only."

"See you the year after next, then," said Lottie.

Jack's face crumpled. In a high, quavering voice, he said, "You are so *mean*, Lottie Perfect. Sometimes I get the feeling you don't even *want* me in this play."

Hannah laughed. Lottie raised her eyes to the ceiling.

Miss Summers called for everyone's attention. Priya looked over and waved to Hannah and Lottie to join her and some other girls in their class. Hannah hesitated. Miranda and her friends were sitting just across from them. But Lottie was already walking towards Priya, so Hannah followed her.

"Thank you very much for coming," said Miss Summers, when everybody had sat down. "It's fantastic to see you all here. Today's meeting will mainly be about backstage work, but first I've got a few exciting announcements to make."

People turned to their friends and started whispering. Miss Summers waited for the room to settle before she continued.

"Firstly, you might remember that I said we were inviting a professional director to judge the house play competition. Well, I can now reveal that we are incredibly lucky that a very well-known theatre director, who has had many successful productions in the West End and around the country, has agreed to come and be our adjudicator. Her name is

Josephine Baxter."

"Ooh!" said Miranda. "How exciting!"

"Just making sure everyone knows she's heard of her," muttered Lottie to Hannah.

"The second announcement," said Miss Summers, "is a rather exciting new development. You know that local estate agents have sponsored our school fair for the past few years. Well, we've just had an offer from another local company to sponsor our very first Key Stage 3 house plays. I'm not able to give any details now, because a representative from the company will be coming into assembly soon to tell you more about it, but I can say that, as well as a rather impressive trophy, they've offered us an additional prize for the winning play – something that involves a day out of school for the entire house."

There was a buzz of excitement all around the room. A day off school was a prize worth winning.

Miss Summers clapped her hands for silence.

"And now," she said, "for the final announcement."

The room quietened.

"When I introduced the house play competition at the beginning of term," said Miss Summers, "I said we would have older students from each house directing the plays." She paused. "Well, the Heads of House and I have had another think about that. The older students have a lot of opportunities to take on responsibility, rightly of course, but we thought it would be rather exciting to hand this project entirely over to Key Stage 3. And so, after a lot of thought,

49

we have decided to choose a person from each house to direct their play."

Lottie nudged Hannah and pointed at Miranda, who was sitting up very straight, looking expectantly at the teacher.

"She thinks it's going to be her," whispered Lottie.

"It'll be a Year 9, won't it?" said Hannah. Please let it be a Year 9, she prayed. Please don't let it be Miranda.

"The people I'm going to ask are all students who have experience in theatre groups," Miss Summers continued, "and, if they're willing to take on the big responsibility of directing a house play, I think they'll do a great job."

Miranda's friend Emily nudged her. Miranda smiled smugly. She had belonged to the Linford Youth Theatre for years, and they always won the Youth Drama competition in the Linford Art Festival.

Lottie turned to Hannah, looking terrified. "She wouldn't, would she? She wouldn't choose her to direct *and* play Juliet?"

"I really hope not," whispered Hannah. The prospect of being directed by Miranda for the next two months as *well* as watching her play Juliet was truly depressing.

"Obviously, I'll be there to provide support and advice whenever they need it," Miss Summers was saying, "but it's a very big job the four directors will be taking on and they will need your wholehearted cooperation."

Miranda was arranging her hair carefully over her shoulders.

"So," said Miss Summers, "without further ado, these are the students we would like to direct the house plays. For Conan Doyle's production of *Macbeth*: Alex Jackson!"

Hannah didn't know Alex, but he was clearly a popular choice, judging by the cheers from Conan Doyle House.

"For Kipling House's production of *The Tempest*: Zara McIlroy!"

Zara looked astounded and delighted. Her friends whooped and hugged her.

The Milne House director was named next, a boy called Gabriel Ince. He went bright red when his name was announced.

"I don't think it will be Miranda," whispered Hannah. "They're all Year 9s."

"Fingers crossed," murmured Lottie.

"And last but not least, Woolf House," said Miss Summers.

Miranda sat up even straighter, looking eagerly at the teacher.

"The person we've chosen is…"

Miranda started to get to her feet.

"Hannah Roberts!"

Hannah stared. What had Miss Summers said?

Lottie hugged her, shouting, "Yes! Yes!"

Hannah sat there, open-mouthed and speechless. People were turning and looking at her, clapping and smiling, but she couldn't take it in. It was as though she were watching the world through a window.

And then she saw Miranda.

Miranda's cheeks were bright red. Her face was contorted with rage.

Miss Summers raised her hands for silence. "I'd like all the directors to stay behind at the end, please. There's no obligation to take on the role, of course, but this is a wonderful opportunity and I hope you'll rise to the challenge."

"She put on a play in a *shed*," spat Miranda to Emily. "In what universe is *that* a theatre group?"

Emily squirmed. "Well, that play was the runner-up at the Linford Arts Festival, so…"

Miranda ignored her. "It must be because Miss Summers feels sorry for her. Just because her mother died, everyone thinks they have to be nice to her. And honestly, that was *years* ago."

As Miss Summers started to explain about rehearsal schedules, Lottie gave a deep, contented sigh. She leaned towards Hannah. "The look on Miranda's face when Miss Summers said your name!" she murmured. "If nothing else good ever happens in my life, I shall die happy, just remembering that."

Chapter Six

Suspicions

On Friday afternoon, Hannah and Lottie, school bags on their shoulders, ducked under the fence at the side of the farm track and walked down North Meadow towards the thicket of thorn trees and bushes in the bottom corner.

Fat ripe blackberries hung from the brambles that grew over the bushes. Hannah picked one and offered it to Lottie.

Lottie shook her head. "No, thanks." She was deeply suspicious of food that wasn't sealed in plastic.

With the tips of her thumb and forefinger, Hannah parted a seemingly impenetrable tangle of brambles. The girls squeezed through the gap. In front of them lay the narrow path through the bushes that they had made last winter.

"We'll have to dismantle the whole set," said Hannah. "We'll need every inch of space to rehearse the big fight scenes."

"We're so lucky to have the theatre for extra rehearsals. Miss Summers isn't giving us anywhere near enough time to rehearse at school."

"If people don't mind coming all the way up here," said Hannah.

"I don't think they'll mind, if it gives us more chance of winning."

"Even Miranda?" Hannah felt a bit sick, as she always did when she thought about directing Miranda.

"Who cares about her?" said Lottie. "Do you really want her to come here anyway?"

Hannah wished she could be as unaffected by Miranda as Lottie was. Miranda hadn't spoken to her since Miss Summers' announcement, but she had taken every opportunity to whisper and snigger with her friends, while throwing sneering looks in Hannah's direction. Hannah tried to ignore it, but it was hard not to let it get her down.

Everything else about the play, though, was really exciting. Since the meeting, Hannah had spent every spare moment thinking about her production. With the birthday money she had saved, she'd bought a purple ring binder and a set of dividers. The first thing she put into the ring binder was a copy of Miss Summers' half-hour version of *Romeo and Juliet*. The script was photocopied on to one side of the paper and the facing pages were blank for Hannah's director's notes on the actors' movements and gestures. The rest of the file was divided into sections: costume, props, lighting, sound, hair and make-up.

"Not that I'll need to write much about costume,"

she told Lottie, "since you're doing everything. I'm so glad Miss Summers put you in charge. I can't wait to see your drawings."

"I'll bring my sketchbook into school tomorrow," said Lottie, ducking an overhanging branch, "if I finish the designs tonight."

The secret path wound around the edge of a long, low wooden shed, covered with ivy and invisible from outside the thicket. It had a corrugated iron roof and a sliding door at each end: a stage door and a front-of-house door.

Hannah felt the familiar surge of joy as she ran her hands over the black metal sign screwed to the stage door. "The Secret Hen House Theatre", it said, in curving wrought-iron letters. The sign was bordered by a pattern of brambles, with the silhouette of a chicken in the bottom left-hand corner. Dad had given it to her as a present for saving the farm last spring.

Hannah slid the stage door open and stepped into the dressing room. A costume rail made from a broom handle was suspended from the beams with baler twine. Against the opposite wall stood their dressing table, an old chest of drawers that the Beans had discovered in a cowshed. Cleaned up, it housed their jumble sale jewellery and the make-up donated by Lottie's mum. An oval mirror was propped on top of it.

The thin wooden walls of the dressing room were bare except for one framed photograph. It showed Hannah's mother standing in North Meadow, holding baby Hannah. Hens pecked around her feet. In the background of the photo was a long, low shed, surrounded by bushes. This shed.

When Hannah's mum was alive, this had been her hen house. After her death, when Hannah was six, it was abandoned. Ivy and brambles had grown up all over it. The shed had been forgotten until Hannah and Lottie had rediscovered it last winter.

They had cleared out all the junk, scrubbed the concrete floor and patched up the disintegrating walls with scraps of wood scavenged from around the farm. Using old fence posts and hessian sacking, they had built wings at the sides of the stage and a proscenium arch at the front. They had made scenery and costumes and entered the Linford Arts Festival with a play that Hannah had written.

"I reckon," said Hannah now, surveying her theatre thoughtfully, "that this whole space is about the size of the school stage. It'll be a perfect rehearsal studio."

"What shall we move first?" said Lottie. "The dressing table?"

"OK. In that corner."

There was a scuffling sound in the auditorium. Ugh. Mice. The only thing to do was to make as much noise as possible and give them time to get away, so you never had to see them.

They pushed the dressing table into place.

"I can't believe we're not allowed scenery in the house plays," said Lottie, dusting off her hands.

"Well, there won't be time to change scenery, not

with four plays one after the other."

"But how's it going to look like Verona, without any scenery?"

"Well, Jack had this great idea of projecting images of Verona on to the back wall of the stage."

Lottie snorted. "Oh, yeah, I'm sure that was Jack's idea."

"It *was*."

"Well, I'll be really interested to see if Jack actually comes up with anything apart from 'ideas'."

Lottie was clearly never going to change her mind about Jack. Hannah changed the subject instead.

"Right, let's move the window. All the bits can go against the wall."

At the side of the stage, a sash window frame, found in another shed, was suspended from the beams. That was one of the great things about living on a farm. There was always loads of junk lying around. You could find anything you needed if you looked hard enough.

"It's a bit sad, dismantling everything," said Lottie.

Hannah untied the baler-twine knots that fixed the top of the window to the roof beam. "I'm sure we'll use it again. It happens at the end of every play, doesn't it? We're turning the theatre into a rehearsal studio for our next production – ooh." She stopped and looked at Lottie.

"What?"

"We should pin your costume designs on the walls. Then it will really look like a studio."

"Oh, yes. And a copy of the rehearsal schedule."

"And the props list, with columns for people to initial if they've got anything we need."

Excitement flooded over Hannah as she pictured her theatre walls covered with sketches and fabric samples, timetables and props lists.

"OK," said Lottie, as they leaned the heavy sash window against the side of the shed, "now the back wall."

The panelled back wall of the stage, built from salvaged wood, was wedged in place between the floor and the roof beams. As the girls grasped either end of it, Hannah heard more scrabbling from beyond the proscenium arch.

The hairs on her arms stood on end. Not rats. Please let there not be rats here.

A stifled giggle came from the auditorium. Hannah and Lottie stared at each other. Then, in three steps, they were through the proscenium arch.

In the corner of the auditorium, with very guilty looks on their faces, huddled Jo and Sam. They clutched sheaves of paper and bundles of coloured pencils to their chests. A piece of paper was pinned to the wall behind them. It said:

Bean Spy Club. Top Secrit.

Hannah's mouth fell open.

"Have you two taken over our theatre?"

"We didn't think you'd be using it," said Jo. "Since you're directing the house play now."

"Well, we are. You've got your own place."

"Daddy needs it," said Sam. "He's getting more pigs."

"Well, you'll have to find somewhere else, then."

"Why don't you use the tractor-shed loft?" suggested Lottie. "That's pretty much empty."

Sam's eyes lit up. He looked at Jo enquiringly but she gave him a warning frown.

"I don't think that would be suitable," she said grandly.

Hannah raised her eyebrows. "Well, if you're going to be that fussy..."

"What are you doing, anyway?" asked Lottie.

"We're making our magazine," said Sam.

Lottie picked up a stapled sheaf of papers from a chair. *Bean Stew*, it said in bubble writing across the top of the first page. *The official magazine of The Great and Mighty Society of Bean.*

Lottie flicked through the pages of articles, recipes, quizzes, letters and comic strips. "*Runner Bean Smashes World Record,*" she read. "*Broad Bean's Diet Tips. Snow White and the Seven Dwarf Beans.*"

"You'll have to do your magazine somewhere else," said Hannah. "We're going to be rehearsing in here."

Jo blew out her cheeks theatrically. "Fine." She started picking up the pencils scattered across the floor.

"What are we going to do with the carpet?" asked Lottie, looking at the rug on the stage.

"Roll it up and shove it against the wall, I guess," said Hannah. Then a thought occurred to her. "No, actually, let's put it in the auditorium. It'll give people somewhere to sit when they're not in a scene."

Jo slid the front-of-house door open and stepped outside. "Come on, Mung Bean."

"We're going to make a bean sculpture," Sam told Hannah. "Out of dried kidney beans and—"

"Sshh," hissed Jo. She poked her head back around the door, her finger to her lips. "Get the notebooks, Mung Bean," she whispered. "Daddy's out there, talking."

"Who's he talking to?" asked Hannah.

"I don't know. It sounds like more than one person."

Hannah looked at Lottie. "*More* visitors?" She moved over to the door and beckoned to Lottie. "Come on."

"Hey, don't push in," hissed Jo. "We're going first."

Sam handed Jo a grubby yellow notebook. The Beans made their way in single file along the secret path. Hannah and Lottie followed them.

At the end of the path, they stopped and peered through the curtain of brambles that screened the entrance to the thicket. Dad was striding up North Meadow with his springer spaniel, Tess, who was his constant companion. But today there was a man and a woman with him, taking two steps to his one to match his pace.

"Who are they?" whispered Lottie. "Do you know them?"

Hannah shook her head.

60

The strangers wore walking boots and carried stout hazel sticks. The man had a bushy grey beard and the woman had a large camera slung round her neck.

"Do you want to come in for a cup of tea?" asked Dad.

Hannah stared at Lottie. What was happening to Dad? He had made more cups of tea this week than he had ever made in his life.

"Oh, that's very kind of you, but we have to get back," said the woman. "Anyway, you've given up enough of your time, showing us around."

"No trouble at all."

"It's such a beautiful place," said the woman.

"And so well preserved," said the man. He stopped and gestured towards where the children were crouched. They drew back their heads. "It's so rare nowadays to find a farm where thickets and copses haven't been rooted out to make way for more crops. They're invaluable wildlife habitats, places like this, impenetrable to humans."

A smile flickered across Dad's face. "This one isn't *quite* impenetrable. My children seem to have found a way in."

The man laughed. "Oh, children always do."

"It's fantastic that you've got things moving with Sophie," said the woman. "She's so lovely."

"Yes, she might be just what we need," said Dad.

Hannah's stomach churned. She could tell Lottie was looking at her, but she couldn't meet her eyes. She didn't want to make the horrible possibility feel any more real than it already felt.

The woman was looking at Dad in a questioning way. She opened her mouth as if about to say something. Then she closed it as though she'd changed her mind. Then she opened it again.

"Look, I know it's none of my business," she said, "but have you told the children yet?"

Hannah stiffened.

Dad hesitated. "Not yet, no."

There was a slight pause before the woman said, "You might need to talk to them soon. You don't want them finding out from somebody else, do you?"

Sam turned to Hannah. Hannah put her finger to her lips and reached out to squeeze his hand.

"It will come as an awful shock if they hear it from someone at school," the woman continued. "And you're not going to be able to keep it secret for much longer."

Jo turned to Hannah with a questioning look and opened her mouth to speak. Hannah shook her head.

Dad started walking again. "Yes, well," he said, in a tone that Hannah knew meant the conversation was over. "We'll deal with that directly. Thank you very much for coming up here. I appreciate it."

"It was our privilege," she said. "This is a very special place. It's been—"

But the rest of her sentence was drowned out by a flurry of barking, and once Tess had calmed down, Dad and his visitors were too far away to be heard.

Hannah felt sick. Was this Sophie person really Dad's new girlfriend? And how come these strangers

62

knew about it and his own children didn't?

Fury rose up inside her. Why did he still not tell her anything?

"You've got to talk to him," said Lottie, as though she had read Hannah's thoughts.

"What was that lady talking about?" asked Sam. "What secret?"

Hannah looked at the Beans. Maybe, if all his children confronted Dad together, it would be harder for him to fob them off with vague replies that told them nothing.

"Come on," she said, parting the brambles and edging out of the thicket. "We're going to talk to Dad."

Chapter Seven

Confronting Dad

Martha was in the kitchen, crouched in front of an open cupboard. She glared at Hannah.

"How come there's never anything to eat in this poxy place?"

"There's a casserole in the larder."

"Not that one we had the other day?"

"There's plenty left."

"Yes, because it was so gross that nobody ate it the first time round."

"Don't be rude. Granny made that."

Their granny, Mum's mother, lived in Middleham. She was old and frail, but she still liked to cook for them, and they always came back from visits to her house with meals for the freezer or tins full of cake.

"I'm making my own tea," said Martha. She reached to the back of the cupboard and pulled out a tin of spaghetti hoops.

"That's not fair!" cried Jo. "How come she gets spaghetti and we have to eat casserole?"

The door to the washhouse, where Dad kept his coats and boots, rattled open.

"Martha, will you leave that for a minute?" said

Hannah. "We have to talk to Dad."

"We? What do you mean, we? What about?"

Hannah spoke quickly. Any minute now, Dad would come into the kitchen. "You know that woman who came up the other day? Sophie?"

"What about her?"

Hannah told Martha what she had overheard in North Meadow. Martha stared. All the colour drained from her face.

"No way," she said at last.

"I swear." Hannah nodded at the Beans. "They heard it, too."

"But what did it mean?" asked Sam. "What's he not telling us?"

The kitchen door opened.

"Tea ready?" asked Dad.

They stared at him.

"What's up with you lot?"

Hannah pulled out a stool and patted it. "Sit down. We need to talk to you."

He sat, frowning at his children. "What's going on?"

They pulled out stools and sat at the table. And everyone, including Martha, looked expectantly at Hannah.

Hannah took a deep breath. "Dad, we know you're keeping secrets from us."

He looked startled for a second. Then he seemed to pull himself together. "What are you talking about?" He turned to the Beans. "Is this that blessed spy club of yours, or whatever it is? Have you been snooping about again?"

"Don't get angry with them," said Hannah indignantly. "We've all seen stuff. It's not exactly difficult. First we come home and there's a strange woman in the house wanting to check out the loft, and you're wearing your best jacket and making her tea, when you've never made a cup of tea in your entire life…"

"Good grief, if I can't make a cup of tea in my own house without facing a court martial from my children…"

"And then we come home and you've got a tea party going on in the sitting room, with a load of women we've never seen before. And just now, you're showing those people round the farm and they're asking you whether you've told us yet. And you said you would do it directly, which we all know means never. So we had to ask you. And we're not letting you leave this room until you tell us what's going on."

Dad's frown had deepened. "What were you doing listening to private conversations? It's none of your business."

"None of our business?" exploded Martha. "Of course it's our business."

Dad hesitated for a second and when he spoke, his voice was gentler. "It's none of your business at the moment, and hopefully it never will be. There's nothing you can do about it so what's the point in getting you worried for nothing?"

"For nothing?" said Martha. "It's not exactly

nothing, is it?"

"It's completely our business," said Hannah, "if we get a strange woman living in our house, putting her stuff in our loft. And what about Mum's stuff? We won't let her throw out anything of Mum's."

"Throw out...? What on earth are you talking about?"

"We know you've joined a dating agency," said Martha. "So I don't know why you're bothering to lie to us."

"A *dating* agency?" Dad's voice was about two octaves higher than usual.

"Wearing your best clothes. Strange women all over the place."

"Are you getting married again?" asked Jo. "Is Sophie going to be our stepmother?"

Dad looked completely bewildered. Then, suddenly, his face cleared and he threw back his head and laughed until the tears rolled down his face.

Hannah stared at him.

"What are you laughing about? There's nothing to laugh about."

"He's gone mad," said Martha. "He needs locking up."

Eventually, Dad stopped laughing, pulled a grubby handkerchief from his jacket pocket and wiped his eyes.

"I'm not getting married again, all right? I've got enough on my plate without that, for goodness' sake. I have absolutely no intention of getting married. Or," he said to Martha, seeing that she had opened her mouth to interrupt, "joining a dating agency. All right?"

They stayed silent for a while, taking this in.

"Really? Definitely?" said Hannah.

"Absolutely definitely."

Oh, thank goodness, thought Hannah. They weren't going to get a stepmother. There was nothing to worry about. Her hunched shoulders dropped and she let out her pent-up breath in a huge sigh of relief.

Sam looked disappointed. "Oh. She was nice."

"Stepmothers always *seem* nice," said Jo darkly. "Until they try to kill you."

Martha was still frowning. "So who were all those people, then? Why were you wearing your best jacket and making tea?"

"They're from the local Ecology Group. They're interested in the farm, that's all. How soon's tea, Hannah? If it's not ready, I've got things to do." He pushed back his stool and stood up.

But Martha's question had stirred up Hannah's thoughts.

"Wait a minute. If Sophie was just interested in the farm, why was she wanting to put stuff in the loft?"

Dad hesitated. Then he said, "Sophie's a chiropterologist."

"A what?"

"She studies bats. We know bats roost in the loft, and she wants to put recording equipment up there so she can identify how many species we have."

"Cool," said Jo, her face lit up with interest. "What was that word you said?"

But it still didn't make sense to Hannah. "But then why did you say she was just what we need? Why do you *need* her?"

"Need? What do you mean?"

"You said she might be just what we need."

"Did I?"

Hannah prickled with irritation. "You're still not telling us the truth. I know you're not. When those other people came round, one woman said something about it being a totally unsuitable site, and you sent me and Lottie out of the room. What's it unsuitable for?"

"And," said Jo, "why did that lady ask if you'd told us yet? What haven't you told us?"

"Yes," said Hannah. "And she said she hoped we wouldn't hear it from someone at school – oh!"

Like a punch to the stomach, she remembered the last time someone hadn't wanted her to find something out from gossip. That time, it had been Granny. And Granny had been warning her that her father had no money to pay the rent and they might have to leave the farm.

Had Dad run out of money again?

"What?" Dad asked Hannah. "What's up with you?"

Hannah glanced at the Beans. She didn't want to scare them, but she had to get the truth out of Dad. This was their chance to get a proper answer, while they had him cornered.

Trying not to sound too panicked, she made herself look her father in the eye. "Is it the rent? Is it the landlord?"

Sam went white.

Jo gasped. "Has the money run out? Is the landlord going to demolish the farm and build houses on it?"

Dad cleared his throat.

"No," he said. "No, it isn't that."

"What is it, then?" said Martha. "Something's going on. You have to tell us."

"We saved the farm," said Jo. "Well, Hannah did. So you have to tell us."

Dad looked at the tabletop and ran his hands through his thinning hair. There was a long pause. Hannah held her breath.

Eventually, Dad raised his head.

"It's not going to happen," he said, "which is why I haven't mentioned it, but I suppose you'd have found out anyway soon. They'll be announcing it any moment now."

"Who?" said Hannah. "Announcing what?"

"The water company. Aqua, or whatever stupid name they call themselves these days."

"The water company? What's the water company got to do with anything?"

Dad took a deep breath, as though he were preparing for a long swim underwater.

"They want to take the farm."

They stared at him. This made no sense.

"Take our farm?" cried Sam. "They can't take our farm. What do you mean?"

"Take it?" said Hannah. "Why? What does the water company want our farm for?"

In a flat voice, Dad said, "They want to flood the farm and turn it into a reservoir."

There was a stunned silence.

"*What?*" said Martha eventually.

"Flood the farm?" asked Sam. "Why would they flood the farm?"

"What's a reservoir?" asked Jo.

Hannah couldn't speak. She had studied reservoirs in geography. She knew what a reservoir was.

She stared at her father. "You're joking. You are joking, aren't you?"

"No. It's true."

"Daddy, what's a reservoir?" said Sam.

Hannah searched Dad's face desperately for a sign that he wasn't serious. But her father didn't make jokes.

"The whole farm?"

"Pretty much."

Hannah couldn't think straight. Her brain didn't seem to be working.

"But … but they can't. Can they?"

"No, of course they can't," said Dad. "It's a ridiculous idea. So don't you worry about it, all right? Now, I need to get round those pigs."

He left the room. The others looked at Hannah.

"What's a reservoir?" demanded Jo.

Hannah felt flat and unreal. It was as though all her feelings had been switched off. In a daze, she rooted through her school bag for her geography book.

"It's a big artificial lake."

"What do you mean, an artificial lake?"

"It's a lake that's made by deliberately flooding a valley. Sometimes they dam a river and sometimes they pump water into the valley."

"But why would they do that?" asked Sam.

"To store water. They take the water from the reservoir and send it through the pipes to houses and factories and whatever."

"But how can they turn our farm into one of those?" asked Jo. Her voice sounded panicky.

Hannah flicked through the pages of her geography textbook. "Look. This is a reservoir in Wales."

They looked at the picture of a large tranquil lake surrounded by green hills.

"Eight hundred acres were drowned to make that. There are twelve farms and a whole village under that water."

"But what about the people who lived there?" said Sam. "Did they drown, too?"

"No, they didn't drown. But they all had to move out of their homes."

"Well, they were stupid, then," said Martha. "They should have refused to go."

"They did. There were loads of protests. We saw a film about it. Marches and banners and chanting. But it didn't make any difference. The government just went ahead and did it anyway."

"Are they going to drown our farm?" cried Sam. "They won't drown our farm, will they?"

"But our farm isn't a valley," said Jo.

Hannah remembered what the woman in the

sitting room had said that day.

It's a totally unsuitable site.

She thought back to the tea party, and Sophie's visit, and those people today. So that was why Dad had invited them to the farm. To help him stop it being turned into a reservoir.

But what if they couldn't stop it? What if the water company was stronger?

In her mind's eye, Hannah saw the sheep grazing in the fields, the new calves in the barn, the ancient cowsheds with their roofs covered in moss and lichen, the swallows' nests and the pigsties and the wildflower meadows and the oak trees, and her own lovely theatre, hidden in the copse. And she imagined a great creeping tide of water spreading over the farm, obliterating every inch of the landscape until the farm was buried beneath it. Forever.

"They can't take the farm," said Sam. "Where would we live?"

"And what about the animals?" said Jo. "What would happen to them?"

Hannah looked at her brother and sister.

"No," she said. "They can't take the farm. They won't take the farm. Because nobody will let them."

Chapter Eight

In the Playground

"Don't be ridiculous, Joanne," said Dad, as they drove to school on Monday morning. "Of course you can't stay up all night." He signalled right as they approached the main road. "Hannah, move your head. I can't see out that side."

"But it's on a Friday," said Jo, leaning forward from the back seat. "We won't have to get up for school the next day."

"I don't care what day it is. You're going to bed as usual."

"Why do you want to stay up all night next Friday anyway?" asked Hannah.

"Because Sophie's going to be here all night," said Sam.

"Is she? How do you know?"

"We heard Daddy talking to her on the phone."

"Oh, there's Lottie," said Hannah, spotting her friend on the pavement.

"She's going to watch the bats flying out of the attic and record them," said Jo. "And we want to help her."

"I bet the last thing she wants is you two 'helping'

her. She probably wants a quiet, peaceful atmosphere, not the poor bats frightened to death."

"We wouldn't frighten them," said Sam. "We are professional batologists."

"*Batologists?*" said Martha. "That's not even a word, you weirdos."

"I thought you were archaeologists," said Hannah.

Jo gave Hannah one of her hard stares. "The Society of Bean has many branches."

"Please can we stay up, Dad?" asked Sam.

"Well, we'll see."

The Beans squealed with joy.

"But it certainly won't be all night, so don't get that into your heads." He pulled in at the school gates to let Martha and Hannah out. "Right, see you later, you two."

Hannah waited for Lottie at the gates, and they made their way across the playground to their favourite bench: the one in the far corner, in the full beam of the morning sun and with a view of the whole playground.

"So you'll never guess what," said Lottie, giving the bench a quick scan and a sweep with her hand before sitting down. "It turns out my dad has known about the reservoir plans for ages."

Hannah stared at her. "What?"

"I told him about it on the phone last night and he said he'd known for months."

"But … how come?"

"He said your dad asked him to step up his bird surveys, so they'd have as much evidence as possible against the farm being flooded. But your dad asked him not to tell me, because he didn't want you knowing and getting worried. He didn't want to burden you with it when it might all come to nothing."

So Dad had known about this for months. No wonder he looked so tired, if he'd been secretly fighting the reservoir plans all this time.

"I wish I *had* known," said Hannah. "At least it wouldn't have been so much of a shock."

"What's a shock?" asked Jonah.

Hannah looked round. "Nothing." She hadn't realised he was right behind their bench. He had gelled his hair into little spikes all over his head. He and Ben were kicking a football against the wall with another Year 9 boy. Matthew Barnes, Hannah thought he was called. He had brown eyes that matched his brown hair, and he always had a football in his hands or at his feet.

"So we're rehearsing at your farm now, as well as at school?" said Jonah.

"Well, six weeks isn't very long," said Hannah. "I thought it would be good to get some extra practice in. Especially with the fight scenes – they're going to be quite complicated. Hopefully the swords will arrive before Wednesday."

"Are you using real swords?" asked Matthew.

"Samurai swords," said Jonah. "Slice you in half like butter."

Hannah laughed. "They're plastic ones Lottie ordered online. They look good, though. At least, they do in the picture."

"So do you get a budget for this play, then?" asked Jonah.

"Yep." Secretly, it was one of the things she found most thrilling. "Fifty pounds to spend on whatever I want."

"Doughnuts at every rehearsal," suggested Jonah.

"I have to keep accounts, though."

"Oh. Spoilsports."

Out of the corner of her eye, Hannah saw Miranda swanning towards them, with Poppy beside her. She steeled herself for the encounter.

"Is Adamson coming?" asked Ben. "To the farm?"

"Oh, yeah," said Lottie sarcastically. "He'd be *really* welcome on Hannah's farm, wouldn't he, after what he did last time he was there?"

"Hi, Hannah," cooed Miranda. "I saw your little note about extra rehearsals at your farm. I'm afraid I won't be able to come."

"On Wednesday? Well, that's—"

"To any of them. I just don't have the time, I'm afraid."

"What do you mean, you don't have the time? You're Juliet!"

"I just feel," said Miranda, flicking her hair back, "that my time could be more productively spent rehearsing at home. And after all," she said, smiling sweetly, "these are *extra* rehearsals, aren't they? They're not compulsory."

Hannah opened her mouth to retort and then snapped it shut again. Why was she trying to persuade

Miranda to come to the farm? The rehearsals would be ten times more fun without her.

"That's no problem. We'll do the scenes you're not in. No problem at all."

Miranda looked slightly taken aback. Maybe she was expecting me to beg her on bended knee, thought Hannah.

"So," said Jonah, "will you still get to live in your house when they flood the farm, or will the house be underwater, too?"

Hannah's stomach somersaulted. "What?"

"What are you talking about?" said Ben.

"This new reservoir they're building at Hannah's farm. It's going to be so cool. Windsurfing, sailing, scuba-diving…"

Hannah's heart started beating very fast.

Matthew stopped kicking the football and looked round. "Diving? Where?"

"Wait a minute," said Lottie. "How do you know about the reservoir? They haven't announced it yet."

"My dad's mate told him. He's on the council. My dad's going to apply for the catering licence. He reckons he'll make a fortune."

Ben stared at Hannah. "They're building a reservoir on your farm?"

"Yep," said Jonah. "It won't be a farm much longer. It'll be a massive great lake."

"Are we really getting a reservoir in Middleham?" said Matthew, tucking the football under his arm and moving closer. "That's awesome. We never get anything good here. Hey, will there be fishing?"

"Bound to be," said Jonah. "They'll probably stock it with trout or salmon or something."

"So are they going to flood your whole farm?" asked Ben. "Where are you going to live? Will you get another farm?"

Hannah couldn't speak. The others kept talking, but their words seemed far off in the distance. Hannah felt sick, and the outside world was a meaningless blur.

So people *wanted* the reservoir. They weren't going to try to stop it. They thought a reservoir would be a great thing to have in the village. They were looking forward to it. They were excited about it.

And, Hannah realised, why wouldn't they be? What did most people in the village care about Clayhill Farm? The only thing the farm offered for everybody else was land to walk on. Whereas a reservoir…

What were a few footpaths and a bit of birdwatching compared with scuba-diving and windsurfing, fishing and sailing?

Lottie's raised voice cut into Hannah's thoughts.

"There isn't going to be a reservoir in Middleham, Jonah, so you and your dad can stop making plans for windsurfing and catering licences."

"There is, actually. You don't know everything, even though you think you do."

"I know they're planning to build a reservoir, but it's not going to happen. The farm's full of wildlife and we're not going to let it be destroyed."

"Oh, wildlife. Big deal. There's plenty of other fields."

"I went windsurfing on Rutland reservoir last summer," said Matthew. "It was so cool. I can't believe we're going to get one here."

"I hope they start soon," said Jonah. "Be great to have something to do in this stinking hole. Hey, if it freezes in winter we could go skating."

"Will you just shut up about it?" said Lottie. "That's Hannah's home you're talking about. And anyway, it's not going to happen."

"Well, they're having a meeting this Thursday about their plans, so we'll find out then, won't we? My dad's going to go. He wants to get the catering contract before anyone else gets in on it."

"But they can't flood your farm," said Ben, "if your family doesn't want to sell it. Can they?"

Hannah's voice came out croaky. "We don't own it. We rent it."

She didn't add: And the landlord will be delighted to sell it. That's exactly what he wants.

"It's very run down, anyway," said Miranda. "It'll be much better to have something there that's actually useful."

Hannah glared at her. "How can you say it's run down? You've never even been there."

Miranda gave a bored shrug. "That's what everybody says."

"Everybody? Who's everybody?"

"Anyway, you can rent another farm, can't you?" said Jonah. "And it will be awesome to have a reservoir in the village, you've got to admit it."

"All you care about," said Hannah, "is your stupid water sports. You don't care at all about the wildlife. You're so selfish."

"Actually," said Miranda, "don't you think it's you who's being selfish, Hannah?"

Hannah shot her a look of loathing, but Miranda didn't seem to notice. "I mean, we need reservoirs, don't we? If everybody had your attitude, where would we get our water from?"

Of course, thought Hannah, with a dull ache inside her. Of course that was how other people would see it. And maybe they were right. Maybe she *was* being selfish.

"Anyway," said Miranda, "it doesn't matter what you think. The water company's hardly going to listen to you, are they? If they want a reservoir, they'll build a reservoir. There's no point trying to stop them."

From the school building, the bell for registration sounded. Hannah had never been so glad to hear it. She couldn't stand this for one more second.

Lottie gave her a concerned look as they walked across the playground. "Are you all right? Don't take any notice of Miranda. She's just being a cow."

"Is she?" said Hannah.

"What do you mean? Of course she is."

Lottie ranted about Miranda all the way to their form room. But Hannah wasn't listening. The conversation in the playground played over and over in her head.

People would love a reservoir, wouldn't they?

And if the village wanted it and the landlord wanted it and the water board wanted it, what possible chance did her dad and a few eccentric wildlife enthusiasts have of stopping their plans?

They had no chance, did they? Absolutely no chance at all.

Chapter Nine

The
Invasion

Hannah took a deep breath of clean Clayhill air as she crossed the road from Elm Lane on to the farm track that afternoon. It was a warm day again, the sky bright blue, dotted with low, grey-white fluffy clouds. But the harvest was nearly finished and the nights were getting colder. There was a definite feel of autumn in the air.

A tractor pulled a seed drill across the freshly turned soil of Brook Field. It didn't look like Dad in the tractor. It must be Adam, his new farm worker. Hannah wondered what he was planting.

Into her head rushed an image of flood waters pouring into the shallow valley, washing away the delicate green shoots. Would there be another harvest at Clayhill?

No. She couldn't let herself think about that.

She rounded the bend in the track, a turn she always loved. It was here that the farmhouse came into view, nestled right in the centre of the land.

But today, as she turned the corner, she stopped dead.

It looked as though a plague of giant wasps had

invaded the farm. Dozens of people in bright-yellow fluorescent jackets swarmed all over North and South Meadows. Some were on their own, some were in groups. Some carried notebooks, some had tools, some held electronic devices and some were taking photographs.

Hannah stood rigid, not even breathing. They weren't starting already, were they? They couldn't be, surely. They couldn't just demolish the farm without permission.

Unless … unless they *had* permission.

What if the landlord had already agreed to this? What if it didn't matter what she or Dad or anybody else thought? What if the landlord just had to sign a piece of paper and they could come in with their bulldozers?

Two of the men strode up North Meadow.

"Heavy clay subsoil with twelve per cent greensand," one of them said.

They wore ID cards clipped to their jackets. They came close enough to Hannah for her to read the words written on their badges, though they took no more notice of her than if she had been one of the sheep grazing in South Meadow.

Aqua, the badges said. *Delivering water to you.*

Hannah remembered seeing other people, wearing the same badges, walking over the fields during the summer holidays. But there were often people at the farm mending pipes or cables, and she had thought nothing of it at the time.

"So there'll be earthworks running right around

the perimeter?" said one of the men.

"That's right," said the other. "Half a million cubic metres of soil. We need to build up the banks to a ten-metre height to get enough depth of water."

"And what's the total area to be flooded?"

"Nearly four hundred acres. Right up to the wood there. It's a perfect site. Only the one house on it. And the landlord's happy. As long as the price is right, of course."

They chuckled.

Hannah started to run. She hurtled down the bumpy track, leaping over potholes, hoisting the strap of her canvas bag back on to her shoulder every few seconds. She had to find Dad. Please, please, she thought, let him be in his office.

As she raced past the gateway to South Meadow, one of the wasp men, absorbed in tapping a number into his mobile phone, stepped on to the track right in front of her. Hannah swerved and knocked his arm. The sheaf of papers he was carrying spilled on to the tarmac. The man swore and stooped to pick them up, the phone still clamped to his ear.

"Sorry," said Hannah, chasing after a couple of pieces of paper which had caught on the breeze and were dancing towards the farmyard.

She grabbed them just before they reached a large muddy puddle, and turned round to give them back. The man was walking up the track, head down, his papers clamped under one arm. He obviously didn't realise that two sheets were missing.

Suddenly he gave a shout into his phone. "*Finally*,

a signal. Listen, Terry, this place is a nightmare for reception so I might get cut off any minute."

As Hannah ran after him, her eye caught the top sheet of paper and she stopped.

It was an aerial photograph of Clayhill Farm. Around the borders of the farm, a thick line had been drawn in black felt-tipped pen.

There was a date at the bottom of the photograph. It was just over a year ago.

Her heart thumping, Hannah pulled out the bottom piece of paper. It was the same photograph, with the same black border, but on this picture, the area inside the border was covered with heavy criss-crossed lines.

Underneath the photograph were the words:

Middleham Reservoir. Area to be flooded.

The criss-crossed lines completely obliterated the farm.

Hannah's throat tightened. She looked across the land, at the pastures, the pig field, the ancient hedgerows full of songbirds, the ponds where the frogs spawned every spring, the veteran oak trees that were homes for owls and bats and countless other creatures, the yard with its centuries-old barn, stables and granary, and their own lovely, ramshackle farmhouse.

Her father and her grandfather and other farmers for hundreds of years before them had spent their whole lives looking after this land. The water company couldn't just destroy it. They wouldn't be allowed to.

Would they?

She became aware of heavy footsteps approaching. She looked up. The man who had dropped the papers was striding back towards her. He stopped in front of her and snatched the papers from her hand. Then he turned back up the track without a word.

For a moment Hannah stood there, too astonished to react. The rudeness of him!

But she had more urgent things to worry about than rudeness. She turned back towards the farmyard and broke into a run.

Chapter Ten

❀ ❀

Letters
and Liars

Hannah dumped her bag on the scullery freezer and ran up the bare wooden staircase. She could hear the clack-clack-clack of typewriter keys from Dad's office. She edged past the dusty filing cabinets in the corridor, dislodging another lump of plaster from the wall, and pushed at the office door. It opened a couple of feet and then ground to a halt against the heap of files stacked on the floor behind it.

Dad was sitting at his desk in the centre of the room. The floor around him was covered with piles of folders and sheaves of paper that had spread and multiplied over the years as though they had a magical life of their own, like the briars around Sleeping Beauty's castle.

"Have you seen all those water people swarming over our fields?" demanded Hannah.

Dad looked up from the big black old-fashioned typewriter that he still insisted on using, even though Adam had recently installed a second-hand computer in the downstairs office.

"Seen them? You could hardly miss them."

"Did you know they were coming?"

He flicked a hand dismissively at the pile of post on his desk. "I dare say they sent one of their stupid letters."

"But you didn't say anything about it. Why don't you tell me anything?"

Dad looked at her with a puzzled frown. "What do you want to know?"

Hannah felt as though she might burst with frustration. "Everything, of course! I want to know everything about it! I want to help, Dad. And I don't want any more horrible surprises."

Dad stared at her. Then he sighed. He pushed his chair back, stood up and walked between the heaps of paper to one of the several filing cabinets randomly scattered around the room, like self-seeded trees. He opened a drawer, pulled out a slim blue ring binder and handed it to Hannah.

"Have a look through that if you like."

Hannah took the folder.

"What is it?"

"It's all in there. Everything I know about the whole darned business."

"Oh. Thanks."

She took the file to her bedroom. Sam was kneeling on the floor, pushing a model tractor and plough very slowly over the threadbare carpet.

"Hi, Sammy. How's the ploughing going?"

"Not bad. The ground's a bit heavy after all that rain, but I've only got two more fields to do."

Hannah propped her pillow against the end of the

bed. "What are you going to plant in here?"

Every room in the house was a field on Sam's farm. He kept a field plan under each carpet with a record of what was planted there.

"Winter wheat." He moved the tractor steadily across the carpet. "It's a new strain. *Farmers Weekly* says it's really good at resisting disease."

"Great," said Hannah. She settled the file on her lap and opened it.

The first document was a glossy brochure from Aqua, one of those incredibly dull quarterly magazines that companies send out to their customers. Hannah's heart sank.

Well, she had asked for more information, and now she had it. So she had better read it.

She opened the brochure. Phrases like "demand management" and "supply side options" swam up from the dense mass of black type on page one. What on earth did it all mean?

She read the first paragraph three times, but it was like trying to read a foreign language she'd barely studied. Half the words made no sense to her at all. If I keep reading, she thought, maybe it will become clearer.

She struggled on, making a huge effort to concentrate. Twice, Sam asked her when tea would be ready and twice she told him vaguely that she'd get it in a minute. She mustn't stop now. Somewhere in all this gobbledegook, surely there would be some information about the reservoir.

But she got to the last page and she still hadn't

found anything. It was just unintelligible water-board jargon. With a sigh of defeat, Hannah closed the brochure and turned to the next document in the file.

It was a copy of a letter from Dad to the landlord's agent, dated five months ago.

Dear Mr Mullins,

Following yesterday's meeting in which you casually told me that Mr Cashmore is planning to sell the farm on which my family has lived and worked for nearly seventy years, and allow it to be destroyed to build a reservoir, I must ask you for more information about this proposed scheme and when the work is expected to start.

Yours sincerely,
A. Roberts

The next letter in the file was also from Dad, dated two weeks later.

Dear Mr Mullins,

I am still awaiting a reply to my letter of a fortnight ago. Your early attention would be appreciated.

Yours sincerely,
A. Roberts

A month later, the land agent had replied.

Dear Mr Roberts,

Thank you for your letter enquiring about Aqua's plans for Clayhill Farm.

May we take this opportunity to reassure you that plans are still at a very early stage and that we do not yet have any detailed schedules of the works to be carried out. We shall of course keep you fully informed of all developments as they occur.

Yours sincerely,
Harry Mullins

In other words, thought Hannah, they're telling him nothing. Horrible people.

After several letters along the same lines, in which Dad asked for information and got none, he seemed to have given up on the landlord's agent. The next letter was to Lottie's dad, thanking him for the "excellent and extremely detailed results of your bird surveys". Then he had written to the Middleham Ecology Group, inviting them to survey the flora and fauna at the farm. This letter had a prompt and enthusiastic reply. They must have been the people at that disastrous tea party.

Hannah had nearly reached the end of the file. The next letter was addressed to "Nick Constable, Assets Director, Aqua".

Dear Mr Constable,

Although my family has farmed this land for nearly seventy years, we have not been informed of the extent of the land you would like to take for a reservoir.

I must now ask that you forward a map without delay showing the exact location of your proposed reservoir.

Yours sincerely,
A. Roberts

As with all the others, this letter was followed by another from Dad, dated three weeks later, asking for a reply to his first letter.

The final piece of paper in the file was from Aqua, dated just a few days ago.

Dear Mr Roberts,

Thank you for your letter of 28th August.

As you are aware, we are about to embark upon a number of environmental surveys at the site, as these are critical in determining whether it is suitable for a reservoir and, if it is, how any reservoir scheme would minimise any environmental impacts while clearly ensuring we have sufficient, available water supplies.

Can I take this opportunity to reassure you that we are not yet at the stage of having a detailed design or, indeed, supporting drawings or maps.

Yours sincerely,
N. Constable

Hannah gasped.

"The liars!"

Sam looked up from his tractor. "Who are liars?"

Hannah didn't answer. She picked up the file, jumped off the bed, ran to Dad's office and shoved the door open as far as it would go.

"Dad, you are going to the meeting, aren't you?"

"What meeting?"

"The one next week, on Thursday. Aqua's meeting about their plans. You have to go. You've got to meet those Aqua people and ask them questions to their lying faces."

He looked at her. "What's got you so fired up?"

"They're lying to you, Dad. In this letter they say they don't have a map of the reservoir, but they do. I've seen it. And it's dated a year ago. You've got to go to that meeting and tackle them face to face. And I'm coming with you."

Chapter Eleven

Stage Combat

"You're joking," said Jonah, staring at the thicket. "This theatre you've told us all about is in *there*?"

Ben laughed. "Is it an invisible theatre?"

"Imaginary theatre, more like," said Jonah. "I reckon Hannah's built it all in her own head."

Hannah said nothing. She pulled the curtain of brambles aside and slipped through the gap on to the secret path.

As the boys jostled and shoved each other into thorn bushes, Hannah began to wonder whether inviting twenty people to rehearse in her theatre had been a really bad idea. And to learn sword fighting, of all things! What had she been thinking?

Each house only had one after-school rehearsal a week in the hall. Woolf House's first slot was tomorrow. Hannah knew it would take a long time to choreograph the fight scenes, so she had wanted a head start. But suddenly she was terrified. What if the boys just went berserk and her first rehearsal turned into a massive fight? What if nobody took the slightest notice of her? After all, why should

Year 9 students show any respect to someone a year younger than them?

She looked at the beautiful sign on the stage door and it gave her strength. She took a deep breath and slid the door open along its metal runners. And when the actors stepped into the long, low shed, the jostling and the laughing stopped.

All along the left-hand wall, Lottie had pinned costume designs for every character. On the opposite wall were several typed sheets under big headings saying **Cast Notices** and **Backstage Notices**. A heading above a large hand-drawn poster on the far wall said **Stage Combat Positions**.

"Wow," said James Talbot, the gangly Year 8 boy playing Mercutio. "Is this really yours?"

"It's amazing," said Amy Perello.

Hannah's heart swelled with love and pride for her theatre. Amy was in Year 9 and so incredibly pretty that Hannah had always been a bit in awe of her. To have Amy praise her theatre was quite overwhelming.

Several people were looking at the diagrams of stage combat positions. Others were studying the costume designs.

"Are our costumes really going to look like this?" asked Marie, trying to extract a thorny twig from her thick blonde hair.

"Yes," said Hannah. "Lottie's brilliant at sewing."

Katy Jones, Marie's tall, dark-haired best friend, was looking at Lottie's sketch for Lord Capulet.

"Wow, these are amazing. Did you really do them, Lottie?"

Lottie looked awkward, as she always did when someone was paying her a compliment. Instead of answering, she pointed to a sketch further along the wall. "That one's yours. It uses some of the same fabric as Lord Capulet's, to show the link between you. And this one's yours, Priya."

Priya turned her attention away from the props list and came to look at the design.

"That's stunning."

"It's a similar design to Lord Capulet's and Lord Montague's," said Lottie, "but because you're the Prince, you show your status by a fuller cloak that trails on the floor and has more jewels on the collar."

"Are you really going to make them all?" asked Marie. "Where will you get the material?"

"Jumble sales and charity shops, mostly," said Lottie, "and then I chop things up and reuse them. Old curtains, throws, dresses, anything. There's a notice on the backstage board to sign up if you want to help with sewing."

Hannah clapped her hands. "OK, everyone, let's get started. So today this space is our fight studio. We're going to learn the basic stage-combat techniques, and then use those moves to choreograph the fight scene at the beginning of the play."

"To do what to the fight scene?" asked Jonah, who had gelled his fringe into a quiff today.

"Choreograph, you plum," said Marie.

Jonah shook his head. "Means nothing to me."

Hannah wrenched open the stiff bottom drawer of the rickety dressing table and pulled out an armful of decorative silver swords made from moulded plastic. Jonah lunged for a sword but Hannah swiped his hand away.

"OK, can everyone sit on the carpet, please?"

"Ooh," said Jonah, "are you going to read us a story, miss?"

People laughed, but they moved away from the costume designs and settled themselves on the big rug in the auditorium.

Hannah had a moment of amazement as she watched all these people, half of them older than her, following her instructions without a murmur. Never in a million years would she have ordered them about like this in normal life. It's like I'm playing a part, she thought. I'm playing the part of director. And when I'm playing that part, somehow I can do this.

She took two swords from the pile and a battered pack of plasters from the drawer, and moved into the auditorium.

"So I'm going to show you the five basic cut targets and two thrust targets, and then I'll teach you the fundamental techniques of the French system. That's the one they use to choreograph fight scenes for films."

She was quite pleased with the way that sounded. No one would have guessed she had only learned it from the Internet last night.

"Can I have a volunteer, please?"

Owen Griffiths, the freckled, red-haired Year 8 boy playing Lord Montague, jumped up, grinning. Owen was always willing to put himself centre-stage.

"OK," said Hannah, "so these are the five basic cut targets. Two here." She stuck a plaster on to each of Owen's upper arms. "A few centimetres below the shoulder. You don't want to aim right at the shoulder, because the sword can easily slip and get the neck."

She peeled another plaster and stuck it on the side of Owen's trousers.

"One either side here, halfway between the waist and knee. These are called the flanks. And the final one is straight down from the top of the head." She stuck a plaster at the top of Owen's forehead, on his hairline. "Although I don't think we'll use that one. It's a bit close to the face, and you must never touch the face."

She stuck two more plasters on Owen, in the centre of the chest and at the belly button. "These are the two point targets, where you would aim to thrust your sword in to kill someone."

Owen pulled a shocked face. "Steady on. I didn't come here to be sacrificed."

"Too late, mate," said Jonah. "You volunteered."

"Right," said Hannah, "now I'm going to show you the seven basic attack and parry moves in the French system. Attack number one is a thrust to the stomach. Keep your sword hand extended and look for your target."

She thrust her sword at the plaster on Owen's belly

button. Owen groaned and staggered backwards theatrically. Several people giggled.

"OK, now you do that, Owen, and I'll show you how to parry it."

She handed Owen a sword. Owen struck a dramatic pose and thrust his sword out. Hannah parried it away.

"See? We'll do it again, in slow motion. Great. Now, you can all take a sword and practise in pairs with the person you'll be fighting with in the scene. When everyone's got it, I'll show you the second move."

An hour later, they had all mastered the seven basic moves of the French system and Hannah asked everyone to sit on the carpet again.

"Now that you know the moves by number, we can choreograph a fight just by using those numbers, you see? And I'll write the numbers down so we have a record for future rehearsals. So can you all choreograph a one-minute fight in your pairs, using those seven moves? When you're done, show me and I'll write down the numbers."

Everyone sprang to their feet again. Hannah weaved her way between the duels, ducking the plastic blades and attempting to write down moves as she tried to keep order.

"Jonah, not near the face!"

"Elsie, extend your arm. You've got to look like you mean it."

"Always look at the target, Nathan."

The theatre was a whirl of parrying and clashing

swords. It wasn't until Lottie tapped her on the arm and said, "Hannah, it's after five," that Hannah even remembered that time existed. She called the rehearsal to a halt and thanked everybody for coming. The cast tumbled out of the theatre, laughing and chatting.

"I don't know why you were so worried," said Lottie. "That was brilliant."

"It was such good fun, wasn't it?" said Hannah, glowing with energy and excitement. "And it felt great, having so many people in the theatre."

But as they emerged from the secret path, her happiness evaporated instantly. A swarm of fluorescent-jacketed wasp people stood a few metres from them, holding equipment and clipboards and gesturing across the fields.

What were they doing now?

"Look at that!" squealed a curly-haired Year 7 girl called Millie.

"Oh, that is the cutest thing I've ever seen," cooed her friend Bea.

Hannah followed their gaze. The Beans were walking up the track from the farmyard, and behind them plodded Jasper, with Lucy swaying on his back.

"Is that really a duck sitting on that sheep's back?" asked Katy.

"What?" said Ben. "No way."

The Beans ducked under the electric fence into the field, followed by Jasper and Lucy.

"He's my sister's pet sheep," said Hannah. "He was an orphan lamb she bottle-fed, and he lived in a stable with a family of ducks. And one of the ducklings kind of adopted Jasper. She started riding around on his back. And she still does it now she's fully grown. It's like they're best friends."

There was a chorus of oohs and aahs from the girls. "That is sooo cute," said Amy. "Can I stroke him?"

"Sure. He's very friendly. Although watch out for my brother and sister. They're a bit loopy."

People crowded round Jasper. "Careful," said Jo. "He bites."

Amy withdrew her hand.

"He doesn't bite," said Hannah.

"He might," said Jo. "I'm just saying be careful, that's all." She approached the wasp woman nearest to her. "Are you the archaeologists?"

"We are," she said.

Hannah stared at Jo. How did she know that?

"Are you looking for treasure?" asked Sam.

The woman smiled. "We're working on behalf of Aqua's environmental consultants. We're doing field walks of the area."

All the girls were cooing over Jasper now. Lucy, unused to crowds, flapped off his back and waddled away to a safe distance.

"If you find treasure," said Sam, "do you get to keep it, or does it belong to us?"

"It's not really about finding treasure. We're looking for any significant surface finds. Then our work will be followed up by geophysic specialists."

"What's that?" asked Jo.

"Well, they use scanning equipment called

magnetrometry, which helps identify any buried archaeological features."

"Like treasure?"

"Generally things like ditches, pits, postholes..."

"Ditches and pits?" Jo screwed up her face in disgust. "You don't need to *dig* to find ditches and pits. There's ditches and pits everywhere."

"Why aren't you digging in South Meadow?" asked Sam. "That's where we found our Roman coins. Look." He grabbed the archaeologist's arm. "I'll show you the place."

The woman looked uncomfortable. She shrugged her arm out of Sam's grip. Jasper licked her shoe and she stepped backwards.

"Do you want to see my coin?" asked Sam.

"Another time, maybe. We need to be getting on now. Nice to meet you." She gave an awkward wave and hurried across the field to join her colleagues.

Sam turned to Hannah. "Do you want to see my Roman coin?"

"Is it the same squashed piece of tin you showed me last time?"

"No, we found another one."

"I'll look at it later, when you've cleaned it."

"You'll have to pay the entrance fee, though," said Jo. "Once it's in the museum."

"What museum?" asked Lottie.

"The Bean Museum of Archaeology, obviously."

"And where's that?"

"In Sam's wardrobe. All our finds are there. It's 50p entrance, or two pounds for a season ticket. We think you'll find that's a very reasonable price."

"Sounds like a bargain," said Lottie. "I mean, the British Museum's free, but what's that compared with the Bean Museum of Archaeology?"

"Exactly," said Jo. "Manu went to the British Museum and he said it's really boring. And nobody's said that about ours. See you later."

They trotted off up the field, with Jasper plodding behind them.

"Wow," said Owen. "They really are wacko."

Hannah bristled. It was one thing for her to question the Beans' sanity, but it was quite another thing for other people to do so.

"Hey, Hannah, is that your granddad?" asked a Year 8 boy called Harry, who was playing one of the Capulet servants.

Hannah glanced to where he was pointing, beyond the wasp people to the ancient oak tree in the middle of the field. Somebody was standing in front of it, dwarfed by the tree's enormous trunk.

Her granddad?!

"That's my dad," she said, and gained some satisfaction from the look of mortification on Harry's face.

"Oh, sorry," he muttered. "He's quite far away. I just thought..." He tailed off.

A couple of people giggled and others glanced at Hannah, looking embarrassed on Harry's behalf.

As they came closer to him, Hannah suddenly saw her father as the others must see him. She had always known, of course, that he was older than her friends' dads, but in his torn and tattered jacket, he looked as windblown and weather-beaten as the hawthorn bushes in the hedge. Hannah felt a sudden rush of guilt. What was she doing, messing about with plays, while he was shouldering all the worry of the threat to their farm on his own?

Well, at least after she had been to the meeting next Thursday, she would know more about what they were up against. Then she could help him fight Aqua's plans.

Dad looked round as they approached. "Ah, Jo, er, Martha, er, Hannah, give me a hand with this, would you?"

He passed Hannah one end of a tape measure. "Hold that firm on the trunk there."

"What are you doing?" Hannah asked.

"I need to measure the girth."

Lottie laughed and Hannah had a sudden vision of Dad fitting the oak tree up with a new frock.

Rags bounded into the centre of the group and planted her front paws on Ben's chest. This prompted another chorus of oohs and aahs, as people surrounded her, patting and stroking her. Delighted by the attention, Rags rolled over on to her back to be tickled.

"Why are you measuring the tree?" asked Hannah, holding the end of the tape measure firm with her thumb as Dad wound it around the trunk. The rough bark was deeply creviced and loose in places. Holes in the trunk looked as though they might be homes for owls or bats. Huge mushroom-type fungi sprouted from one side of it.

"It's a good way to tell the age, they say." He read the measurement at his end of the tape. "Six metres twenty-eight centimetres."

He took a little blue notebook from his coat pocket and wrote the number down.

"Six metres?" repeated James, who was slightly less distracted by the puppy than most of the others. "Six metres around the trunk? That's massive!"

"So how old does that make the tree?" asked Hannah.

Dad took a folded piece of paper from his other pocket and straightened it out. It was a photocopied page from a book.

"One of those ecology people gave me some information."

He ran his finger down the paper. "Here we are. Six metres twenty-eight centimetres means this tree dates roughly from the time of Elizabeth I."

Lottie gaped at him. "Elizabeth I? Really?"

"So this tree was alive," said Hannah, "when Shakespeare was writing *Romeo and Juliet*."

"Wow," said Priya. "Imagine that."

"Imagine what?" said Jonah, straightening up from playing with Rags.

"This tree is over four hundred years old," said Hannah. "Imagine all it's lived through, all it's seen."

"It's probably seen a lot of grass and cows. It looks half dead, anyway."

"It is half dead. Oak trees take hundreds of years to grow and hundreds of years to die."

"Are you cutting it down?" Jonah asked Dad, his eyes lighting up. "Do you want some help with the chainsaw?"

Dad turned to him with a look of horror. "Am I *what*?!"

"Of course he's not cutting it down," said Hannah. "Old trees are habitats for masses of rare wildlife."

"All right," said Jonah, "keep your hair on."

"It's amazing when you think about it, isn't it?" said Lottie. "We just take trees for granted, but a tree lives longer than anything else on earth. Did you know there are yew trees still living in England that were planted when the Romans were here? Isn't that amazing?"

"Yeah, well, if they could talk, it might be interesting," said Jonah. "But as it is, they're never going to tell us anything, are they, so what does it matter how old they are?"

Dad was frowning at Jonah as though trying to place him. Suddenly his frown cleared.

"Are you Jim Hadley's son?"

Jonah looked surprised. "Yes."

"So Ted Hadley was your grandfather."

"Yes. Why, did you know him?"

"Knew him well. Used to come up here in my father's time and help with the harvest. Old Middleham family, the Hadleys. Been here generations."

"So your great-great-grandfather might have climbed this tree," said Hannah. "Imagine that."

Jonah looked up into the leaf canopy far above

them, tinged with orange and gold. "I guess so."

"And yet Aqua want to destroy it." She turned on Jonah with a fierce rush of anger. "But that's OK, isn't it? Because you'll have all the windsurfing and scuba-diving you could want, right on your doorstep. So everything's fine."

Jonah shifted his gaze.

"Nobody would allow a seven-hundred-year-old cathedral to be destroyed, would they? But this farm," Hannah said, and she flung out her arms to take in the hedgerows full of berries, the enormous parkland oaks and the sweep of meadows leading up to the ancient wood, "this farm has been here at least that long. And if things turn out the way you want, every single tree, every hedge, every plant you can see right now will disappear forever. Do you really think that's right?"

Chapter Twelve

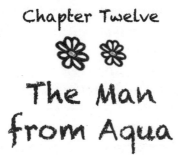

The Man from Aqua

Hannah looked at her watch. "It's two minutes to seven. Isn't anyone else going to come?"

Lottie glanced up from an information board headed **Water Resources Demand Management Strategy**. There were several of these boards placed around Croxton Village Hall. For all the sense Hannah could make of them, they might as well have been written in Ancient Greek.

"Well, it's hardly the most fun way to spend an evening, is it?" said Lottie. "I mean, would you be here if it wasn't about your farm?"

"No, I wouldn't. But that's the whole problem, isn't it? Who else is going to care?"

There were four other people, including Hannah's dad, looking at the information boards. One of them was the excitable fuzzy-haired woman who had been at Dad's tea party. Several rows of plastic chairs had been set up to face a trestle table and screen at the front of the room. Apart from one old lady in the second row, every seat was empty.

"Well, I'm here, aren't I?" said Lottie.

"Yes, you are. And I'm really grateful."

"There's nothing about the reservoir on these boards. Maybe they won't even mention it."

"It'll probably be just like that brochure," said Hannah.

A glossy Aqua brochure had arrived in the post on Tuesday. On the cover, in bold black lettering, were the words: **Draft Water Resources Management Plan**. The photo showed a laughing girl in shiny wellies splashing in a puddle. The puddle water sparkled with cleanliness. There wasn't a speck of mud anywhere.

Hannah had flicked through the pages, looking for information about the reservoir. The brochure was full of graphs, tables and columns of print with headings like **Supply Demand Balance** and **Base Deployable Output**.

Wow, she thought. They're really doing everything they can to make sure people don't understand what they're up to.

When she did eventually find the one tiny paragraph about the reservoir, all it said was that Clayhill Farm had been identified as a possible site and investigations were being carried out.

She had brought it to that day's rehearsal to show Lottie, but Lottie had seen it already.

"They must have sent them to every house," said Katy.

"Yeah, my dad was reading it at breakfast," said Jonah. "No idea how. It's the dullest thing I've ever seen. And I do geography with Mr Turner, so you can imagine."

Now, the village-hall door opened and a tall, slim man with thick shiny dark hair walked in and sat at the trestle table. He wore a smart black suit and he looked very pleased with himself. He took a laptop from his briefcase and opened it up.

"If you'd all like to take a seat," he said, in a smooth voice that made Hannah prickle with irritation, "then we'll make a start."

Lottie and Hannah went to join Hannah's dad, who had sat, as he always did, in the back row.

The door banged and another man walked into the hall. He looked vaguely familiar.

Hannah nudged Lottie. "Who's he?"

Lottie looked at him. "Jonah's dad," she whispered.

Of course. He wanted to find out more so he could get the catering contract. So did everybody else here support the reservoir plans? Hannah felt even more depressed.

"Thank you for coming along to this Public Consultation Evening," said the man at the front, with a smile that didn't reach his eyes. "I'm Nick Constable, Aqua's Assets Director."

He pressed a button on his laptop. A slide appeared on the screen. It said: **Supply and Demand Analysis**.

Lottie groaned. "Just kill me now."

Hannah's heart sank. This might turn out to be the longest evening of her life.

Nick Constable didn't mention the reservoir. Instead, he droned on about "demand forecasts" and "projections" and "long-term strategic planning."

"I'm actually going to die of boredom in a

minute," Lottie muttered.

But Hannah forced herself to concentrate. He *wants* us to switch off, she thought. He's using these words on purpose, so we won't understand. But I *have* to understand.

Nick Constable put up a slide showing a graph. He said that people were using a lot more water than they used to, and that there was also a big demand for more houses in the south-east of England, so even more water would be needed to supply those houses. Millions and millions more litres of water every day.

"And so, as part of our strategy to meet projected demand, we are proposing to build a new reservoir on the outskirts of Middleham, three miles east of here."

Hannah's stomach contracted. She nudged Lottie and sat up very straight.

"This proposed reservoir will be an extremely valuable resource, providing the essential extra fourteen million litres of water per day to the local area."

Hannah was filled with a deep, dull despair. It was exactly as Miranda had said, wasn't it? People needed water, and this reservoir would provide that water. What right did they have to object to that?

Nick Constable clicked the remote again to show a picture of a beautiful lake on a summer's day. Geese pecked on the banks and weeping willows trailed their leaves in the water. Smiling couples strolled around the perimeter.

"The reservoir will also," he said, "provide

excellent leisure opportunities, as well as being a highly attractive landscape feature."

He clicked the remote to show a happy group of windsurfers.

"We envisage the reservoir as a focal point of the community in terms of leisure and relaxation."

The next slide pictured children in sailing boats. The one after that showed anglers fishing from the banks. With each slide, Hannah's despair deepened.

"The land on which we are proposing to site the reservoir," he continued, "is currently a tenanted farm."

Another slide appeared. Hannah frowned. It was a photo of Springbank Meadow, a field below the wood. In the spring and summer, it was a mass of wild flowers. But this picture had clearly been taken in midwinter, and the field looked like a sea of mud.

"As you can see," he said, "the land is of poor quality and unproductive."

He clicked to another picture, this time of Bracken Field, again bare and muddy.

"That's so unfair," Hannah hissed to Lottie. "If they showed those fields in summer they'd be completely different."

The next was of Stream Field in the same state.

"The site," he said, "is currently unattractive..."

Hannah gasped in indignation.

"...as can be seen here."

Up flashed a slide showing the heap of junk behind the old cow stalls, a rusting mess of tangled barbed wire, old plastic containers and scrap metal.

Hannah seethed with rage. How dare he just show the mud and the mess? All farms had mess. All farms were muddy in winter. What about the hedgerows full of blossom, the sheep with their lambs, the kingfishers by the stream?

The next slide showed an area of ground covered with ash and blackened steel struts. It was the remains of the burned-out barn.

"The buildings are neglected," he said, "and the house is practically uninhabitable."

Up flashed a series of pictures of the farmhouse: close-ups of the exterior, showing peeling paint, loose guttering and crumbling mortar.

Uninhabitable? How *dare* he?

Hannah glanced at Dad's profile. His cheeks were red and his eyes were creased in a deep frown.

The next photograph showed the muddiest gateway on the farm, the one where half a gate hung jagged off its hinges and the ground was completely churned up by animals' hooves.

"As can be seen," Nick Constable drawled, "what we have here is poor-quality, poorly maintained agricultural land…"

Poorly maintained! Hannah thought of how hard her dad worked every day of his life to look after his farm and she wanted to punch Nick Constable very hard where it would hurt him most.

"…but which, being a heavy, clay-based soil, is ideal for water storage."

Ideal for water storage? Hannah felt sick.

"In conclusion," he said, "the site has been

carefully chosen to have minimum impact on the environment and the local population."

Hannah wanted to scream at him. Minimum impact! What right did he have to stand up there and say things like that?

But a part of her, a part she didn't want to listen to, knew there was some truth in his words. It wouldn't really affect anyone except them, would it? She could see why, in many people's eyes, it would be an ideal site for a reservoir.

"We are, of course, still at the beginning of the process," continued Nick Constable. "The surveys which we are undertaking may well identify further social and environmental benefits which a new reservoir scheme could deliver."

Dad snorted. "Environmental benefits, my foot," he muttered.

Up flashed the opening picture again, the one of the tranquil sunny lake surrounded by happy couples and frolicking water sports enthusiasts. Nick Constable left it on the screen while he turned to the eight people in the audience.

"And now," he said, "I shall be delighted to answer any questions you may have."

Jonah's dad raised his hand.

"What I want to know," he said, "is what opportunities there are going to be for local people to get involved in this reservoir project. Are there going to be jobs?"

Nick Constable smiled. "That's an excellent question. Thank you, sir. And yes, I'm happy to say that there will be many jobs created in the construction of the reservoir. It's a multimillion-pound project and will provide considerable employment opportunities."

"In the short term, maybe," Dad called out, making Hannah jump. "But those jobs won't be there any more once the reservoir's built."

"I would appreciate it," said Nick Constable, "if anybody wishing to comment could raise their hand." He turned back to Jonah's dad. "And, of course, the leisure facilities that the reservoir provides will also create long-term employment opportunities, providing a real economic boost to the local area."

The fuzzy-haired lady raised her hand.

"The land that you want to destroy to build your reservoir is absolutely full of wildlife as well as being a productive working farm. There's no way a reservoir could possibly provide any 'environmental benefits' that outweigh what's already there."

Nick Constable smiled his fake smile again. "We are of course undertaking extensive surveys of flora and fauna at the site. To date, however, our findings have shown no wildlife of any significance."

"No wildlife?" whispered Lottie. "What about the birds?"

Hannah felt deflated. Maybe the birds that Lottie's dad raved so much about weren't so rare after all. Maybe every farm had the same sort of birds.

Dad stood up.

"Having spent all my life farming the land you're proposing to flood," he said, his voice tight with anger, "I'd be very interested to see these surveys."

Nick Constable smiled again. Hannah itched to smack his smooth, smug face.

"As our surveys are still ongoing," he said, "we are unable to make any results available to the general public as yet."

"I'm not talking about the general public," said Dad. "I'm talking about common courtesy. That land is my home and my livelihood. It was my parents' livelihood. It ought to be my children's livelihood."

Nick Constable's mouth was fixed in a thin smile. "As soon as the findings are properly analysed, they will of course be made available to all interested stakeholders. And we shall, of course, actively seek to maximise the opportunities that a reservoir presents to create wildlife habitats and enhance the biodiversity of the area."

Dad gave an incredulous snort. "Enhance the biodiversity of the area! You're talking rubbish and you know it."

Jonah's dad put up his hand. Dad sat down and folded his arms.

"Will there be fishing?" asked Jonah's dad.

Nick Constable's smile widened. "Absolutely. We are proposing to stock the reservoir with a large number of freshwater fish, thus providing an unrivalled environment for anglers."

The couple in the third row, who had been quiet so far, turned towards each other, and Hannah saw the interested looks on their faces.

"And windsurfing and sailing?" asked the youngish

man in the middle of the room.

"Indeed. Our past experience indicates that there is likely to be considerable support for the enhanced leisure opportunities that a reservoir can provide, not to mention the enormous benefit to the local economy in a rural area like this."

"*Leisure* opportunities?" said Dad, in a tone of utter disgust. "It's a working farm, not a leisure opportunity."

Hannah sat silent, buried in misery.

The old lady in the second row raised her hand.

"Yes?" said Nick Constable. His smile made Hannah want to knock his gleaming white teeth out.

"There's been a leaking mains pipe at the end of my road for more than three months now. Shouldn't you be fixing your leaks before you destroy a farm to build a reservoir?"

Nick Constable's reply was full of technical terms and figures and statistics. Hannah didn't listen. She couldn't get the picture out of her head of her farm buried underwater.

Dad stood up again.

"Are you going to show us the map you've drawn up showing exactly how much land you're planning to take for your reservoir?"

"We're still at a very early stage of our investigations," said Nick Constable smoothly. "As soon as we have any map, we will obviously make it available to all interested stakeholders, but, as yet, we don't have any detailed design or maps."

Hannah sprang to her feet. "Liar!" she shouted.

Nick Constable's smile disappeared.

"I beg your pardon?"

Every face had turned to Hannah.

"I know you have a map," she said, "because I've seen it."

The thin smile returned. He spoke as if he were talking to a five-year-old. "I don't think you have."

Hannah trembled with anger. "I live at Clayhill Farm and one of your survey people dropped some pieces of paper. I picked them up and they were maps showing the borders of the reservoir. So I know you have maps. You just don't want to show them to us."

He gave a fake laugh. "I think you must be mistaken. You've clearly misinterpreted something you saw."

"There was writing at the bottom," said Hannah. "It said, *Middleham Reservoir. Area to be flooded.*"

Everyone looked at Nick Constable. He gave a short laugh.

"I think you must have misread something and taken it quite out of context. Our surveyors may have made some tentative sketches, perhaps, but certainly nothing concrete. I don't think there's any need to waste more time over this."

But Hannah was beside herself now. How dare he belittle her and make her look stupid? She *knew* what she had seen.

"And it's not true that there's no significant wildlife at the farm," she cried. "There are some really rare birds. My friend's dad's seen them. What are you going to do about that?"

He smiled indulgently. "Your friend's father has seen rare birds?" he repeated in a mocking tone. "Well, how can our expert surveys possibly compete with that sort of evidence?"

Lottie jumped up. "There *are* rare birds. My dad's been surveying them for years. And he's not just some random amateur; he's a member of the British Ornithological Society."

"Well," said Nick Constable, looking as though he was enjoying himself now, "how selfish of us to disturb the birds by trying to ensure that the people of Sussex have an adequate supply of running water to their houses." He paused, putting on a thoughtful look. "I wonder what we should do about those birds. If only they could fly. Then they would be able to find other places to live." He smiled broadly at the audience, and this time his smile seemed thoroughly genuine. "Wouldn't it be nice, ladies and gentlemen, if birds could fly?"

There was a ripple of laughter. Nick Constable looked extremely pleased with himself.

"If there are no more questions, I think we'll draw things to a close. Thank you all very much for coming. I hope you've found the evening interesting and informative."

* * *

Hannah tried to read Dad's face as they walked to the car. What was he feeling?

"Were you upset?" she asked eventually.

"Upset? What do you mean?"

"By all those horrible things he said about the farm, of course." She couldn't bear to repeat the actual words, but they were burned on her brain. *Poor quality … poorly maintained … unattractive … uninhabitable.*

Dad gave a contemptuous snort. "Oh, that's just the way these people behave."

"But what if everyone believes them?"

"Well, that's why we're getting all this evidence together. Bats and birds and the like."

"But they'll just say their surveys are right and yours are wrong, won't they?"

Dad stopped. "Blast, I left my jacket in there. You get in the car. I won't be a second."

He headed back to the hall and the girls got into the car.

Footsteps sounded on the tarmac. The locks on a nearby car clicked open and the lights flashed. They heard Nick Constable's voice, speaking into a mobile phone.

"Oh yes, very straightforward," he was saying. "Just a few locals with nothing better to do. Absolutely nothing to worry about. Like I said, it's the perfect site. And with the landlord in favour, too…"

There was a pause while he listened to the person on the other end of the phone. He laughed.

"Yes, old Farmer Giles was there. Brought his kids along, would you believe? Oh, he wittered on a bit, but he's got enough to do holding that mess of a farm together. He's not going to have the energy to put up a fight."

Hannah stared at Lottie, fury bubbling up inside her. Lottie sat motionless, listening.

The person on the other end of the phone was speaking again. Nick Constable laughed. "It'll be a piece of cake, this one. Easiest reservoir deal I've ever made."

He opened his car door, the phone still held to his ear. But as he was about to get in, Hannah sprang out of the car and marched over to face him. He looked briefly startled, but he quickly rearranged his features.

"We heard every word you just said," said Hannah, her voice unsteady with anger. "You think you know everything, don't you? But you don't know us. We're not some stupid country bumpkins you can trample all over. We're going to fight you every step of the way. You'll see. You're not going to win this one."

"I'll call you later," said Nick Constable into his phone. He removed it from his ear and put it in his pocket.

"Did you hear what I said?" asked Hannah. "You won't win."

The patronising smile was back on his face. "You were at that meeting. You saw as well as I did what the situation is. So I think you'll find that we've already won. Now, if you'll excuse me, I'm going home."

He slid into the driver's seat and pulled the door shut. The engine started up.

Hannah marched back to Dad's car, tingling with adrenalin. Lottie was standing by the car door, staring at her.

"No one's going to fight it, huh?" said Hannah. "That's what *he* thinks."

Lottie paused. Then she said, "Well, who is, though, really? I mean, he's kind of right, isn't he? Look at that meeting tonight. It doesn't seem like many people care."

"Well, I care. They think they can lie to us and do whatever they want and no one's going to have the guts to stand up to them. We can't let them get away with it."

"How can you stop them, though?"

"I don't know. But you saw what he was doing tonight. The water company's only telling one side of the story. I'm going to have to tell the other side. Because nobody else is telling it."

"What about your dad? He's protesting against it."

Hannah made an impatient gesture. "He's written a few letters and he's asking people to do surveys, but Aqua don't care about that, do they? No, I'm going to have to think of another way."

Lottie looked at the ground. She thinks I'm mad, thought Hannah. She thinks it's pointless. And maybe it is. But I can't just sit around doing nothing while Aqua destroys the farm.

Lottie raised her head. "I'll help you."

Hannah stared at her. "Really?"

"Don't sound so surprised. Of course I will."

Hannah threw her arms around Lottie and hugged her tight. "You're such a good friend."

"But what can we do?" asked Lottie, when Hannah let her go.

"I don't know yet," said Hannah. "But we have to stop them somehow. Because if we don't…"

She couldn't finish that sentence. The picture flashed into her mind, of her farm buried beneath a cold grey sheet of water. She forced it away. Into her head came something her granny had once said to her.

"We'll think of something," she said. "We'll find a way."

Chapter Thirteen

Rehearsing Miranda

From the centre of the school hall, Hannah cast a critical eye over the stage.

"Millie, could you take a step forward? Great. And, James, go down on one knee? Grace, move stage right of Harry. Perfect. And Miranda will stand there, when she turns up."

It was Wednesday lunchtime and the entire cast, except Miranda, was assembled on stage. They took up the whole space, in an arrangement carefully designed to look casual. Some people stood, some knelt. Some were in clusters, some in pairs, some on their own. All had their backs to the audience.

"Right," said Hannah. "Jack will play some Elizabethan music – where is Jack, by the way?"

She glanced over her shoulder in case he had shown up since she last checked.

He hadn't.

"Anyway, it's the start of the play, the curtains will be closed, you'll all come on stage and get into position exactly as you are now, backs to the audience, looking at the floor. Then the curtains will open, the lights will go up and, on Jack's sound cue, you turn to face the audience, raise your heads and start the Prologue in unison. As we haven't got the music, I'll count you in this time."

On the count of three, all twenty-five people turned to face the audience, raised their heads and began Shakespeare's Prologue to *Romeo and Juliet*.

"Two households, both alike in dignity,
In fair Verona, where we lay our scene,
From ancient grudge break to new mutiny,
Where—"

The rest of the line was drowned out by a burst of deafening rock music played through the speakers at top volume.

"Jack!" yelled Hannah.

Jack looked up from the sound system, turned the music down and raised his hand in greeting.

"Hey, Roberts. Was that the sort of thing you wanted?"

"Oh yes, it's perfect. It's only wrong by about four centuries, that's all."

Jack shrugged. "Oh well, if you're going to be that fussy..."

"Have you actually found any Elizabethan music?"

"Not exactly. I thought this might liven things up a bit."

Hannah could feel Lottie's I-told-you-so look burning into the back of her head. Blast Jack. Why did he always have to prove Lottie right?

"Jack, we don't have much time. Are you going

to do the music properly or should we ask someone else?"

"All right, chill out, I'll find you some boring stuff."

"Do you have the projections of Verona for the back wall, at least?"

"Ah, yes," he said, opening his laptop. "Give us a minute. You carry on, don't mind me."

Hannah turned back to the actors, hoping she didn't look as flustered as she felt. "Right. From the top."

Everyone turned to face the back wall again.

"On the count of three," said Hannah. "One, two…"

A huge projection flashed up on the back wall of the stage. Everyone burst out laughing. Lottie leaped from the stage and hurtled to the back of the hall.

"You *idiot*! Turn that off right now!"

A home video of an infant-school nativity play was playing on the screen. A round-faced, gap-toothed Lottie, dressed as Mary, dangled the baby Jesus upside down by one leg while lisping "Away in a Manger".

"Oops, sorry," said Jack, grinning. "I must have accidentally opened the wrong file." He stopped the film.

"You idiot," spat Lottie. "Where did you get that?"

Right behind Lottie, the hall doors opened and Miss Summers appeared. "Is everything all right in here?"

With a huge effort, Hannah smiled brightly. "Yes, fine, thank you. We're just rehearsing the Prologue."

"Oh, lovely. I'll sit and watch for a minute, if I may."

Miss Summers settled herself on a chair at the side of the hall. With a warning look at Jack, Hannah turned back to the stage. "OK, I'll count you in."

Bang on cue, the actors spun round to face the audience and began the Prologue in perfect unison. Hannah felt a surge of gratitude towards them. At least the cast could be trusted.

The doors beside the stage opened and Miranda sauntered in.

"Where have you been?" muttered Hannah, as she approached. "You're twenty minutes late."

Miranda widened her eyes. "Am I? Aren't you rehearsing the Chorus parts first?"

"But you're in the Chorus. Everybody is."

Miranda puckered up her mouth. "Hmm. I'm not sure that's a good idea. I think, as Juliet, I need to make a proper entrance."

"Oh, do you?"

"Yes, I do. I've discussed it with my parents and they think so, too."

The Prologue finished. Miss Summers clapped as she walked towards the stage. "Well done, everyone, that's going to be a really effective start to the play. And the fight scenes are shaping up beautifully. I was very impressed with what I saw yesterday."

"Thank you," said Hannah. "We're going to do Juliet's potion scene now. In Room 2, because

Kipling need the stage."

"I'll leave you to it," said Miss Summers. "I'm going to see how Conan Doyle are getting on. Well done again, all of you. I'm really looking forward to your production."

"Thank you so much, everyone," said Hannah. "That was great."

As the cast left the stage, Miranda cocked her head to one side and gave Hannah a sympathetic look.

"It must be so hard for you, Hannah, doing this."

"Why?"

"Well, you know, trying to organise a big cast and direct experienced actors like me. I mean, I know you've done a play in your little shed, but never a real production with an actual audience, have you?"

"Oh, that's not quite fair," said Jack, strolling to the front of the hall, his laptop under one arm. "I heard there were three pigs and a cow at their last show. I mean, granted, the pigs did get bored and leave in the interval, and the cow demanded its money back, but still..."

Hannah laughed. Miranda looked disconcerted for a moment. Then she said, "Oh, by the way, Hannah, I've got some really exciting news!"

"What?" asked Hannah, hoisting her school bag on to her shoulder and tucking her purple ring binder under her other arm.

"So," said Miranda, as they walked into Room 2, "my mum's friend runs a costume hire company and she's offered to lend us all the costumes for *Romeo and Juliet*! Isn't that amazing?"

Hannah felt herself tensing up all over.

"Lottie's doing our costumes, you know that."

"Oh, don't worry. My parents will pay for the hire. You won't have to fund it from that pathetic fifty pounds the school gave you."

The classroom door opened and Jade and Martha walked in. Oh, great, thought Hannah. It would have to be them, wouldn't it?

"Sorry, you two," she said. "I know this is your form room, but it's booked for our rehearsal this lunchtime."

"All right, keep your knickers on," said Martha. "I just need to get my hockey kit from my locker. If that's OK with you?"

Hannah sighed. "Fine. Right, Miranda, let's do the potion scene. From when the nurse leaves and you're alone on stage."

"Now, where's my locker key, I wonder?" said Martha.

With infinite slowness, she settled herself on a chair, put her bag on the table and, at the pace of an ancient snail, inched open the zip.

"The point is," said Miranda, "we can get proper professional costumes. Like Kipling will have. You know Zara's mum's designing theirs, and she's a professional designer."

"The point is," said Hannah, "that we've got Lottie making our costumes, and she's amazing and she's in our house. I don't care what Kipling are doing. Anyway, Miss Summers said we'd get credit for doing things ourselves, remember, so it might actually help us win."

"No, it's not in that pocket," said Martha. "Where did I put it, then? Maybe in this pocket? Hmm, let's see."

"Don't you think it's a bit selfish of you to expect Charlotte to make all the costumes herself?" said Miranda. "Think of the trouble you'd save her if you hired them."

"It might be hard for you to understand, Miranda, but Lottie actually *wants* to make the costumes. She's done all the designs and they're amazing."

Miranda sniffed. "Anyone can *draw* a costume. The point is, can she actually *make* what she's drawn, or are we all going to be laughing stocks? I mean, we saw what you turned up in for your audition."

Hannah felt her cheeks heating up. "That was a beautiful costume. It wasn't Lottie's fault it got covered in oil and piglet wee."

Miranda curled her upper lip. "Priya said Charlotte goes to *jumble sales* to get the fabric for her costumes. If you really think we're going to win with *jumble sale* clothes…" She shuddered.

"Our costumes are going to be awesome," said Martha. "The designs are so cool. Did you know Zara's mum's an actual designer?"

"Are you still here?" snapped Hannah. "You could have sewn yourself a hockey kit by now."

"Hi." Lottie was standing in the doorway, a long white floaty dress draped over one arm. "I thought you might like to have the costume for this scene, Miranda. To help you get into character."

Miranda recoiled. "Is that the dress Hannah wore for her audition? The one that disgusting pig…" She wrinkled up her nose as if she couldn't even say the words.

"Yep," said Lottie. "The very same. I haven't even washed it. Have a sniff. Mmm."

She thrust the costume at Miranda's nose. Miranda shrieked and jumped backwards.

"Oh, don't be so ridiculous," said Lottie. "I've made this especially for you."

Miranda gave her a suspicious look. She took the nightdress between her fingertips and held it up at arm's length. She wrinkled her nose.

"It's very shapeless, isn't it? But I suppose a shapeless dress is easier to make."

"I can make clothes any shape I like," snapped Lottie. "This is a nightdress, that's why it's this shape."

Miranda rubbed the fabric between her thumb and forefinger. She made a disgusted face. "I can't wear this. It's synthetic. It's probably a fire risk."

"Nobody will be able to tell what fabric it's made from when you're up on stage," said Hannah.

"Anyway, I'm allergic to synthetic fibres."

"No, you're not."

"And white's not a good colour on me. I have to be very careful what I wear, with my hair and complexion, you see. White washes me out."

"The whiter the better, then," muttered Lottie.

"What did you say?"

"I said, wear the costume someone's made for you

and be grateful."

"Oh, I didn't mean to be ungrateful. It's very kind of you, of course. But I don't want you to have to go to any more trouble for me."

"It wouldn't be any trouble," said Lottie, "if you didn't make it trouble."

"Anyway, my mum's friend has a costume that's perfect for Juliet. Well, five, actually. One for each of Juliet's scenes. So it's really nice of you to go to all that trouble, Charlotte, but I won't be needing you to make my costumes."

Lottie's eyes were very dark. "You can't just wear whatever you want, Miranda. It's a play, not a fancy dress party."

Miranda smiled a patronising smile. "I can see how you'd worry about professional costumes showing up your work, Charlotte, but think how much it will help you. If you don't have to spend time on my costume, you'll have more time to work on everyone else's."

"I'm not worried about the time. Or about anything showing up my work. I'm worried about these costumes you're bringing in having a completely different look from the rest of the costumes."

"We're so lucky, aren't we, Jade," said Martha, "having a proper designer doing all our costumes."

"And a proper choreographer," said Jade.

"What?" said Miranda.

"Jade! That's a secret!" hissed Martha.

Jade clapped a hand to her mouth. "Oops. Sorry."

"What do you mean, a proper choreographer?" asked Miranda.

"Oh, nothing," said Martha. "It's just a friend of Zara's mum's who's helping a bit with the spirits' movements. Come on, Jade." She stuffed her kit into her bag and dragged Jade out of the door.

Miranda rounded on Hannah.

"You see? They're having all this professional help and we're getting nothing! They're going to win and it will all be your fault. Well, I'm not wearing her costumes, even if everyone else is. I've got proper costumes and I'm going to wear them."

"You—" began Lottie. But Hannah put a hand on her arm.

"Fine. Bring in your costumes and let Lottie see them. Then we'll decide."

Lottie gaped at Hannah, her eyes flashing with fury.

Miranda smiled at Lottie. "You'll love them. They're fabulous."

Just humour her, Hannah mouthed to Lottie.

Miranda's eyes lit on a sheet of paper in Hannah's open ring binder. "So you're writing letters to the newspapers about this reservoir, are you?"

Hannah slammed the ring binder shut. "That's none of your business."

"You know it's a complete waste of time, trying to fight the reservoir plans, don't you? My dad says it's a done deal. They pretend to consult the public and listen to objections, but really it's all decided already. My dad says these big companies do exactly what they want. They just bribe the government if they have to."

"Oh, that's a great attitude," said Lottie. "So we should all just sit around letting terrible things happen and not even try to stop them?"

"Just get on with your life, that's what I'm saying, instead of wasting time on pointless protests."

"But this *is* my life," said Hannah. "It's my farm that's going to be flooded, isn't it?"

"Exactly."

"What do you mean by that?"

"Well, this is all just selfish, really, isn't it? You wouldn't care about the reservoir if it was on someone else's farm."

Hannah could think of no answer to this. She was sure in her heart that it would be wrong to flood Clayhill, even if it wasn't her farm, but she knew she wouldn't be able to convey what she wanted to say to Miranda.

Miranda gave her a triumphant glance. "Anyway," she said, "I thought we were supposed to be having a rehearsal. Are we going to do this scene, or not?"

Chapter Fourteen

An Equivalent Farm

As she walked into the farmyard with Lottie on Friday afternoon, Hannah saw their land agent's shiny black BMW parked in front of the tractor shed. She felt a sudden, sickening jolt in her stomach. A visit from the land agent was never a good thing.

"Why's he here? The rent's all paid until December. I checked with Dad."

Lottie pointed towards the pigsties. "Listen."

At first, all Hannah could hear were the grunts and snuffles of contented pigs. Gradually, though, she started to make out the sound of men's voices.

"Maybe it's about the reservoir," said Lottie.

Hannah took a deep breath and clenched her fists. "Come on. Let's find out."

Between the yard and the pigsties was a straw-strewn path, bordered by the pig shed on the right and a thick blackthorn hedge on the left. Dad stood at the end of the path, his back to the girls, beside a wheelbarrow heaped with ripe-smelling dung. Two men were with him, also facing away from the girls. On Dad's left stood the landlord's agent. Hannah recognised his slicked-back dark hair and his stocky

136

figure in the black suit he always wore. A taller man in a grey suit stood to Dad's right.

"In here," whispered Hannah, ducking through a gap in the blackthorn hedge.

Lottie looked horrified. "No way!" she whispered. "My clothes will get torn to pieces."

"There's a really wide tunnel inside," whispered Hannah. "I'll hold these branches."

Very cautiously, Lottie squeezed in through the gap Hannah had made. They crouched in the hollow hedge.

The agent held out a fat brown envelope to Dad. Dad made no move to take it.

"We sent the compensation package a fortnight ago," said the agent, in his grating voice, "but since we've had no reply, I thought I'd bring you a copy, in case you hadn't received it."

"Oh, I received it all right."

"Well then, you'll have seen that we're making you a very generous offer. You'd be a fool to turn it down."

"A generous offer?" Dad gave a bitter laugh. "It's all about money with you, isn't it? I'm not interested in your compensation package. I care about this farm and I'll see it destroyed over my dead body."

"Well, let's hope it doesn't come to that, eh?" said the agent.

Hannah gasped. Lottie was open-mouthed with outrage.

The other man shifted so the girls could see his face. Hannah drew in her breath.

"It's him!" she whispered. "The Aqua man! Nick Constable."

"As you know, Mr Roberts," said Nick Constable in his oily voice, "this is Aqua's preferred site. And the fact is that the wildlife findings at Clayhill have been much lower than at the other potential sites we've surveyed."

"Oh, have they?" said Dad. "That's very convenient for you, isn't it? And can you show me these wildlife surveys?"

"I'm afraid not," said Nick Constable, in a voice even smoother than before. "The raw data is still being analysed and the results are not publicly available yet."

"No, of course they're not."

Hannah, squatting on the balls of her feet, leaned a bit too far forward and grabbed at a branch to keep her balance. The branch snapped and Hannah tumbled forwards. A shower of broken twigs and dead leaves fell all around her.

"Have you got rats?" asked the agent, frowning at the hedge. "I hope you're taking appropriate measures to keep the rodents down."

"There's only two rodents I can see right now," said Dad, "and I'll be taking appropriate measures to get rid of them, don't you worry."

Lottie almost let out a snort of laughter. She clapped her hand over her mouth.

"The important thing," said Nick Constable, his voice positively creamy with concern, "is to come to a genuinely positive solution for everyone concerned."

"You mean a positive solution for you."

Nick Constable gave Dad a patronising smile that made Hannah want to throttle him.

"I can see how difficult this is for you, Mr Roberts. I understand that you're attached to this place."

Dad snorted. Nick Constable moved smoothly on. "So we're trying to make sure that you and your family are properly looked after. The compensation package we're offering is above and beyond what we're legally obliged to do. I'm sure you'd like to have something to pass on to your children, wouldn't you?"

In an unsteady tone, which didn't sound at all like Dad's usual voice, he replied, "I'd like to pass this farm on to them."

The agent gave a short bark of a laugh. "I'm sure you would, but we're dealing with reality here. You know perfectly well what the situation is."

"What situation's that?" asked Dad, and his voice was harsh now.

The agent made an impatient noise. "Because of your late rent payments, Mr Roberts, you're now on a short-term farm business tenancy, as you know. That's not something you can pass on to your children. So there's no guaranteed future for your family here, whatever you might like to think."

Hannah felt cold inside. She hadn't known that. She stared at Lottie. Lottie reached for her hand and squeezed it.

Nick Constable spoke again, in a tone that was clearly trying to be gentle and understanding. "The thing is, Mr Roberts, people need water. That has to be our priority. And there's a limited number of places we can put a reservoir. I mean, you wouldn't want us to destroy a whole village, would you?"

"Of course I wouldn't. That's not the—"

"So I'm sure you can see, if you can manage to put your own feelings aside, that this place is ideal."

"I've told you once and I'll tell you again," said Dad, "this farm will be flooded over my dead body."

Nick Constable's voice was like clotted cream.

"Mr Roberts," he said, "we have to face facts. This area desperately needs another reservoir. More houses are being built every year and people use a lot more water than they used to. They want power showers, sprinklers, jet washers, all those things. And as your water company, we have a statutory duty to provide that water. We're responsible for more than six hundred thousand households, not just your family. Those are the hard facts. As a reservoir location, this place has everything going for it. It *will* happen. Clayhill *will* be flooded. And what we now need to focus on is securing the best possible outcome for you and your family."

Paws skittered on the path and a blur of wet fur and waving tails shot past the hedge. Tess and Rags had clearly been swimming. Mud and pondweed clung to their saturated coats.

Nick Constable indicated the thick brown envelope in the agent's hand. "I'd think very carefully before you reject this, if I were you."

Rags skidded to a halt in front of the men and

shook herself vigorously, sending pond water spraying in all directions. Tess bounded up to the agent and planted her filthy front paws squarely on his chest.

The agent yelped and stepped backwards. "Call your dogs off me!"

"Rags, Tess, sit down," called Dad, but he didn't seem to be trying very hard.

Tess gave the agent's hand an affectionate lick. He made a disgusted noise and looked around in vain for something to wipe it on. Rags nibbled at the bottom of his trouser leg.

"Will you get your dogs under control!" he yelled.

"Rags, Tess," called Dad again, and this time the dogs knew he meant business. They sat down beside him. He ruffled the backs of their heads. "Good girls," he murmured.

The agent swiped at his suit with his hands.

"Sooner this place is underwater the better," he muttered.

Dad whipped his head up.

"Give me that envelope." His voice was harsh.

The agent smiled. "I knew you'd see sense."

He handed the envelope, now soggy and mud-spattered, to Dad.

Looking him hard in the eye, Dad ripped the envelope in half.

"What the heck are you doing?" spluttered the agent.

Dad tore each half of the compensation package in half again. He screwed the sodden pieces into a ball and tossed it on the dung lump. Then he pushed his wheelbarrow right between the two men, forcing them to jump aside, and emptied the barrow full of manure on top of the ball of screwed-up paper. He righted the barrow and faced the men.

"I won't have anything to do with your weaselly compensation package," he said. "If this farm drowns, I'll drown with it. Now, get out."

There was a pause before Nick Constable said, "You might want to rethink your attitude before it's too late, Mr Roberts. I don't think you'll have many allies. From past experience, I can tell you that I think you'll find the village will be very supportive of Aqua's plans."

Dad's voice had a hard edge to it. "You think so, do you?"

"What the reservoir project will achieve, you see," said the agent, "is to transform this place from a third-rate farm into a first-rate leisure facility."

Hannah gasped. Powered by the force of her fury, she burst from the hedge, scattering twigs and leaves all around her, and ran to Dad's side.

"How dare you?" she said to the startled agent. "How dare you call this place a third-rate farm? This is a first-rate farm and we're not going to let you destroy it."

"And there's loads of wildlife here," said Lottie, emerging from the hedge. "We know that and we can prove it."

Nick Constable's mouth was hanging open. The agent stared into the blackthorn, as if to see how many more children were hiding there.

"You're all a bunch of thieves and liars," said Hannah. "But you can't steal from us and lie to us and get away with it. You'll see."

They turned and marched down the path, leaving all three men staring, speechless and motionless, after them.

Hannah was shaking as they strode to the house.

"How dare they come up here and say that stuff to Dad? Third-rate farm? How *dare* they?"

"We should make leaflets," said Lottie. "Post them through everyone's doors. Tell the whole village what liars they are."

Hannah slowed down. "Yes, that would be good. But we need more evidence. All we've got is your dad's bird lists and my word against theirs about the map. It's not enough. We need evidence that this isn't the right place to build a reservoir – that it would actually be wrong to flood this land. Otherwise people like Miranda can just say we're being selfish." She opened the back door and threw her school bag on the freezer. "I printed out a newspaper article I found on the Internet. About whether we actually need reservoirs at all. I'll read it tonight."

In the kitchen, the Beans were spreadeagled on the tiles, drawing comic strips.

"What we really need," said Lottie, stepping over Jo, "is more evidence that there's loads of wildlife here. To prove their surveys are wrong."

Hannah was rummaging for biscuits in the cupboard. "It's pretty suspicious that they're not showing anyone their survey results, isn't it?"

"Totally," said Lottie. "My dad's seen over a hundred species of birds on this farm. And that's because your dad hasn't killed the soil with chemicals and he's left all the old hedges and trees. Dad says it's a perfect habitat. And if it's a perfect habitat for birds, it must be the same for other wildlife. Some of the birds that live here are globally threatened, Dad told me."

"Globally threatened?"

"Yes. They're on the international red list. Red for danger. So they're really rare."

"Like the bats," said Jo.

"What about the bats?" asked Hannah.

Jo picked up a green pencil. "Sophie thinks there might be really rare bats living here."

"Really? How do you know?"

"She told us. Because we're professional batologists. That's why she's doing this survey tonight. She said it's an incredible habitat. It's because of all the old oaks and hedgerows. What did she say the hedgerows were, Bean? Wildlife something."

"Wildlife corridors," said Sam, who was colouring a kidney bean with a purple felt-tip.

"Yes, wildlife corridors. Animals use the hedgerows to travel from the Downs through the fields into the wood. The hedgerows protect them from predators, you see. If the hedges were destroyed then the bats wouldn't be able to roam. And they need to roam to hunt for food."

"But Aqua said their surveys didn't find any rare

wildlife," said Hannah.

"Probably looking in the wrong place," said Sam. "Like the archaeologists."

"Those archaeologists are so stupid," said Jo. "We keep telling them they should be digging in South Meadow. But they're just digging by the wood."

"Oh, and you would know," said Lottie, "because you two are professional archaeologists, right?"

Jo gave Lottie one of her hard stares. "That's right."

Lottie laughed. But Hannah was frowning.

"What?" asked Lottie. "What are you thinking?"

Hannah said nothing for a minute. Then, still frowning, she looked at Lottie.

"What if," she said slowly, "the surveyors are looking in the wrong places on *purpose*?"

Lottie's eyes widened. "You mean, because they don't actually *want* to find anything."

"Exactly. Because if they *did* find rare birds or bats, they might not be allowed to flood the farm. So they're *deliberately* not finding stuff."

"Do you really think they'd do that?"

"Of course they would. We know they've lied about the map, don't we? It's exactly what they'd do."

"But even if they are, how could we prove it?"

"We have to get evidence. We know some stuff already. All your dad's bird surveys are written down. And Sophie's doing a bat survey tonight. That's the kind of evidence we need. So that people know what's really here. Not just – what did Nick

Constable call it? – an unattractive, poor-quality, poorly maintained farm. Horrible man."

"Is that what he said?" asked Sam.

"Oh, don't be upset, Sammy. He's just a nasty liar."

"Sounds like he was talking about himself," said Jo. "He looked very unattractive and poor-quality to me."

"Exactly," said Hannah. "And what we need now is the evidence to prove it."

Chapter Fifteen

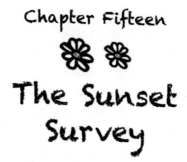

The Sunset Survey

As Hannah said goodbye to Lottie in the yard after tea, a little red hatchback came bumping down the track. Hannah remembered Sophie's last visit and guilt washed over her.

The Beans tumbled into the yard, both talking at once.

"Where's your equipment?" asked Jo as Sophie opened the car door.

"Are you going to be staying all night?" asked Sam. "Can we stay up with you?"

"Hello, everyone," said Sophie, smiling as she got out of the car. "Well, not *all* night. I'm going to do a sunset-emergence survey of the colony – that's to count the bats leaving the attic – and then I'll be going home for some sleep, but I'll be back before dawn to do a sunrise-re-entry survey."

Now that Hannah knew Sophie wasn't a potential stepmother, she thought what a nice face she had. Sophie smiled at her and she felt even more guilty.

"So you're not staying all night?" asked Sam, clearly disappointed.

"No. Sorry. But I do have some very cool equipment."

She opened the boot and took out a large plastic box. "Come into the garden and I'll show you everything." She looked them up and down. "First, though, we're going to be in the garden for a good couple of hours, so you'll need to wear warm clothes. As soon as the sun goes down, it'll get pretty nippy."

"I'd better get home," said Lottie. "I'd love to help, but my mum's expecting me. I really hope you find rare bats."

Hannah gave Lottie a meaningful look. She knew the real reason Lottie was leaving. Lottie wasn't at all keen on flying mammals.

"Right, let's get set up," said Sophie. "We need to start fifteen minutes before sunset."

Martha was sitting at the kitchen table, reading a magazine.

"Do you want to do the bat survey, Martha?" asked Sam. "We're going to count the bats flying out of the attic."

Martha looked at Sam as though he'd just invited her to feast on tarantulas.

"Are you *mad*? Bats are evil."

"Bats are amazing," said Jo. "I've been reading about them. Their wings are actually hands they've adapted for flying, so they're really flexible."

"Really?" said Hannah.

"Yep. They're even better at flying than birds."

Martha shuddered. "Hands turned into wings? That's like a horror film."

148

"So cool," said Sam. "If I could choose a superpower, it would definitely be flying."

"Bats are gross. They're just flying mice."

"Actually," said Jo, "they're more closely related to humans than to mice."

Martha snorted. "To you, maybe. Not to me."

"And they can live up to thirty years," said Jo. "Mice only live about two years."

"Thirty-year-old bats?" shrieked Martha. "That is *so* disgusting." She shuddered. "Imagine a thirty-year-old bat tangled in your hair."

"There's no way a bat would get tangled in your hair," said Jo. "If they can sense a teeny-tiny insect in pitch darkness, they're hardly going to miss your massive head, are they?"

"Whatever," said Martha, turning back to the problem page. "Have fun with the rodents, weirdos."

"Shall I catch one for you?" asked Jo. "A long-eared one. It would be such a cute pet."

"Get lost," said Martha, head down in her magazine.

The others went outside. Dad was standing by the garden gate talking to Sophie.

"Are you going to be helping with the bat survey, too?" asked Sam.

"I certainly am," said Dad. "Should be very interesting."

Sophie smiled round at them all. "So, what I propose is that we split into two groups and stand at opposite corners of the house. That way, we should be able to see most of the bats flying out. But don't worry if you can't count every one. I'll be doing several more surveys. This is just to give us an idea of how many bats roost here."

She crouched down and opened her box. The Beans peered in. Sophie took out a pair of headphones plugged into something that looked like a TV remote control. She gave it to Jo.

"That's for you two." She handed a clipboard to Sam. "You can take turns with the bat detector and the clipboard."

Jo looked at the black object in her hand. "Is this really a bat detector? How does it work? Has it got a camera?"

"I'll show you how to use it. I've got one for your dad and Hannah to share, too. But actually your most important piece of equipment is the clipboard." She handed one to Hannah. "I'd like you to make a note of the time you see the first bat, and then record, using a tally chart, how many bats you see. Arthur, if you and Hannah could station yourselves at the opposite corner of the house, we'll cover this side. Oh, one more thing."

She handed Hannah and Jo a sheet of paper each. It had six different silhouettes of bats on it, with information about their flight patterns. "That might help you identify the species. Write it down if you think you know what species it is, but don't worry too much about it. It's the kind of thing that takes practice. Same with interpreting the calls on the bat detector. But it's fun to have a go."

The bat detectors had two dials on the front. Sophie explained that one was a volume dial and one was a frequency dial.

"It's actually a myth that bats are blind. They can see nearly as well as we can. But because they fly and hunt for insects in the dark, they use a high-frequency system called echolocation. They make calls as they fly and they listen to the returning echoes to build up a sound map of their surroundings. The bat can tell how far away something is by how long it takes for the sound to return to it."

"That's so clever," said Jo.

"We can't normally hear their calls because they're too high for the human ear. But the bat detector catches them and translates them instantly to a frequency we can hear."

"So we'll be able to hear the bat calls live?" asked Hannah.

"That's right. And the bat detector also records the calls, which can be very useful. This one can pick up most bats within about ten metres. Now, different species of bat echolocate at different frequencies, but to make it simple, I've tuned your detectors to the frequency at which you can hear the most common bat, the pipistrelle. Its echolocation call is a kind of snapping sound."

She looked at the pink-tinged sky. "OK, sunset's in about fifteen minutes. This is a waiting game, I'm afraid. We may not see any bats until half an hour after sunset, but we want the survey to be as accurate as possible, so we need to be prepared."

"Do we have to be completely silent?" asked Hannah.

"You can talk quietly. Just no loud noises if possible. Good luck! We'll see you in a couple of hours."

Hannah and Dad made their way to the far corner of the house, by the orchard and the farmyard.

"Do you want the clipboard or the bat detector?" Hannah asked Dad.

"Whichever you like."

Curious to hear what a bat might sound like, Hannah took the detector and placed the headphones on her ears. But then she realised there was no need to put them on until the first bats emerged. She should take this opportunity to talk to Dad.

"Lottie and I were thinking," she began, "that maybe we could make leaflets about the wildlife on the farm and deliver them round the village. So people know what will be lost if they flood the farm. We don't trust Aqua's surveys, you see. We thought people should know what Lottie's dad's seen in his bird surveys. And put other things in, too, like the age of the trees, that sort of stuff."

He nodded. "Good idea. Once we've got these bat results."

"Do you know when that will be?"

He shook his head. "Sophie's putting a lot of survey equipment in the loft and in some of the oak trees. Depends how long it takes her to go through everything once she's got the recordings, I suppose."

He started rummaging in the inside pocket of his

jacket. "Right, better find a decent pen, if we're going to record these bats."

Hannah sighed. It looked as though the process of fighting Aqua's plans might take a very long time.

The last trace of the sun sank behind the hills. The sky was reddish pink above the blue-grey outline of the Downs. The landscape had flattened in the evening light, so that only the shape of things was left.

Hannah was starting to think that maybe they wouldn't see anything at all when Dad said softly, "There it is."

Hannah followed his gaze just in time to see the black silhouette of a bat flutter into the orchard. Dad looked at his watch and wrote on the clipboard, "First bat 7.36pm. Pipistrelle."

Hannah looked at him in surprise. "How can you tell?"

"Well, it's the right shape. And see the way it flies, with those downward swoops and turns. Now that one's come out, there'll be plenty more."

Hannah put the headphones on. A couple of minutes later, another black creature fluttered past them. Through her headphones, Hannah heard the most extraordinary series of loud popping noises. She turned to Dad, lit up with excitement. "I can hear it echolocating!" she whispered.

Dad looked just as excited as she felt. "Really?"

Hannah slipped the headphones off and handed him the bat detector, swapping it for the clipboard. Just as she took the clipboard, another bat flew past, and then, immediately after, another and another. She added the lines to the tally chart and then looked at Dad. His face as he listened through the headphones was lit up with excitement. He caught Hannah's eye and grinned like a little boy. "Incredible sounds they make," he murmured. "Completely different from birds. I've never heard anything like it."

Painted across the pale-blue sky were deep red-pink streaks and strips of watery grey clouds. As the bats continued to emerge, the red faded like a fire dying down to its last embers, leaving only the domed silhouettes of the oaks standing tall above the hedgerows. Birds chattered in the orchard. Rooks flew out of the wood. A dog barked. From the main road came the distant hum of traffic. And from under the overlapping roof tiles, bats continued to fly out of the attic.

Dad handed the headphones back to Hannah and she put them on. They were filled with popping, clicking, lip-smacking, tocking sounds, which meant nothing to her but were enabling the bats to navigate the world so accurately that they could hunt down and eat the tiniest insect on the wing. It was as though she had been handed a key to the world of night.

The sky was grey now. A full moon, huge and white, hung over the wood. The sky around it glowed silvery-gold. From close by came the screech of a little owl and, from further away, the *toowit-toowoo* of a tawny.

After two hours, just as Hannah's toes were beginning to freeze and she was desperately wishing she'd worn gloves, Sophie appeared around the corner of the house. She smiled at them.

"How long ago did you see your last bat?"

Hannah glanced at the clipboard. "About twenty minutes ago."

"Good," said Sophie. "Us, too. That's all of them, then."

"How many did you see?" asked Hannah.

"Shall we go into the kitchen and compare notes?"

Hannah imagined pulling off her boots and resting her feet on the warm Aga.

"Ooh, yes. I'll make hot chocolate. There might even be biscuits, if Martha hasn't eaten them all."

* * *

It was bliss to be sitting in the cosy kitchen, warming her hands around a mug of hot chocolate. The Beans were huddled over their tally chart.

"We saw thirty-seven bats," said Sam. "How many did you see?"

Hannah had already tallied her figures. "Twenty-nine." She looked at Sophie. "Is that good?"

Sophie smiled. "That's not just good, it's really impressive."

"Are any of them rare, though? Rare enough to stop the reservoir?"

"Sophie doesn't know yet," said Jo importantly.

"I was telling Jo and Sam," said Sophie, "that seventeen species of bat breed in this country. The six on the sheet I gave you are the most common. And from what I've seen I think you have all of them here."

"So which are the rare ones?"

"The rarest are the Bechstein's and the barbastelle. The Bechstein's is one of the rarest mammals in the country. And the barbastelle is exceptionally rare, too – there may be as few as five colonies in England."

"And do we have any of those?"

"Well, they both roost in trees, not houses. The barbastelle likes woods with meadows around it, and the Bechstein's particularly likes old oaks. So that's why I'm surveying the trees and woods as well as the house."

"And have you found any?" Honestly, thought Hannah, some people take forever to get to the point.

"Not yet. But they're both really tricky to detect with bat detectors. The Bechstein's echolocation calls are very quiet, and the barbastelle is easily missed, too, because its calls aren't very distinct and they're often masked by the louder and more repeated calls of other species. So you have to listen to your recordings really carefully."

Hannah remembered her conversation with Lottie earlier.

"So it would be easy for a survey to miss those bats?"

Sophie nodded. "Very easy."

"And if we had those species, would Aqua have to stop the reservoir?"

"Well, they might say they could minimise the impact on the bats. But in fact, that wouldn't be possible. The landscape you have here, with the buildings and old trees providing roosts, the woods and meadows providing foraging habitats and the hedgerows providing safe commuting habitats, is absolutely perfect for bats. It couldn't be better. And your father – " she smiled across the table at him – "is so careful, too, to maintain all the wildlife habitats and not poison the land with chemicals. That's so important. Do you know how many insects one bat can eat in a single night?"

"Fifty?" said Hannah.

"A thousand?" said Sam.

Jo made a face at him. "Don't be crazy. A hundred?"

"Actually," said Sophie, "Sam was the closest. Bats have huge appetites. The common pipistrelle can eat over three thousand tiny insects in one night."

They stared at her. "Three *thousand*?" said Jo.

"That's right. So the presence of bats is a sign of a healthy environment. Bats are often at the top of their food chain. If there are plenty of bats, then all the little creatures below them in the food chain, which are so important to the environment, must be alive and well, too."

"Not the ones that have been eaten by the bats," said Sam.

Sophie laughed. "Well, no. But there must be a thriving population."

"Can we do the sunrise survey with you, too?" asked Jo.

"That's up to your dad."

The Beans turned to Dad with pleading eyes. "Can we, Dad? *Please?*"

Dad narrowed his eyes at them. Then he looked at his watch.

"If you two scuttle up to bed right now and go straight to sleep, and if I don't hear a peep out of you when I come up to check, then yes, I'll wake you up in the morning for the sunrise survey."

"Yay!" they squealed. "Thank you, Dad. Thank you so much!"

"Oh, and by the way," Sophie said to Dad, "I've got the licence to do a catching survey."

The Beans stopped in the doorway and turned round enquiringly. Sophie smiled at them.

"That's one you can't help with, I'm afraid. It's very specialised. But it's the best way to find the really rare ones, if there are any."

Oh, let's hope there are, thought Hannah. Please, please let there be rare bats living at Clayhill.

Chapter Sixteen

Hannah Takes
a Stand

"Sam, this one's got a maggot in," said Hannah. "Do you really want maggot crumble for tea?"

She took the maggoty apple out of Mum's basket and threw it into the long grass. A stout little piglet trotted across and snaffled it up. Hannah was pretty sure it was the one who had ruined her audition, but it was so cute that it was impossible to bear a grudge.

It was Thursday afternoon, and a perfect autumn day. Granny had taught Hannah to make crumble last weekend, so she and the Beans were taking advantage of today's teachers' strike to pick the late apples in the orchard, before the cast of *Romeo and Juliet* arrived for an extra rehearsal.

Ten sleek piglets, pink with black splodges, rooted at the children's feet. Dad normally brought his sows indoors to give birth, but this one had farrowed early, so the piglets had been born in the field. The weather was warm and they were all healthy, so Dad had left them outdoors and they had the run of the farm. They spent their days trotting around the yard in a happy

159

gang, digging up grass with muddy snouts, their tails waving with pleasure and their floppy ears flapping.

Hannah reached for an apple on a high branch and another piglet started sniffing at her boots. Hannah shooed it away. As cute as the pigs were, she wasn't about to let them chew the purple DMs that were her pride and joy. Lottie had spotted them in a charity shop, Hannah's size and hardly worn, and had given them to Hannah for her birthday. They were, without a doubt, the best birthday present she had ever received.

Beyond the orchard, the thicket in North Meadow was full of birdsong. The leaves had fallen from the hawthorns, leaving dozens of nests exposed. Fieldfares and redwings feasted on the blood-red berries. Hawthorn berries are a rich source of antioxidants, Lottie's dad had told Hannah, which is why so many birds eat them.

A tractor rumbled up the track. It had some sort of mowing machine fixed to the back of it.

"That's not Daddy's tractor," said Sam.

The tractor turned into North Meadow and bumped down the field. It stopped in front of the thicket. The driver jumped out and started fiddling with the machine.

"That's not Adam," said Sam.

The driver climbed back into the cab, revved up the engine and turned the tractor round so the machine faced the thicket. Sam stood on the orchard railings to get a better look.

"It's a mulcher."

"A what?" asked Hannah.

Sam's reply was drowned out by a roar of machinery and a whir of blades.

"No!" Hannah screamed. "Stop!"

But the tractor reversed right into the thicket. Their thicket. The thicket where the Secret Hen House Theatre lay hidden from view.

Hannah stared, paralysed, as the mulcher crunched its way through the thicket, screeching and scraping, crushing and flattening every tree and bush in its path. Birds flapped and scattered in all directions. Rabbits and squirrels bolted from the undergrowth.

She watched in horror as the machine backed deeper and deeper into the bushes. Its shining metal teeth spun round and the mulcher ripped and roared as it sucked the hawthorns, the blackthorns, the willow and the brambles into its jaws.

When it reached the other side, the driver shifted gears and the tractor drove forwards over the flattened trees. As the mulcher moved back over them, it sucked the branches in, chewed them into tiny pieces and spat the dusty splinters into the air in a great brown spray.

Sawdust and leaves rained down on the children, into their eyes and noses and mouths. Hannah coughed and blinked and rubbed her eyes as the tractor emerged into the field again. It shifted its angle. It was pushing back into the thicket to mow down another line of trees.

"The theatre!" she screamed. "It's going to crush the theatre!"

Hannah raced to the orchard railings, scrambled over them and jumped down into North Meadow. Out of the corner of her eye, she saw Sam starting to climb the fence.

"No, Sam, get back!"

She ran through the pile of leaves and splinters that, one minute ago, had been trees and bushes and birds' nests. She had to stop the machine.

The tractor was reversing into the thicket again, the blades of the mulcher whirring round manically in a silver blur, crushing the trees with a jarring, scraping, screeching, roaring noise that drowned out every other sound in the world.

Hannah reached the driver's door and beat her fists on the glass. "Stop!" she shouted. "Stop!"

But the driver was facing the other way, looking out of the tractor's back windscreen, watching the machine plough its way through the vegetation. Hannah stumbled round to the back of the mulcher, yelling for him to stop, although she could barely hear her own voice above the grinding of the great beast's jaws and the cracking of branches.

Suddenly the driver saw her. His eyes widened in shock. He shouted and gestured, and although she couldn't hear a thing, she knew he was telling her to get away.

"No!" she yelled. "No! I'm not moving! Turn it off!"

His eyes looked panicked. He flapped his hands

wildly for her to go away. Hannah stood rooted to the spot. "No!" she screamed. "Turn it off!"

With a look of terror, he turned to the dashboard. The tractor engine cut out. The blades slowed to a halt. The silence was deafening.

The man wrenched open the door of his cab. "What do you think you're playing at, you little idiot?" he yelled. "You could have got yourself killed."

Hannah was shaking. "What do you think *you're* playing at, you horrible man? You're destroying our farm!"

His expression changed from fury to annoyance and then to mild amusement. "Well," he said, "the tree-huggers are getting younger and younger."

Jo and Sam ran up to Hannah. Sam threw his arms round her and burst into sobs. "I thought you were going to be killed."

Hannah hugged him back, but she didn't take her eyes off the man.

"Who sent you?" she demanded.

"Water board. They want the land cleared for a site office. Not that it's any of your business."

"It's totally my business," said Hannah, beside herself with anger. "I live here."

"Did you tell our dad you were going to do this?" Jo demanded.

"Nothing to do with me. I'm working for Aqua, not your dad, whoever he is."

"Were you going to demolish the theatre, too?" asked Jo.

"The what?"

"The theatre in those bushes."

The man looked at her as though she was a lunatic. "Theatre? What are you talking about?"

Hannah pointed to where the near corner of the theatre could just be seen, inches away from the edge of the mulcher.

He frowned. "They never said anything about a building."

"Well, they wouldn't have. They don't know it's here."

"Derelict, is it?"

Hannah felt like she might explode with hatred. "No, it is not derelict. It's in use the whole time."

He rolled his eyes and swore. "Typical," he muttered. "Idiots. Never do anything properly."

"What haven't they done properly?" asked Sam.

"Needs a whole different set of forms if there's a building involved. Nightmare load of paperwork. Else people start suing, see, if you demolish a structure without permission."

"So you won't be demolishing the theatre?" said Sam.

"Not without the paperwork. They'll have to put their office somewhere else, if they're in that much of a hurry." He shook his head. "What a waste of a journey."

"But you're allowed to just destroy all these trees, are you?" asked Hannah.

The driver gave a derisive laugh. "You talking about this bit of scrubland?"

"It's not just a bit of scrubland. It's an incredible

wildlife habitat. A hawthorn tree can support more than three hundred species of insect, did you know that?"

He snorted. "Insects? So what?"

"So, those insects nourish the soil and provide food for birds and bats. The hawthorn and blackthorn blossom make nectar and pollen for bees, and then the pollinated blossom becomes berries, which are more food for birds. The leaves feed hundreds of caterpillars, which turn into butterflies. Plus, the thorn trees make perfect safe nesting grounds for birds. Nothing can get them in here. Except you, with your tree-eating machine."

He grinned, as though she had paid him a compliment.

Hannah looked at the desiccated splinters at her feet that were all that remained of the butchered trees. She felt a prickling behind her eyes.

"Do you know how long a hawthorn tree can live?" she asked the man.

"I haven't a clue," he said, "but I'm sure you're going to tell me."

"Over seven hundred years," said Hannah, and he actually did look surprised. "Seven hundred years these trees might have been growing, and in a few seconds your machine can mow them down and chop them into a thousand pieces. Not to mention all the birds and the nests and the voles and the wood mice and every other creature you've just killed."

"It's a powerful bit of kit all right," said the man. "Does a beautiful job. Now, have you finished with the hippy talk? Because if I can't do anything else here today, I've got another job to go to."

"Destroying more trees?" asked Sam.

"That's right, sonny. See ya."

He climbed back into his cab and revved up the engine. With a jolt, Hannah suddenly became aware of people behind her. It took her brain a few seconds to refocus on the cast of *Romeo and Juliet*, staring in bewilderment at the destruction.

"What's going on?" asked Ben. "What's happened?"

The tractor roared back up the field.

"It's started," said Hannah. "Look at it. This is just the beginning. They've started to destroy the farm."

Chapter Seventeen

Hannah's Idea

Nobody said anything. Priya bent down and picked something out of the debris. It was a tiny blue eggshell, crushed to pieces.

Marie, crouched on the ground a few feet away, gave a gasp of horror.

"What?" said Katy, moving over to her.

Marie pointed to the heap of splinters at her feet. Half buried in the shards was the mangled body of a robin. There were cries of pity from around the group.

Hannah ran her finger over the raw jagged stump of a hawthorn branch.

"You know," she said, "hawthorn blossom is incredibly beautiful, but there's an old superstition that it's bad luck to bring it into the house. People believed it was connected with death. And then, recently, scientists discovered that the chemical that produces the scent in hawthorn blossom is one of the first chemicals that's produced in a dead body."

"Wow," said Amy. "Really?"

"So?" said Jonah.

Hannah didn't speak for a moment. She was sure

this was important, but she didn't quite know how to put it into words.

"I don't know. It's just…"

The others looked at her expectantly.

"It just shows that … maybe, sometimes, people just know something. Instinctively. We don't know why we know it, but we just know something."

"Is it really true that hawthorns can live for seven hundred years?" asked Ben.

"Yes. Seven hundred years of growing and giving food and shelter and protection to hundreds of thousands of creatures, and then somebody who probably doesn't know or care if it's a hawthorn bush or a privet is allowed to come along with a machine and destroy it in less than a minute. That *can't* be right. Can it?"

"No," said Lottie. "It can't."

"So was he going to demolish the theatre, too?" asked Millie.

"He would have done if he could have."

"But Hannah stopped him," said Sam.

"But he'll come back, won't he?" said Hannah. "It's only a matter of time. He'll come back next week or the week after, with a piece of paper giving him permission. And then what?"

"We can stand in front of the machine," said Sam. "Like you did today."

"But we'll probably be at school. You saw that machine – it could destroy this whole thicket in five minutes."

In her mind's eye, she saw the mulcher reversing

into her theatre, rolling back over it and spitting it out in tiny pieces. Her mother's hen house. Another part of Mum gone forever. She felt sick.

"Come on," said Sam, tugging at Jo's arm. "Let's go and find Daddy. He'll tell them they can't come back."

The Beans ran up the field towards the track. Hannah stared at the devastation.

"This is it, isn't it? This is what they're going to do to the whole farm. Flatten it and flood it."

She bent down and picked up a handful of dust and snapped twigs and chopped-up bark.

"Just think how many creatures had their homes destroyed in that one minute. And then multiply that by thousands. All of this – " and they followed her gaze as her eyes took in the oak trees, the meadows and the ploughed fields, the hedgerows, the stream and the little pigs snuffling in the orchard – "this whole farm will be gone forever."

"What about your dad?" asked Ben. "Isn't he doing anything?"

Hannah sighed and shuffled her feet in the debris. "He's had people up here to do surveys, which is great, and he's written letters to the landlord and Aqua, but the landlord wants to sell the land to Aqua, and Aqua just ignore his letters, so nothing's really happened. I think…" and she hesitated, because she didn't want to admit this, "I think he doesn't really know what else to do, and he's so busy just running the farm that he doesn't have the time or energy to do much else."

"We should get up a petition," said Priya. "Loads of people would sign it."

"My dad says they don't take much notice of petitions," said Lottie. "It's so easy to sign a petition, you see, so it doesn't mean much, unless you get hundreds of thousands of signatures."

"Well then, what can we do?" said Jonah.

Everyone stared at him.

"*We?*" said Hannah.

"What are you looking at me like that for?"

"But … you're all in favour of the reservoir."

"I was. But this…" He gestured around at the destruction. "They can't be allowed to just come on to your farm without even asking permission from your dad, and start destroying his land. That's crazy. There must be some way of stopping them."

"Letters," said Lottie. "My dad said letters are really powerful. If enough people actually take the trouble to write a letter, they can change things."

"But Dad's written all those letters and got nowhere."

"Maybe he's been writing to the wrong people. Dad says you have to write to the government. The Environment Minister. She has to give permission for a new reservoir to go ahead and apparently she really does take notice of letters, if she gets enough of them. Well, that's what my dad says, anyway. He's already written."

"But loads of people think the reservoir's a good thing," said Katy. "So how many people are really going to write?"

170

Hannah remembered Nick Constable's words after the Croxton meeting.

Absolutely nothing to worry about ... piece of cake ... easiest reservoir deal I've ever made ... we've already won...

He was right, wasn't he? If nobody could be bothered to oppose the reservoir, he *had* won.

"If we care," said Hannah, "then we're going to have to fight. And we're going to have to make other people care, too. Make them care enough to write letters. After all, Jonah's changed his mind. Maybe other people would, too, if they knew what was going on."

"Everyone who uses the farm," said Lottie, "Scouts and Guides who camp here, walkers, horse riders – they should all be writing."

"So how do we tell everyone?" asked Ben.

"We should make leaflets," said Lottie, "like I said. Put them through everyone's doors."

Marie wrinkled her nose. "People get leaflets through their doors all the time, though, don't they? And they mostly just chuck them in the bin."

"Well, have you got a better idea?" snapped Lottie.

"Call a meeting?" suggested Owen.

Ben laughed. "Who's going to come to a meeting called by us? No one likes going to meetings, so why would they turn up just because we asked them to?"

"We need a captive audience," said Katy. "Literally. Penned in a room so they *have* to listen."

A spark of an idea flashed into Hannah's mind. She drew in her breath.

"What?" said Lottie.

Hannah said nothing. But her mind was whirring so fast she couldn't keep up with it.

A captive audience...

The house plays...

Hundreds of people would be there. Students, teachers, parents. Half the village would be there.

What if...?

"Hannah!" said Lottie. "What are you thinking?"

But Hannah still couldn't put it into words. Images whirled around in her head.

What if...?

In her mind's eye, she saw the cast of *Romeo and Juliet*, waiting behind the closed curtains, ready to begin the Prologue. She saw the darkened auditorium, filled with the hush of expectation. She saw the stage lights go up and the cast turn to face the audience. She saw them raise their heads, open their mouths to recite the opening lines of *Romeo and Juliet*. And then...

What if...?

"What *is* it, Hannah?" asked Marie.

Finally, Hannah looked at her friends.

"I don't know if we can really do it," she said, "but I might have thought of something."

"Well, tell us, then," said Priya.

"You might not want to do it. It could get us into massive trouble."

Lottie made a noise that was remarkably like a growl. "Hannah, you're driving us all mad here."

Hannah drew herself up to her full height and

took a big breath.

"OK. Come into the theatre and I'll tell you. But you'll all have to swear, whether you want to be a part of it or not, that you won't breathe a single word of what I'm about to say. Not to anyone. Not to a single soul. Is everyone OK with that?"

Chapter Eighteen

The Special Guest

It was only ten past nine on Friday morning, but Mr Collins seemed to have been droning on for hours. He stood at the front of the hall, beside a table on which was displayed the enormous new House Play Shield. The guest speaker was late, and Mr Collins had decided to entertain the Key Stage 3 assembly with a lengthy reminder of the school rules.

When Hannah's class had walked into the hall and caught sight of that trophy, Miranda had shot Hannah a poisonous look that clearly said: *If we don't win this prize, it will all be your fault.*

Hannah pretended she hadn't seen the look. But she felt queasy. She couldn't believe how enthusiastic the others had been about her plan. But the idea would only work if they could get rid of Miranda. And how could they possibly do that?

Hannah had spent half the night going over and over the problem in her mind, and she still had no idea what to do about it.

Now, trying to avoid Miranda's evil looks, Hannah turned her head as if looking for someone in the row behind her. Jack caught her eye and winked. She turned back to face the front, desperately hoping he hadn't seen her blush.

Apart from Miranda, Jack was the only member of their group who hadn't been at the farm yesterday. Lottie had considered this a great opportunity not to tell him at all.

"There's no way we can trust Jack Adamson with something this important," she had said.

"Do you *really* think he'd grass us up to the Head?" said Jonah. "Adamson's the last person in the world who'd do that and you know it."

"But he'll mess it up, won't he? Like he messes everything up. I mean, has he done one single thing right for *Romeo and Juliet*?"

There was no answer to this. Jack had not done one single thing right for *Romeo and Juliet*.

"But actually," said Hannah, "this is better. We'll only need really basic lighting. Lights up, lights down. Even Jack can't mess that up."

Lottie looked doubtful, but Hannah could tell she was slightly reassured. Jonah had said he'd tell Jack the plan that evening. Hannah wondered now what Jack had thought of the idea. What had that wink meant?

"It has also been brought to my notice," Mr Collins was saying, "that some students have been coming to school wearing jewellery which expressly contravenes the uniform policy laid out in the Student Handbook."

Hannah looked at her Head Teacher and suddenly wondered how she could have been so stupid. She had been so excited by her idea that she hadn't allowed any doubts to creep in. She had even managed to carry the rest of the group along on the tide of her enthusiasm.

She must have been mad. There was no way on earth they would get away with this. Mr Collins would stop them the moment they started. And then they'd get into massive trouble and they'd probably all be expelled.

What on earth had she been thinking?

"And may I remind you all," Mr Collins said, "that trainers, irrespective of their colour, are not an acceptable form of footwear except in PE lessons."

The Deputy Head, Mrs Young, walked into the hall and made her way towards Mr Collins in an exaggerated tiptoe, so her heels didn't clack on the wooden floor.

"And furthermore…"

Mrs Young whispered in Mr Collins's ear. His face brightened and he rubbed his hands together.

"I am delighted to announce that our special guest has arrived."

People sat up a bit straighter and looked towards the double doors. Hannah didn't bother. She had more important things to think about. She really wasn't interested in some "representative from a local company".

"Will you please give a warm welcome to the sponsor of our inaugural house plays: from our water company, Aqua, Mr Nick Constable!"

Hannah gaped. Surely not.

Lottie's eyes were enormous. "No. No way."

But there he was, striding into the hall in a black suit with a pink shirt and a purple tie, lapping up the dutiful applause with his creamy smile.

"Good morning, everybody, and thank you very much for your warm welcome. As your local water company, Aqua is delighted and proud to be sponsoring Middleham Community College's house plays."

"I don't believe it," muttered Hannah to Lottie. "Of all the people..."

"We're very keen," Nick Constable continued, "to become more involved in the local community, and I always enjoyed drama at school myself, so this was a cause close to my heart." He smiled his oily smile. "We put a lot of thought into what we could give as a really exciting prize to the winning house, and I hope you'll agree that we've come up with something worth competing for."

He paused. "But before I get on to that, I'd like to say a little bit about what we do." He smiled the slimy smile again. "Of course, in a sense, we at Aqua are in your homes every day."

"Ugh," muttered James, who was sitting behind Lottie. "I wouldn't have him in my home. Creepy old git."

"By which I mean," said Nick Constable, with a chuckle, "that every time you turn on a tap, that water has come to you courtesy of Aqua."

"Shame we can't turn him off like a tap," whispered

Priya. "What a slimeball."

"So we're very keen to get more involved with the local community and raise awareness of what goes into bringing you clean water, since it's something we all use every day."

Lottie gasped and her eyes grew even rounder.

"What?" said Hannah.

But Lottie put her finger to her lips.

"However, I'm sure you don't want me rambling on like this," he said, with an ingratiating smile. "I'm sure you're all waiting to hear what the prize will be."

There was a murmur of anticipation from around the hall.

"As well as this rather splendid Aqua House Play Shield," said Nick Constable, gesturing to the trophy, "every member of the winning house will have a day off school next term for an all-expenses-paid trip, courtesy of Aqua, to one of the country's top theme parks."

An excited burst of chatter broke out.

"So *that's* why he's here," said Lottie.

"What do you mean?"

"Don't you see? He's trying to bribe us. He wants to make everyone love Aqua, so we'll all support the reservoir."

Hannah's mouth fell open. "So *that's* why he's sponsoring the plays."

"I'm glad we don't have a chance of winning his stupid prize. I wouldn't touch it."

But Hannah glimpsed Bea and Millie, a few rows

in front. Everyone else in their class was chattering excitedly, but they were whispering to each other and looked distinctly depressed.

"I don't know if everyone's going to feel that way," she said.

"They will," said Lottie, "when they realise why he's doing it."

Mr Collins called for quiet and Nick Constable started talking about how much he was looking forward to watching their plays and what a marvellous thing school drama was. Hannah looked at him, so smug and pleased with himself, and all her doubts about her crazy plan were smothered by a burning desire to see this man publicly humiliated.

I wish we could get him up on stage, she thought. I wish we could put him under a spotlight, so the whole school could see his smug fat face when we expose his lies. I wish we could put him on trial, in front of everybody.

And then a really crazy thought sprung into her mind.

I wonder, she thought.

Could we pull it off?

I wonder.

Nick Constable finished his speech and Mr Collins moved forward to thank him and order another round of applause. With a final reminder to remain silent until they left the hall and to walk on the left at all times in the corridors, they were dismissed.

The Year 7s, under the watchful eyes of their form tutors, began to file out. Nick Constable was talking to Mr Collins.

How long would he stay? She would have to catch him while he was still in the hall.

The second row started to leave. Two rows to go. Mr Collins and Nick Constable were laughing together now.

The third row stood up. Hannah felt sick. She couldn't do this, could she? It was completely mad. It would definitely get her expelled.

And yet, if it worked…

She had to try, didn't she? What choice did she have? They couldn't wait for adults to act. There wasn't time. They had to act now.

Their form tutor, Mr Richards, gestured for Hannah's row to stand. They started to file out of the double doors. But Hannah turned and walked over to the table at the front where Mr Collins and Nick Constable were chatting like old friends.

"Hannah, what are you doing?" whispered Lottie. "You're not going to hit him, are you?"

Hannah burst out laughing. "*Hit* him?"

"Well, you hit Jack that time."

"Charlotte, Hannah, could you stop talking and leave the hall, please?" called Mr Richards.

"I just want to ask him something," whispered Hannah. "I'll tell you later. Say I have to see Mr Collins, will you?"

Lottie shrugged, looking slightly put out. "OK."

"Thanks."

Hannah walked towards the two men and waited, at what she hoped was a respectful but insistent distance, for them to finish their conversation.

The Year 9s were straggling out now. But Jack was ambling across the hall towards Hannah.

"Oh dear, Roberts, called up to see the Head? What have you done now?"

"Nothing," said Hannah. "I need to see Mr Constable. How about you?"

Jack shrugged. "Collins seems to have some sort of problem with the fact that I'm allergic to French homework. Fascist."

Mr Collins turned towards them, frowning. Nick Constable followed his gaze. He started slightly when he saw Hannah but he quickly rearranged his face into its usual smug mask.

"Go and wait by the door, please, Jack," said Mr Collins. "What is it, Hannah?"

"I'm sorry to interrupt, sir, but I just wondered if I could ask Mr Constable something?" said Hannah in her politest voice.

Mr Collins frowned. "Well, quickly, then."

Hannah looked up at Nick Constable through lowered eyes.

"Mr Constable," she said, in what she hoped was a tone of overawed reverence, "I just wanted to say I'm so sorry for misunderstanding you before, about the reservoir. I hadn't thought properly about it and I was just overreacting because it was our farm, but I've thought about it now and I can see you're right. We do need a reservoir and I was just being selfish. So I hope you'll accept my apology."

A benign smile suffused Nick Constable's features.

"That's very mature of you, Hannah. I appreciate your coming to say that. And of course I accept your apology."

Out of the corner of her eye, Hannah noticed Jack, a few feet away, leaning against the doors that led to the dining room, looking at her curiously. She tried to ignore him.

"Oh, thank you," she said. "That's really nice of you." She paused. "Er … there was one other thing … I was just wondering … if I could ask you a favour?"

Mr Collins glanced at his watch.

"Please do," said Nick Constable.

"Well, I'm directing the Woolf House play – *Romeo and Juliet* – and … you might not want to do this, and please say if you don't, but you were saying how much you'd enjoyed drama at school, and so I just wondered … it would be such an honour … if you might actually come up on stage and act a small part in our play? Just a few lines. We could send them to you, so you wouldn't have to rehearse or anything. I thought maybe you might like the opportunity to be really involved, you know, rather than just watching?"

Mr Collins was looking alarmed. "I'm not sure that's—"

But Nick Constable raised his hand, palm up, to stop Mr Collins.

"What a charming idea. I'm very flattered that you'd like me to be in your play. Of course I'll do it."

"Oh, thank you *so* much. The others will be so pleased."

"So do I get to wear a costume?" He chuckled.

"Lottie will sort all that out for you. She's our wardrobe mistress. It will just be a cloak or something that you can wear over your suit. She'll give it to you on the day."

Nick Constable took a small card from his jacket pocket and handed it to Hannah.

"All my details are on there. Just email me with the lines and anything else I need to know."

Hannah took the card. "Thank you so much."

"Well, that's very community-spirited of you, Mr Constable," said Mr Collins, with a forced smile. "Rather you than me. Off you go, then, Hannah."

Hannah turned away from the two men to leave the hall and her face broke into a huge grin.

"Over here, please, Jack," called Mr Collins.

As Hannah passed Jack, he muttered, "What are you up to, Roberts?"

"Nothing," said Hannah airily. "Nothing at all."

Chapter Nineteen

Jack Makes an Offer

Lottie had a piano lesson at lunchtime, so Hannah headed across the patio to the library. She had science homework to finish before this afternoon's lesson.

Jack was playing table tennis with Jonah on one of the outdoor tables. As Hannah passed them, Jonah smashed the ball across the table and Jack leaped sideways, whacked it back and crashed into Hannah's shoulder. She staggered across the paving stones, trying to keep her balance.

Jack turned and grabbed her shoulder to steady her. The sudden contact made Hannah's heart thump.

"Sorry, Roberts. His rubbish shot."

Jonah was rummaging in the bushes for the ping-pong ball.

"So," said Jack, "what's with asking Mr Creepy to be in the play? What's the cunning plan?"

Hannah looked at him. He would hear about it soon anyway. She had already told Lottie, and she would be telling everyone else at the next rehearsal.

So she told him. He listened in silence. When she finished, she braced herself for the sarcastic retort.

"Wow," said Jack. "That is genius."

"Look, I know it sounds mad, but it's a desperate situation and—"

"Roberts, I'm not being sarky. I do think it's genius."

Hannah stared at him. "Really?"

"It's a brilliant plan. Once he realises he's been set up, he's stuck. Caught in the spotlight. If he walks out, he totally loses face."

"Well, that's the idea."

Jack spun his bat between his fingers. "Have you thought about using multimedia?"

"What do you mean?"

"Got it," called Jonah, emerging from the foliage with the ball in his hand. "Ready for my world-beating serve?"

Jack sauntered back to the table and struck a pose. "Bring it on, Hadley."

Hannah watched them bat the ball back and forth. What exactly had Jack meant?

"Hey, Hannah."

It was Lexie and Amber, both in Hannah's tutor group and both in Woolf House.

"How's the play going?" asked Amber.

Hannah felt herself going red.

"Oh, er, yes, not bad, thanks."

They seemed to be waiting for more, so she added, "Everyone knows their lines now. And the costumes are amazing."

Well, at least that bit wasn't a lie.

"You'd better make sure we win," said Lexie.

"Imagine if we had to watch everyone in Kipling skipping off to a theme park while we spend the day in school."

"I bet we'll win," said Amber. "Vishali says it's really good."

Jack sprang sideways for the ball and landed squarely on Lexie's foot.

"Ow!" she screeched.

"Oops, sorry," said Jack.

Lexie hopped up and down clutching her foot. "You idiot. I think you've broken my toe."

Amber grasped her arm and steered her over to a bench.

Jonah was searching for the ball again. Hannah grabbed her opportunity.

"What did you mean before? About multimedia?"

Jack tossed his bat from hand to hand. "Just that you can use other stuff as well as words to make your point. Projections on the back wall: visuals, statistics, quotes. And music to underscore your meaning."

"Like what sort of thing?"

"Well, at that meeting you went to, you said the water guy was using images of the farm that made it look run down, yeah? So you can do the opposite."

"Show the good side of the farm?"

"Yeah, but also you can show they're lying, by quoting their own words alongside images that *show* the opposite. Ironic juxtapositions, see? So when the water-board guy says this is an unproductive farm, the images you're projecting behind him show crops being harvested, fields full of cows, that sort of thing."

"And when he talks about there being no wildlife," said Hannah, seeing possibilities now, "we can project pictures of the birds and trees and wild flowers."

"Exactly. And you can flash up text, too, that contradicts what he's saying."

"Like Lottie's dad's bird results. Yes, that would be great."

"You should use old photos of the farm, too. Film footage would be perfect, if you've got any. With some kind of emotional music playing in the background. Show people the history of the place. You have to approach it from all angles, you see."

Hannah looked at Jack curiously, as though he had turned into somebody completely different.

"That sounds amazing. How do you know all this stuff?"

Jack shrugged. "I like film."

"Hey, Adamson, are we playing or not?" called Jonah.

Jack turned back to the table-tennis table. Jonah served. Jack sliced the ball back across the table and it bounced off the edge. Jonah lunged for it but Matthew, who was standing watching, caught it and threw it to his friend Ethan. Jonah pounced on Ethan and they started scuffling.

Jack turned back to Hannah. "Tell you what, Roberts. I could come up to the farm if you like. Take some photos, do a bit of filming. Then I could make you a sample. Put some images and music together, see what you think."

For a moment, Hannah was overcome with gratitude. She opened her mouth to thank him.

"If your dad wouldn't mind," Jack said.

Hannah froze with her mouth still open.

What would Dad think if he saw Jack at Clayhill? What would he think of Hannah inviting the boy who had burned his barn down to come to his farm and take photos?

But if it was to save the farm?

Would Jack even produce anything worthwhile, though? What if he just messed about? After all, that was all he'd done so far. So why on earth should she trust him now?

Most terrible of all, what would Lottie say if Hannah invited Jack to the farm?

Hannah could imagine exactly what Lottie would say, and it wasn't a conversation she wanted to have.

Ethan freed his arm from Jonah's grasp and threw the ball to another boy behind Jack. Jack intercepted it. He turned to Hannah.

"Listen, Roberts," he mumbled, looking at the ground and tossing the ping-pong ball from one hand to the other, "I really am sorry about the fire. I never meant it to happen, you know that. And this plan of yours sounds like a laugh. So if I can help, that's cool, you know?"

Hannah glared at him. "It's not a *laugh*. It's deadly serious."

"Yeah. That's what I meant."

"And the show's in two weeks. There's so much to do. We don't have time for anyone mucking about. And it's not like you've done anything so far."

"Fair point."

"And it's got to be good. Really good. It's the only way we'll get away with it without being expelled. I can't let everyone down. I'm going to be getting people into enough trouble as it is."

Jack looked into her eyes. "I promise I'll be good, miss."

Hannah made the mistake of meeting Jack's gaze. Her insides melted.

"Well … OK, then. If you really promise."

"Cool."

"Come on, Adamson, what are you playing at?" called Jonah. "Your serve."

Jack turned back to Jonah.

"I hope you're ready for this, Hadley."

He tossed the ball in the air as if to serve, but then he caught it again and spun round to face Hannah. "Last Saturday of half term? Around two?"

Hannah felt herself blushing. "Yes, thank you, that would be great."

Jack turned to the table.

"Oh, but Jack?"

"Yeah?"

"Don't mention it to any of the others yet, will you?"

"Sure. Whatever you say."

He raised his bat to serve. "Right. Game on."

Chapter Twenty

Costumes and Coins

It was the last Saturday of the October half term. Hannah was brushing her teeth after breakfast when, from the bathroom window, she saw Lottie, Priya, Marie, Katy, Ben and Jonah walking up the farm track. Her stomach flipped at the sight of Lottie. If she found out who was visiting that afternoon...

But there was no time to worry about that now. Anyway, there was no reason Lottie would find out. Not yet, anyway. Not until Jack had actually produced something. And, knowing Jack, he probably wouldn't even turn up.

She shoved her toothbrush in the mug and ran down the back stairs.

Nobody else had eaten breakfast. The Beans were busy with their archaeology museum and Martha was engaged in some top-secret project in the dining room. She had slammed both doors and threatened them all with death if they disturbed her. Whatever the project was, it had put Martha in an even worse mood than usual.

"Hi!" called Lottie, as she and the others appeared at the garden gate.

Hannah stepped outside and closed the scullery door behind her. You never knew when the Beans might be spying.

"I know you said to go straight to the theatre," said Priya, "but as we were early, we thought we'd call for you."

"Marie's bottling out," said Jonah.

"What?" said Hannah.

Marie glared at Jonah. "I'm not bottling out. I'm just not sure it will work. I mean, even with the Aqua bloke being in it, I still think Collins will stop us when he realises what we're doing."

"Oh, I had an idea about that," said Hannah. "Lottie, could you ask your mum to sit next to him at the play? We all know Collins fancies her – he practically drools every time he sees her – and she can use her famous charm."

Lottie looked as if she were about to throw up. "You're asking me to *encourage* my mum to flirt with the teachers?"

"It will mean you'll have to tell her what we're going to do. Not in detail, but you'll have to prepare her a bit. She won't tell on us, will she?"

"Of course she won't. She's completely against the reservoir. But I'm not sure she'll be able to—"

The kitchen window flew open and Jo's head appeared. "Hannah, will you make me an omelette?"

"Make it yourself," called Hannah.

"But yours are nicer than mine. Please?"

"Sorry, Jo," said Hannah. "I'm busy."

Jo sighed and her head disappeared back inside the kitchen. Through the open window, Hannah heard Dad's and Martha's raised voices.

"It's more likely," said Lottie, "that Nick Constable will walk out once he realises he's been stitched up."

"He needs a minder," said Katy. "Someone to keep him on stage."

Jonah's eyes brightened. "A security guard?"

"No, idiot. Charm, not force. Someone to stand next to him and smile at him and make him feel like everything's going to be all right."

Everyone's eyes turned to Amy. Amy recoiled in horror.

"Me? No way! He gives me the creeps."

"He gives everyone the creeps," said Katy.

"Stupid, stupid thing!" shouted Martha from the dining room. "How am I supposed to do it by myself?"

"Well, I don't know why you're asking me," said Dad. "I haven't got a clue."

"Fine! I'll just throw it all in the bin!"

Dad's footsteps sounded on the tiles.

"Let's go," said Hannah, glancing at her watch. "The others might be there already."

"Hannah!" shouted Dad.

Hannah raised her eyes to heaven. "What now?"

Dad wrenched the scullery door open.

"Oh, there you are. Come here, will you?"

"But we're having a rehearsal."

"Just come here a minute. Martha's having problems with some costume or other."

Hannah sighed. "Coming. Just give me a second, OK?"

Dad glared at her and stomped back into the house.

Hannah handed a folded piece of paper to Priya. "Listen, can you start without me? Exactly the same as before except with this."

Priya started to unfold the paper. "What is it?"

"Not here!" hissed Hannah, glancing at the open window. "It's the new Prologue. There's only one copy. I'm really scared of anyone finding it."

"How can we all rehearse from one copy?"

"How about you read a couple of lines and everyone repeats them? We'll have to learn it by heart. It's too dangerous for everyone to have a copy."

"Hannah!" yelled Dad.

"Coming!"

"Shall I stay?" Lottie asked Hannah. "Maybe I can help. If it's a costume thing."

"Oh, thank you. That would be great. See you in a minute, guys."

They walked through the kitchen. Sam stood at the sink, sloshing his hands about in a bowl of bubbly water. Jo was grating cheese on to a board. Butter sizzled in a frying pan on the Aga.

At the dining-room table, Martha sat with her head in her hands, her shoulders heaving with furious sobs. Mum's sewing machine stood in its case on the table. Pieces of blue fabric and sheets of paper were strewn all around it. Dad stood by the door, looking bewildered.

"What's going on?" asked Hannah.

Martha ignored her.

Lottie picked up a sheet of paper. "So you're making a costume for *The Tempest*?"

Martha continued to sob. Hannah picked up another piece of paper. "Water spirits," she read.

"Water what?" asked Dad.

"Spirits. Martha's playing a water spirit in *The Tempest*."

Dad shook his head in disbelief. "Right, well, I'll leave you to it. Must see to those calves."

Lottie held a piece of paper out to Hannah and pointed to the words at the top.

"Dear Parents," it said, followed by a letter explaining that simple instructions for constructing a spirit costume were attached.

"They don't look simple to me," muttered Hannah.

Lottie held up a piece of fabric, frowning. "This one's got staples in it. Have you been *stapling* your costume, Martha?"

Martha's head jerked up. "How else am I supposed to make the stupid thing? I can't even get the lid off the poxy sewing machine."

She gave the plastic case a swipe.

"Don't do that!" cried Hannah. "That's Mum's sewing machine."

Lottie pressed the clips at either side of the case, raised them and lifted the lid off. "There you are."

Martha shot her a look of loathing. "Oh, well done. Lottie Perfect can open the sewing machine.

How's that supposed to help? I don't know how to use the stupid thing, do I?"

"But I do," said Lottie.

"Well, good for you."

Lottie glared at her. Then she spread out the pattern sheets and examined the pieces of fabric. "No wonder you couldn't do it. They haven't given you big enough pieces for the skirt panels."

Martha mumbled something.

"What?" asked Lottie.

Martha muttered something unintelligible again.

Lottie gave an exasperated sigh. "Martha, if you want me to help, you're going to have to talk to me."

Martha shot her head up. "I said I might have cut them in half, all right?"

"You cut the skirt pieces in *half*? Why on earth did you do that?"

"Because I was trying to make the stupid top, wasn't I?" yelled Martha. "How was I supposed to know those pieces were for the skirt? So now I can't make any of it and Zara won't let me be in the show any more." She burst into tears again.

"Isn't Zara's mum supposed to be a West End costume designer or something?" said Hannah. "Why isn't she making the costumes?"

"She can't do everything," snapped Martha. "Zara gave us this bag with all the stuff in and said could we ask our mums to make it."

"She said to ask your *mum* to make it?"

"That's what I said, stupid. Are you deaf or something?"

Hannah felt a surge of anger towards Zara. Why were people so thoughtless? Why couldn't they just check before they sent things home for people's mums?

Lottie was folding the fabric pieces. She picked up the empty bag from the floor and put the fabric in it. Then she tucked the pattern sheets into the side of the bag.

Martha snatched the bag from her. "Don't pack it away! If I don't have the costume done by Monday, I can't be in the show."

"So do you want me to make it or not?" asked Lottie, holding out her hand for the bag.

Martha's mouth fell open. "What?"

"I said, would you like me to make your costume for you?"

Silence. Martha stared at the table.

Lottie shrugged. "Well, if you don't want me to…" She started to leave the room.

Martha stood up and pushed the chair back so hard that it skidded across the tiles. "Fine. Whatever. Since you're so desperate to."

Without making eye contact, she shoved the bag at Lottie and stomped out into the hall.

"You're welcome," called Lottie after her, as the door slammed. "Really, don't mention it."

Hannah turned to her friend. "That's so nice of you."

"It's no problem," said Lottie, as they walked back through the kitchen. "I can't believe Zara did that."

"I know."

196

"Did what?" asked Jo.

"Nothing."

"Look at this, Hannah," said Sam. "We've found another Roman coin."

"Great."

"Wait a second, I'll dry it."

Jo cracked an egg on the side of a jug and pulled the two halves of the shell apart. The egg plopped on to the table.

"Whoops. Missed."

The egg slithered off the edge of the table and on to the floor, where the yolk broke and oozed into the white.

"Get a cloth and clear it up," said Hannah.

"I've got a better way than that." Jo walked to the scullery door and called, "Rags!"

Rags bounded into the house, her tail wagging furiously.

"Here, Ragsy, here!"

Rags scampered across the kitchen and gobbled up the pool of broken egg.

"See," beamed Jo. "She has so many uses."

"Wow," said Sam. "This is a really good one. Look, Hannah."

He was scrutinising a small metal disc lying on a tea towel. To Hannah's surprise, it did actually look like an old coin.

She picked it up. Lottie peered at it over her shoulder.

It looked like it had been cut by hand, by somebody who wasn't that good at cutting. There was a circle marked on the metal, but on one side of the circle the coin had been cut outside the lines. Inside the circle were what looked like symbols, but Hannah had no idea what they represented. One of them seemed to be a pear with fronds growing out of the top where the stalk should have been.

"Did you really dig this up, Sam?"

"You know we did. In South Meadow, where we found the other things."

Hannah turned it over. She drew in her breath. Stamped on the coin's face, as clear as if freshly minted, was a beautiful image of an elephant. And underneath the elephant, in capital letters, was stamped one word.

CAESAR.

"*Caesar?*" said Lottie.

Hannah stared at the Beans, her mind racing. "And you've found other stuff, too?"

"If you ever took any notice," said Jo, "you'd know."

"Where is it?" asked Lottie. "The stuff you've found?"

"In our museum."

"Show us."

Hannah and Lottie started up the back staircase.

"It's 50p entrance, remember?" called Jo, running up the stairs behind them.

"I haven't got 50p," said Hannah, "and this is too important to mess about."

"It's not messing about. These are valuable treasures."

198

"Careful in here," said Sam, as Hannah opened the door to his room. "I'll get it. There's winter barley in this field."

He tiptoed around the edge of the frayed carpet, took a green shoebox from the bottom of his wardrobe and brought it to Hannah. She lifted the lid.

Inside the box, on a bed of tissue paper, sat two coins and three tiny model animals. Hannah picked up the first coin. It was very worn but she could make out the figure of a man. He must be an emperor. There were letters around the edge, but she couldn't read them.

She looked at the coin Lottie was examining. This one was much less worn. It showed the figure of another man. At the side, Hannah could clearly read: HADRIANVS.

"Hadrian?" she said. "As in Hadrian's Wall?"

"Wow," said Lottie. "I can't believe you really found these."

"The animals are the best," said Sam.

Very gently, he picked from the box a little metal tortoise and placed it in Hannah's palm.

"Where did you get this?" she asked.

"In South Meadow. Near where we found the coins. I found this cockerel there, too, and this ram. I think they're olden-days toy farm animals, like Grandfather's ones that Daddy has in his office. Only I think these are newer. Grandfather's are made from lead and lots of the animals' legs have got snapped off."

"They're very sweet," said Hannah, replacing the tortoise, "but these coins are amazing. Imagine, they might be two thousand years old. And those archaeologists said they'd found nothing?"

"They were looking in the wrong place, you see," said Jo. "We did tell them."

Hannah and Lottie looked at each other.

"More evidence," said Hannah. "This is brilliant."

"We need to show them to an archaeologist," said Lottie. "Not one of the Aqua ones. A proper one. To tell us if they're genuine."

"How will we find an archaeologist?"

"You could ask Sophie," said Jo. "She works at the university, doesn't she?"

Lottie and Hannah stared at her.

"That is actually a really good idea," said Lottie.

"I know. How much are you going to pay us?"

"Honestly," said Lottie. "You two are obsessed with money."

"So would you be," said Jo, "if you didn't have any."

"Will you get Sophie's contact details from your dad?" said Lottie, as she and Hannah clattered down the back stairs. "Then we can get in touch today. Come round to mine this afternoon if you like."

Hannah's stomach tightened.

"Oh, er, thanks, but I … I can't, you see. Someone's … er … someone's coming up this afternoon."

"Oh? Who?"

Hannah squirmed. She knew from experience that if she wasn't honest with Lottie, there would be dire consequences.

"Jack," she muttered.

"*Jack?* Why?"

"I didn't invite him," Hannah said desperately. "He offered. To take photos of the farm. And film footage. To make a sample. To see if we wanted to use it in the play, you know? He's offered to put together some music and images to help get across our points. And I think that might work really well. You know, to tell the story of the farm?" She knew she was babbling now. "Jack's really good at film stuff. Jonah said. And he offered..."

She tailed off, wilting from the force of Lottie's scowl.

"So," said Lottie, "you're trusting Jack to come to the farm, after he practically destroyed it last time, and you want him to have a massive part in our play, even though he's completely unreliable and a total waste of space?"

"Don't be like that. I know we said we wouldn't let him come here, but this is different, isn't it? He's coming to help."

"Help!" Lottie gave a scornful laugh. "Listen to yourself! Wasn't he meant to be helping with *Romeo and Juliet*? Wasn't he meant to be putting together music and images? And did he do anything? Did he do one single thing to help?"

"But this is different."

"Too right it's different. This is a play that we're doing to save your farm. It's a play that could get us all expelled. And just because you fancy him, you've told Jack he can practically run the show."

"I do not—" Hannah began, but Lottie's glare stopped her from finishing the sentence.

"And if he ruins the play? And gets us all expelled? How are you going to feel then?"

"He promised he'd be good." Even as she said this, Hannah realised how lame it sounded.

"Oh, *did* he? Well, that's all right, then. I'm *completely* reassured."

Lottie walked out into the yard. Hannah followed her.

"Listen," she said, desperate not to fall out with her friend, "it's only a sample. He might not even turn up. You know what he's like. It might not be any good. And if it's all rubbish, or if he just messes about, we can ditch him, can't we? It's just that he had some really good ideas, and if they work, it could be amazing."

Lottie quickened her pace.

"Fine. You do whatever you want. I'm going home. I've got a costume to make."

Chapter Twenty-One

The Site Office

Hannah's mood for the first fifteen minutes of Jack's visit veered between tongue-tied awkwardness, pinch-me-I'm-dreaming exhilaration and sudden plunges into guilty misery when she thought about Lottie. But once she settled down and got used to the fact that Jack was actually here, on her farm, walking around chatting to her and taking photographs, she became fascinated by this whole new side of him that she was seeing. Because the Jack behind a camera lens was a completely different Jack from the one she had always seen at school.

They started in North Meadow, where Jack took long-distance shots, panoramas and close-ups.

"Mmm, blueberries," he said, when they came to a cluster of blackthorn bushes covered in dusky-blue sloes.

"Try one," said Hannah innocently. "They're really nice."

She held her breath as Jack popped one into his mouth.

A second later, his face creased up in disgust and he spat the remnants of the berry violently out on to the grass.

"Ugh, what the heck was *that*?" he spluttered.

Hannah was doubled up laughing. "Your face! It was a sloe, you dingbat. Have you never tasted a sloe before?"

"Well, I never will again," said Jack, shoving her shoulder. "Thanks a lot, Roberts."

"Hey! You nearly pushed me into the hedge."

"Would've served you right. That was the most disgusting thing I've ever eaten. It's sucked every bit of moisture out of my mouth."

"Sorry. That must have been a bad one. They're not usually that bitter. Here." She plucked a plump sloe from the bush. "Try this one."

Jack flicked it out of her hand. "What do you think I am, some kind of idiot?"

"Sorry. No, I really am. Here, try a nettle. They're delicious."

"Ha ha." Jack crouched down and lifted his camera. "Nice view of the stream here."

"We get kingfishers along it, but you don't see them that often. We should go to a couple of the ponds as well."

"How many ponds are there?"

"Eleven. And they're full of wildlife."

"I'll take some pictures of the trees, too. Those ones over there are massive."

They walked up to the wood, down through the fields, past two of the ponds and back across North Meadow, Jack taking film footage and pictures all the way.

"So, how's the stealth play coming on?" he asked.

"I don't really know. I mean, it's so weird, writing a play where the person with the main part doesn't have a script. I'm writing all these lines and then leaving blanks. But what if he doesn't say what we want him to say?"

"He will, if you ask the questions right. You know the kind of thing he's going to say, don't you? You said the stuff in that brochure they sent round was exactly the same as what he said at the meeting you went to. So he'll probably say exactly the same stuff again."

Hannah laughed. "Yes, you're right. He *does* have a script, doesn't he? All that stuff he spouts, it's all scripted. We just have to prompt him."

Jack stopped to photograph a towering holly tree, its deep-green leaves and bright-red berries so shiny they looked as though they had been polished.

"Can you take some footage of the animals in the yard now? They're all rare breeds and they're all farmed properly, no horrible battery cages or anything. And the calves are so photogenic, with those lovely big eyes."

Jack hesitated. "What about your dad? Won't he mind me being in his farmyard?"

"No, it'll be fine," said Hannah, sounding a lot more confident than she felt. Dad was probably in the yard somewhere and she had no idea how he might react to seeing Jack.

On the way to the calves, Hannah suddenly had a thought that made her insides freeze.

The burnt-out barn! It was right next to the calves' barn.

What should she do? It would sound weird if she suddenly told Jack they shouldn't film the calves after all. But if she took him to the burnt-out barn, would it look as though she was deliberately making him face the consequences of what he'd done?

And so he should, said Lottie's voice in her head, and she felt another twinge of misery at how she and Lottie had parted.

But Lottie shouldn't be so ridiculously anti-Jack, should she? If she could see how helpful Jack had been today...

They turned the corner. And there it was, right in front of them. The blackened shell of the burnt-out barn.

All that was left were the steel uprights. The rest was just a flat empty concrete space. Nettles had already pushed their way up through the gaps in what had been the floor.

Jack stopped dead. Hannah didn't breathe.

After what seemed like minutes, she risked a glance at him.

His face was white. He looked frightened.

"I didn't realise..." he said, and Hannah had to strain to hear him. "I didn't think it was so big..."

He took a step across the soot-blackened floor into the vast empty space.

And then, around the corner, a bucket in each hand, came Dad.

Hannah's stomach contracted. What would Dad

do when he saw Jack? What would Jack do? Would he run away, like he had done when the fire started?

Dad barely glanced at them. He carried on walking towards the calves' barn.

And then, to Hannah's amazement, Jack walked right up to her father.

"Hello, Mr Roberts."

Dad looked at him blankly. He didn't seem to recognise Jack. He seemed to be looking right through him.

"I'm Jack Adamson. It was me who burned your barn down. Me and Danny."

Still Dad didn't react.

"I never apologised to you. I ... I don't know why. I've just seen it. I'm so sorry."

Dad grunted. "Bit late for that now."

"He's trying to make up for it," said Hannah. "He's taking photos of the farm. To show people what will be lost if it gets flooded."

"Oh, is he? Well, he'd better take a photo of that, then."

He jerked his thumb to the left, towards the pig field. Hannah looked, and drew in her breath. In the corner of the field stood a huge white portacabin, as big as a bungalow.

"What is it?"

"See for yourself. They've stuck a sign up."

Hannah walked towards the portacabin. Taped inside one of the windows was a large piece of paper. In massive black capital letters, it said: **SITE OFFICE**. In the top right-hand corner was the Aqua logo.

So Aqua had decided to set their office up here.

For a moment, Hannah felt only relief. They weren't going to demolish the theatre!

When she glanced at her father's drawn, tense face, though, guilt flooded over her. What was she doing, feeling relieved?

But then the guilt turned to anger. Why should *she* feel guilty? *She* wasn't the one who had dumped a massive great building on her dad's pig field.

"When ... when did it come?" she asked. As if the time of arrival mattered. But she couldn't think of anything else to say.

"Articulated lorry brought it up this morning," said Dad.

"And didn't you know?"

He gave a bitter laugh as he picked up his buckets. "Oh, they don't need to tell *us*. The landlord's granted permission and that's all that matters."

The clomp, clomp, clomp of his boots echoed across the yard as he walked away. Jack stood motionless. The silence seemed to go on forever.

"Do you want to take some photos of the swallows' nests?" asked Hannah, and she hated how high and fake her voice sounded. "They're amazing. Did you know the swallows come back to the same nests every year, all the way from Africa? How do they do that? It's like a miracle, isn't it?"

"Actually, I'd better go. Homework and all that."

"Oh, yes, sure," said Hannah, who knew perfectly well that Jack made it a point of honour never to do homework. "Well, thanks so much for coming."

"No problem. See you."

He mooched off up the track, head down, hands in his pockets.

Hannah suddenly felt exhausted. But she needed to speak to Dad.

He was leaning over the wall of the pigsties at the bottom of the yard, the buckets at his feet, scratching his favourite sow behind the ears.

"There you are, Gertie," he was saying, as the pig grunted with pleasure. "Good girl. Good girl."

Hannah stood beside him.

"It's going to be all right," she said. "With the reservoir, I mean. I've got a plan."

"Have you? What's that, then? Yes, that's right, old girl, you like that, don't you?"

"I can't tell you exactly, but it's good."

He gave her a brief sharp look before turning back to his pig.

"You're not going to do anything stupid, are you?"

"Of course not."

"Good. Because I've got enough on my plate at the moment without you getting into trouble on top of everything else."

Hannah crossed her fingers firmly behind her back.

"Don't worry, Dad. Everything will be fine. I promise."

Chapter Twenty-Two

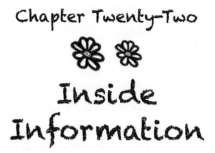

Inside Information

In a classroom off the hall, Miranda was in full flow.

> *"Good night, good night. Parting is such sweet sorrow,*
> *That I shall say 'Good night' till it be morrow."*

She placed one hand on her heart and, with the other, blew an extravagant kiss to Ben, who winced.

"Great!" said Hannah. It was so much easier to direct Miranda when the actual performance was never going to happen. "That was perfect."

"I know," said Miranda, arranging strands of hair around her face with her fingers.

Behind them, somebody gave an enormous sniff. They all turned. In the doorway, wiping imaginary tears from his eyes, stood Jack.

"I'm sorry," he gulped. "That was just so moving."

Ben threw his script at Jack. "Shut up, Adamson."

Jack ducked. "What? It *is* moving. Or is that just me? Is it meant to be a comedy?"

"Jack, get out," said Hannah. "We're trying to rehearse."

Jack looked thoughtful. "Maybe it *is* just me. I'm very easily moved. I cry at cat-food adverts. If, you know, the cat looks really hungry, or has really big eyes."

"Jack! We're having an important rehearsal here."

"Go ahead, don't mind me. I only came to give you this."

He handed Hannah a memory stick. She took it, her heartbeat speeding up as her fingers brushed his.

She looked at him. "Is this…?"

"Just a sample of the kind of thing you might have in the background. Sounds, visuals, you know – what we were talking about on Saturday."

"Oh, brilliant. Thank you so much."

Miranda looked curiously at the memory stick, and then at Jack's and Hannah's faces, and Hannah could have sworn she saw a flash of something very like jealousy pass across her features.

Miranda Hathaway, jealous of her and Jack? Could it really be true?

"When do you need this back?" she asked.

"That's OK, you keep it. It's all on the hard drive."

Miranda looked from one to the other of them, her eyes narrowed.

"Effects for the play," Hannah told her. "It's going to be amazing."

"Yep," said Jack. "The stuff on there will blow your mind."

Matthew appeared in the doorway. "You have got to see this, mate. Look what she's getting them to do."

He dragged Jack out into the hall, where Zara's choreographer was holding a dance rehearsal for the spirits in *The Tempest*.

Lottie appeared in the doorway, holding an embroidered jacket.

"Can you try this on, Ben? In case it needs any last-minute adjustments."

She didn't look at Hannah, and Hannah felt the misery of it like a weight in the pit of her stomach. For a few minutes, the rehearsal had taken her mind off the hideous fact that Lottie had acted all day as though she didn't exist.

Hannah had tried to explain again but Lottie had totally blanked her. How long would she keep it up? What if she went through the whole play like this? What if she never spoke to Hannah again?

Hannah couldn't bear even to think about that.

Miranda looked at Ben's jacket and curled her upper lip. "Are we finished? Because I do have other things to do."

"Er ... yes," said Hannah. "That scene's perfect now. Thanks so much."

Miranda elbowed past the others, her expensive bag whacking Hannah on the leg. She stopped in the doorway. Then she spun round and glared at Hannah.

"Look at that!"

"What?"

"That," spat Miranda, flinging out an arm in the direction of the stage, "is what you get when you have a proper choreographer and a proper costume designer. Not a bunch of amateurs like we've got here. I don't know why we're even bothering."

With a final look of disgust at Hannah and Lottie, she strutted away.

"What are you planning to do about her?" asked Ben. "We'd better think of something soon. We're running out of time."

Hannah and Lottie were silent. Jack walked back into the classroom, unzipped his bag and pulled out a laptop.

"Now she's gone, take a look at this."

"If it's to do with you-know-what," said Hannah, "it's too risky to watch it here. Anyone might come in."

"It's nothing incriminating. Just a bit of film footage. I don't know if you've ever seen it, that's all."

Hannah shot a sideways glance at Jack. He sounded so mature. He hadn't even said anything rude to Lottie. And he clearly had been working on the projections. She had been so right to trust him. Why couldn't Lottie admit that?

Jack double-clicked on the mouse pad and turned the laptop round so they could all see the screen. Ben moved closer. Lottie was fiddling with the jacket, pretending not to be interested, but Hannah knew she was watching.

Up flashed the animated body of a chubby garden gnome, with Lottie's head superimposed on it. The Lottie gnome was dancing to synthesised music.

"Jack!" yelled Hannah.

Lottie made a grab for the computer. "You idiot! Turn that off right now."

"I am *so* sorry," said Jack. "I totally did not mean for that to happen. I have no idea how it got there."

"Delete that this second," spat Lottie. "No, give it here and let me delete it."

"Hey, get your hands off my computer. Look, I'll delete it and you watch, OK? Jeez, some people are so touchy."

Lottie turned to Hannah, her eyes blazing. "See? Do you see now? Or do you *still* think he should be part of our play?"

Hannah felt as though she was going to explode. Emotions boiled up inside her: fury with Jack for making a fool of her, hatred of herself for being so stupid, and utter misery at ruining her friendship with Lottie.

She rounded on Jack.

"How *dare* you do that? You promised! You promised you'd take this seriously and look what you've done. I *trusted* you and you've made a complete idiot of me, and my best friend won't even speak to me. Don't you care about *anything*? You said you wanted to make up for what you'd done, and all you've done is make things worse. The farm's going to be destroyed and all you can do is make videos of dancing gnomes. You are a complete—"

"Hannah," said Lottie.

There was something in her voice that made Hannah look up.

Lottie glanced towards the door with a warning

look. Hannah turned round. Miss Summers was standing in the doorway.

"Oh," said Hannah. "Hello."

Miss Summers stepped into the room.

"I just came to see how your rehearsal was going. Is everything all right?"

Lottie broke the awkward silence.

"Yes, thank you. We've finished the balcony scene. Hannah and Jack were just having a bit of a disagreement about the projections for the backgrounds, that's all."

"I see." She looked hard at Hannah and Jack. "Will you be able to resolve your differences, do you think? Without coming to blows?"

Hannah said nothing.

"I think so, miss," said Jack. "I've got some other stuff she might prefer."

"Right. Well, I'll leave you to it, then. But if you have any problems that are too difficult to resolve by yourself, Hannah, come to me, will you, and we can chat about them. Don't let things get on top of you."

With a last look at Hannah, she left the room.

Hannah turned to her friend and took a deep breath.

"I'm *so* sorry, Lottie. You were completely right and I was completely wrong. He is an idiot."

"Hey, I am here, you know," said Jack.

"Yes, and you're an idiot. Just go away. You've ruined everything."

"Well, I'm glad you've finally realised what a loser he is," said Lottie. "It took you long enough."

Hannah looked at Lottie. Her voice sounded normal again. Could she ... might she ... be forgiven?

Jack was fiddling with his laptop. He turned the screen out to face the others again.

"What are you doing?" asked Hannah. "I told you to go away."

"Just look at this one thing, will you? I'm sorry about the gnome. Just look at this and then I'll go away if you want me to."

A picture appeared on the screen. A flickery, slightly faded, black-and-white film of farm workers harvesting a field of corn.

The camera zoomed in slightly. Hannah gasped.

Grandfather! He had died before she was born, but she recognised him immediately from the photos around the house. He was driving an old combine harvester. He had stopped it next to the grain trailer and the freshly harvested corn was pouring from the combine's chute into a slithery golden heap in the trailer.

She turned to Jack. "Where did you get this? I've never seen it before."

"There's an old bloke down my road who used to work at your farm. Tom Robson? I asked him if he had any photos of it in the old days and he brought me this. He had a bit of a thing about photography, he said. He took this with his first video camera."

The camera panned out to show the tractor pulling the grain trailer.

"Wow, that tractor's tiny!" said Ben. "It hasn't even got a cab. And look at that exhaust funnel."

Hannah wasn't looking at the exhaust funnel. She was looking at the tractor driver.

"Is that your dad?" asked Lottie. "He looks so young."

"His fashion sense hasn't changed, though," said Jack. "He's still working that flat cap and checked shirt combo."

There was no sound on the video but you could tell that Dad and his father were sharing a joke as the corn spilled in a steady stream into the trailer.

"He must be young," said Hannah. "Grandfather died when Dad was fifteen."

"What year was this film taken?" Lottie asked Jack.

"1973, I think he said."

"Oh!" cried Hannah.

"What?" asked Lottie.

Hannah was staring at the screen. "Grandfather died in 1973. In the autumn. He was doing some tractor work for another farmer, up on the Downs, and his tractor rolled over on the hill and crushed him."

"Ouch," said Jack.

Ben gave him a look. Lottie shuddered, even though she had heard the story before.

Hannah looked at the image of her father, so relaxed and carefree up on his tractor seat, with no idea that his world was about to change forever.

"Cool to have some footage of him," said Ben.

"Yes. I wonder if Dad's ever seen it."

The picture cut out suddenly and the screen turned

to flickery greyness.

"I thought it would be good to show this kind of thing," said Jack. "To show the continuity of the same family farming it for all that time."

"It's amazing," said Hannah. "Thank you so much for finding it."

"There's more on that memory stick. And I've set the pictures I took on Saturday to music, so they make more of an impact. Anyway, watch it and see what you think."

Hannah looked at Lottie. "What do you think? Should we give him one last chance?"

Lottie narrowed her eyes. "I don't know. He may have got hold of that film, but he's still an idiot."

"Tell you what," said Hannah. "You and I will watch it together." She turned to Jack. "And if it's *really* good, and if you absolutely swear that you won't mess about, then we *might* let you stay in the team."

Jack looked as though he were about to make a sarcastic retort, when the door opened. He closed his laptop.

"It's OK," said Hannah. "It's only Jonah."

"Charming," said Jonah, walking in and shutting the door. "You won't be saying, 'Only Jonah' when you hear what I'm about to tell you."

"Really? What?"

"This reservoir, yeah? You're not going to believe it."

Hannah made herself focus on Jonah. "Believe what?"

"You know my dad's got this mate who's a local councillor?"

"Yes, you said something about it."

"Well, my dad asked him a while back to find out as much as he could about the reservoir."

I bet he did, thought Hannah. Trying to see how he could make money out of it.

"Anyway, this guy's a retired engineer and he's been looking into all the technical stuff. And he rang back this morning and guess what he's found out?"

"What?"

Jonah looked round at the others dramatically. "You are not going to believe this. I was totally gobsmacked when my dad told me. After everything they've been saying, and all those photos in their brochure. I'm telling you, when we tell everyone, there is going to be a riot in that hall."

Chapter Twenty-Three

Lottie
Investigates

The first lesson for 8M on Friday was geography. They were supposed to be reading information in their textbooks about locations for industry. Lottie was bent over her book, the picture of concentration. If you hadn't known better, you would have taken her for a model student. But Hannah did know better, and Hannah knew that Lottie, like her, was actually reading Aqua's Draft Water Resources Management Plan.

They had decided they must read the Aqua brochure properly if they were going to tackle Nick Constable in public. They had also decided the task would be easier to bear if they did it together. Geography was ideal for this, partly because the brochure fitted neatly inside their textbook, and partly because their geography teacher, Miss Purcell, was both lenient and unobservant.

Hannah looked at the first page. The words swam before her eyes. However many times she tried, it didn't get any easier to read. As soon as she attempted to focus on the brochure, other thoughts popped into her head.

"I emailed Nick Constable's lines to him last night," she whispered.

"Oh, great. I've nearly finished his costume, too. Just a cloak and hat, since I don't have his measurements."

Hannah shuddered. "Well, no, you wouldn't want to get that close, would you?"

"It's quite fancy, so he'll feel really important."

Hannah snorted. "What, even more important than he feels already?"

"Girls," said Miss Purcell, "can we have less talk and more work, please?"

They went back to the brochures tucked into their textbooks. After a few minutes of silent contemplation, Lottie suddenly started skimming through the pages, running her finger down the columns, a frown knitting her brows.

"You're reading fast," whispered Hannah.

"I'm not reading, exactly. The way they write this stuff's so awful, I thought I'd look at the numbers instead. We know they just use words to lie, but maybe it's harder to lie with numbers. Maybe the numbers will actually tell us something."

"Right, class," said Miss Purcell. "Now that you've read the introductory paragraphs, could you all look at the Points for Discussion in the box on page 38? I'd like you to discuss Question 9 in pairs and make a list of at least five points in favour and five against."

Lottie turned to the next page of the brochure. "Here we are. Some actual figures at last."

She pointed to Paragraph 72. The combination of words and figures seemed, to Hannah, even more intimidating than the paragraphs without figures.

Maybe if she read it aloud she would be able to understand it better.

"*The dry year annual average per capita consumption of Aqua's domestic customer base as a whole is forecast to be 166 l/hd/d...*" she muttered. "What the heck is that supposed to mean?"

"I think it means they predict each person in the area will use, on average, 166 litres of water per day in a dry year."

Hannah stared at Lottie as though she had just translated the sentence from Ancient Greek.

"How on earth did you work that out?"

"It's not hard, really. You just need to use your brain a bit."

"But what's all that *l/hd/d* stuff?"

"Litres per head per day, I think."

Hannah gazed at Lottie in awe.

"You just have to work out the abbreviations," said Lottie. "It's really not that difficult."

"Not if you're a genius."

"I'm not a genius. I just try to work things out."

Hannah tried to do the same, but she couldn't tune out Miranda's voice from across the aisle, discussing Christmas plans loudly with Emily. Hannah always found the build-up to Christmas difficult. There was nothing more guaranteed to make you feel the lack of a mother than Christmas.

"So because we're going to the Seychelles for

Christmas and New Year, we're going to have our Christmas party on the first Saturday of the holidays," Miranda was saying. "Can you come? It's going to be the best ever."

"Well, we're not going away for Christmas," said Emily, "so I'm sure—"

"You have to come in costume. We're doing a Victorian theme. Oh, and also you need to bring a piece to perform. It's going to be exactly like a real Victorian Christmas." She caught Hannah's eye across the aisle and put on her sweetest voice. "Oh, I'm so sorry, Hannah. I mean, I'd love to invite you, but I can't have everybody, you see."

"Oh, I wouldn't be able to come anyway," said Hannah airily. "I'll be frantically busy with the Tudor banquet we're giving."

Miranda gave her a suspicious look.

"Oh, didn't I mention it?" said Hannah. "I'm so sorry I can't invite you, but we only have room for our five hundred closest friends. We're roasting ten pigs and seven oxen. My dad's dressing up as Henry VIII. I'm going to be Elizabeth I, and guess what? I'm going to be wearing the *actual* Crown Jewels. My dad has a friend who works at the Tower of London and he said I can borrow them. He says no one will notice if he puts them back the next day."

Emily smiled.

Miranda gave Hannah a sour look. "Ha ha, very funny."

"Girls, there seems to be a lot of talking over

there," said Miss Purcell. "I hope it's all about the question."

Hannah turned back to her desk. Lottie was scribbling down numbers in the back of her exercise book.

"Anything useful?"

Lottie frowned. "They're trying to hide the figures," she murmured. "They stick them right at the back in little tables and they make them look as dull as they possibly can."

"Well, they've done a great job."

"But if they're trying to hide them, then maybe that means they've got something to hide."

Miranda leaned across the aisle. "Oh, by the way, Charlotte?"

Lottie didn't look up. "What?"

"I've brought in a couple of my costumes for *Romeo and Juliet*. They might give you an idea of the sort of standard you'll need to aim for, if you want to be a costume designer."

Lottie remained hunched over the brochure.

"My mum's friend who runs the hire company was saying it's *so* hard to get into professional costume design. Hardly anyone makes it. Apparently, most of the people on her course are working as shop assistants now. If they've got a job at all."

Lottie grabbed her calculator and started stabbing buttons. Hannah envied her ability to shut out Miranda's voice.

"Anyway," said Miranda, apparently talking to Emily, but in a voice clearly meant to be heard by Hannah, "Mum says even though the house play's going to be rubbish, at least my acting will stand out. She says it's a great opportunity to get noticed by a top professional. The judge will probably pass my name on to agents for film roles, you see."

A spark lit up in Hannah's brain. She turned to Lottie, who was frowning over her page of figures.

"I've got it!"

Lottie stared at her notes. "That can't be right." She picked up her calculator again.

"Lottie," Hannah whispered, "I know how to get rid of Miranda. Without force or anything. We just need the right person to do it." She looked around the classroom and her eyes lit on a fair-haired girl at the front. "Jess. She'd be perfect. As long as she agrees. But she'd never tell on us, even if she didn't want to do it. And we'll need other people as back-up. But that—"

Lottie gasped. Hannah turned to her.

"What?"

Lottie was staring at the numbers on her calculator. "If that's right," she murmured, "it's unbelievable." She shook her head. "I must have got it wrong."

She bent over the figures again. She ran her fingers through her hair. She flicked through the brochure and checked something against her notes. Then she turned to another page and did the same.

"It *seems* right," she said, "but it can't be."

"What can't be?"

"Girls, are you OK back there?" called Miss Purcell.

"Fine thanks," said Lottie.

"I'm going to shake you in a minute," whispered Hannah. "What is it?"

"I can't tell you until I know. I might be completely wrong. I'll get my mum to look at it when she comes back from her conference. She's brilliant at maths." She turned to Hannah, her eyes sparkling with excitement. "It seems too crazy to be true. But if it does turn out to be right, it could be the most important piece of evidence we've got."

Chapter Twenty-Four

Backstage at the House Plays

The clapping and cheering and the sound of feet thundering down the backstage stairs faded away as the cast of *The Tempest* left the stage. In a French classroom further down the corridor, Hannah closed the door behind the small group of conspirators: herself, Lottie and Priya, Katy and Marie, Jonah and Jack.

Hannah's body was pumping with adrenalin. She couldn't believe this day had finally come and she couldn't believe what they were about to do.

Even beneath the heavy stage make-up liberally applied by Vishali and Anna in Year 9, Hannah could see how nervous the others were. She hoped her own nerves didn't show too badly.

"Right," she said, "*Twelfth Night* is about to start. We've got ten minutes max before we need to get into costume, so this will have to be quick. Lottie, you go first. If anyone comes in, I'll start talking about *Romeo and Juliet*."

Lottie glanced at the door, then took a bulging envelope from her rucksack and handed it to Jack.

"There's four hundred in there. My dad printed them at work. And I can't believe I'm trusting you with them."

"Can we have a look?" asked Katy.

Lottie pulled a bunch of leaflets from the envelope and handed them round. Hannah had seen it before but she took one and studied it again, her heartbeat speeding up at the thought that, if their plan worked, every member of the audience would have one of these in their hands in an hour's time.

The leaflet was a piece of A4 paper folded into three. On the front it said, in bold black capitals: **GIANT RESERVOIR IN MIDDLEHAM?** Beneath the headline was a photograph of the farm, with a big black cross right through it.

Inside the leaflet, Lottie had summarised the main arguments against the reservoir, with pictures of rare birds, flowers and animals. On the back page, in large bold type, she had written: "Do add your own opinions, but most importantly, **PLEASE WRITE**." Then she had printed the address of the Environment Minister.

"It really does count if the government gets a lot of letters, Dad says. It can make a massive difference."

"Who's handing out the leaflets?" asked Marie.

"Jonah and Jack have organised people to be at all the exits," said Hannah.

"Yep," said Jonah. "Our highly trained team of security guards."

"*Security* guards?" said Priya.

"We have recruited," said Jack, "the entire Under

14 Rugby squad. They are totally up for it. Legalised violence is meat and drink to them."

"They're supposed to be handing out leaflets," said Lottie, "not rugby-tackling people who try to leave."

"Whatever it takes, my friend," said Jonah. "Whatever it takes. They're very versatile people."

"All right," said Hannah. "So leaflets are sorted."

"Oh, yes," said Lottie sarcastically. "Nothing could *possibly* go wrong with that plan."

Priya's face looked strained. "I can't believe we're really doing this."

"I still think he might storm out," said Marie. "Once he realises he's been set up."

Jonah rubbed his hands together. "I think you'll find our security team will see to that."

"Oh, please," said Lottie.

"He's not going to storm out, is he," said Jack, "when he's standing centre-stage with a spotlight on him? It would make him look a total idiot. Once he's up there, he's trapped."

"Well, let's hope so," said Hannah. "Because it's all we've got."

"Oh, I dunno," said Jack. "He's a fair-sized guy, but I reckon we could wrestle him down."

"Sure," said Lottie, "if you really do want to get expelled *and* done for assault. Which, by the way, is absolutely fine by me."

Jack's face crumpled into mock tears. "You are a mean, mean, *meanie* of a girl, Lottie Perfect."

"How could you?" said Jonah, rounding on Lottie.

"You just made Jack *cry*."

Lottie rolled her eyes.

"And Jess knows exactly what to do with Miranda?" said Katy.

Hannah's stomach lurched.

"Ye-es."

Lottie frowned at her. "Why did you say it like that?"

"Oh, I don't know," said Hannah. "It just seems a bit … mean, that's all."

There were incredulous exclamations from everyone.

"Mean?!" cried Lottie. "You're worried about being *mean*? To *Miranda*? After how vile she's been to you at every single rehearsal? Not to mention how vile she is in general."

"Yes, but she has learned all her lines and everything, hasn't she? She's expecting to be in a play and now she's not going to have the chance. That seems a bit mean."

"The thing I'm worried about," said Priya, "is how her parents are going to react. I saw them coming in and I just thought, what are they going to do? They're expecting their little darling to be the star of the evening and instead, she's nowhere to be seen. They'll probably sue us all."

There was silence. Everyone looked at Hannah.

"Oh, lord," said Hannah. "I hadn't even thought of that."

"Leave it to me," said Jack. "I'll handle them."

"So," said Lottie, "your security guards will be

throwing them to the ground, too, will they?"

"Actually, I thought I'd use psychological tactics."
Lottie cackled.

Jack ignored her. "When *Twelfth Night* finishes, I'll go over to Miranda's parents and tell them we're doing something a bit more radical and experimental, and that Miranda has the star part, but it's right at the climax of the play."

Hannah stared at him, her eyes wide. "That's *brilliant*. So they'll sit there all quiet, just waiting for their daughter to come in and steal the show."

"And when she doesn't?" said Lottie. "Then what?"

Jack shrugged. "Then it'll all be over and they won't have interrupted."

"They could still sue us afterwards."

"Well," said Hannah, "there's no point worrying about that now."

"Oh, and, Roberts?" said Jack.

"Yes?"

"I've put in a bit of extra film footage."

"You're telling me that *now*?" Hannah almost shrieked. "How's that going to work with the timings?"

"All right, chill out. It'll be fine."

"But it might mess everything up. What is it, anyway?"

"It won't mess anything up. When it starts, you can all just stand still while it plays. It's only a short clip."

"But what is it?"

The door opened. Hannah's stomach somersaulted. Everyone's heads whipped round.

Vishali put her head round the doorframe.

"It's OK, we're coming," said Hannah. "We've all had our make-up done, anyway. We just need to get into costume."

"You'd better come right now," said Vishali. "You won't believe what Miranda's trying to do."

Hannah's stomach somersaulted again.

"Oh no, what?"

"Just come and see. You're not going to believe it."

Hannah turned to the boys, her insides churning. "Go and get changed. Meet you in the corridor in ten minutes."

The girls hurried after Vishali to the music classroom, which had been temporarily converted into the girls' dressing room. The Kipling House girls, including Martha, were changing out of their *Tempest* costumes and hanging them back on the rails at the sides of the room. Vishali's friend Anna, who was helping with hair and make-up, was on her hands and knees under the teacher's desk, picking up discarded blobs of grubby cotton wool and dropping them in the bin, which was already overflowing with cotton buds, cleansing wipes and crisp packets. The teacher's desk was littered with make-up, sponges and brushes.

"Oh, Charlotte, here you are," said Miranda. She had had her hair and make-up professionally done and was dressed in the first of her five hired costumes.

"I was just telling them you wouldn't mind."

She gestured behind her and, for the first time, Hannah saw a rail of unfamiliar costumes in the corner of the room. Standing in front of the rail, looking hunched and miserable in heavy brocade dresses, stood Bea, Millie, Elsie and Grace.

Hannah stared, speechless. Lottie's dark eyes smouldered.

"What on earth are you playing at, Miranda?"

Miranda smiled sweetly. "My mum's friend was so kind, she sent all her Shakespearean costumes for us. I mean, we ought to do everything we can to win the competition, shouldn't we? And we need all the help we can get at this stage. So I knew you'd understand. I mean, you can always use yours in one of your little chicken shed plays, can't you?"

"Oh, I understand," said Lottie in a dangerously quiet voice. "I understand perfectly."

"We all understand," said Hannah, stepping towards Miranda, rage filling every cell of her body. "And we're all wearing Lottie's costumes. So you can just take those hired ones right back where they came from."

"Oh, look," said Marie loudly. "Here's Jess."

The sound of Marie's voice, unnaturally loud and bright, made Hannah stop. She wanted nothing more than to punch Miranda, but that would not be a good move. There were more important things to be done.

"Hi, Miranda," said Jess. "Oh, you look amazing."

"Thank you," preened Miranda.

Marie put one hand on Hannah's shoulder and the other on Lottie's. "Deep breaths," she murmured.

"Hey, guess what?" Jess said to Miranda. "The judge just asked me to give you a message."

"What, the guest judge?" said Miranda. "The director?"

Out of the corner of her eye, Hannah noticed Amy slip out of the room, a bundle of purple velvet under her arm.

"Yes," said Jess. "Josephine Baxter. She said she'd love a word with you before the show."

Miranda beamed. "Really? Where?"

"In Room 16. I think you'd better go now so you're there when she comes. She won't have much time."

"Ooh," said Vishali, looking up from the desk, which she was wiping with kitchen roll. "What do you think she wants, Miranda?"

"She must have heard about my acting," said Miranda, with a smug glance at Hannah. "I expect she knows someone from my youth theatre. And of course there was that amazing review in the *Linford Gazette* after the festival."

She smoothed down her bodice, flicked back her hair and made for the door. "See you on stage!" she trilled over her shoulder, with a little wave.

"Do you know what?" said Hannah, as the door closed behind her. "I don't feel one bit guilty about her any more."

"Ssh," said Lottie warningly.

Hannah bit her lip. She scanned the room to make

sure the cast of *The Tempest* had all left.

"It's OK," said Vishali. "They've gone to watch the rest of *Twelfth Night* from the back of the hall."

"What if she escapes, though?" said Katy. "And gets the show stopped?"

Hannah's heart pounded. Now that Miranda had gone, there was no pretending any more. What they were about to do was actually real.

Lottie turned to the Year 7s. "OK, take those off and get your proper costumes on, quickly."

"We didn't want to wear these," said Millie.

"I know," said Lottie. "It's not your fault."

"Miranda bullied them into it," said Vishali.

"Lottie's costumes are so beautiful," said Marie, gazing admiringly at Katy's perfectly fitting dress, with its huge puffed sleeves and frills of lace at the wrists. "It seems awful that we're hardly going to wear them."

"I know," said Priya. "But at least the cloaks will be worn."

"You do all have tops and leggings underneath, don't you?" said Lottie. "Unless you're planning to give the audience even more of a surprise than they're going to get already."

"Hannah, are you all right?" asked Katy. "You look weird."

"I'm fine," said Hannah. "Everybody ready? Let's go."

They walked down the corridor towards the doors that led backstage. The boys were already waiting. As they got closer, Hannah saw that Ben was sitting on the floor, huddled against the wall, his head in his hands. Jonah and James were crouched either side of him.

"What's wrong?" she asked, hurrying up to them.

"Oh, phew, you're here," said Jonah. "He's having a panic attack or something."

Ben looked up. His face was white. "We're not really going to do this, are we? It's mad. Collins is sitting in the front row. We're all going to get expelled."

"They can't expel us for doing a play," said Hannah. "You don't get expelled just for changing the words of a play."

"It's a bit more than that, isn't it? We've got, like, the director of Aqua or whatever he is coming. What if he sues us for inviting him to be in a play on false pretences? What if everyone walks out and there's a massive fight with the bouncers? Then we'll definitely be expelled. And no other school will take us and we won't get any GCSEs and I'll have a criminal record and—"

"OK, OK," said Hannah, crouching in front of him. "Slow down, Ben. Deep breaths. You can't think about all that stuff. One step at a time. We're just doing a play, that's all. A slightly different play from the one they're expecting. And if the audience wants to leave, we let them leave. There won't be any fights. Jonah's told the security guys that. And this was all my idea and I'm taking responsibility for it. If anyone's going to get expelled, it'll be me. But that's not going to happen.

OK? Deep breaths."

Ben took a long, juddering breath. Looking at him, Hannah felt terrible. She stood up and turned to the rest of her cast.

"Listen, everyone, you've all been absolutely amazing, agreeing to this. But there is a good chance we'll get into massive trouble. I'll do my very, very best to make sure I take all the blame, but I can't guarantee anything. So if any or all of you want to back out, just walk away now and I promise I'll never say a single word about it. I can do it on my own if I have to. I know all the words."

Nobody moved.

"Are you sure?" said Hannah. "Are you completely sure?"

"Yes," said Katy. "It's the right thing to do. Aqua's just spreading lies. We have to go out there and tell everyone the truth."

From the hall came whooping and cheering.

"Oh, help," said Priya. She looked terrified. "*Twelfth Night*'s finished."

Suddenly, Hannah started to shiver.

Lottie looked at her. "Are you OK?"

Hannah's palms were sweating. She gripped Lottie's arm. "Do you really think we should do this?"

"Just remember," said Lottie, "it's to save your farm. If you didn't try now, you'd regret it for the rest of your life."

Hannah's legs trembled. She took a deep breath, which came out more like a shudder.

Lottie squeezed her hands. "He's here," she muttered.

Hannah looked up. And there was Nick Constable, swaggering down the corridor in the purple cloak and the velvet hat with an ostrich feather that Lottie had made, accompanied by Amy, wearing her Lady Montague dress and her sweetest smile.

"Well, hello, team," he said, beaming around at them. "Aren't we all looking splendid?"

Hannah forced a bright smile. "Are you all clear about everything?"

"Absolutely, boss," he said, with a mock salute. "Learned all my lines, done all my homework." He flashed a smile around the group. "I have to say, I've been very impressed with the standard of the plays so far. Do you think this one has a chance of beating them all?"

"Well, it should do," said Jonah. "With you as our secret weapon."

Nick Constable smirked. "I'm not sure about that." But he definitely looked flattered.

"You know we've changed a few lines," said Hannah, her heart thudding beneath her bodice. "You could probably tell from your script."

"Well, yes, I did wonder where the 'players of Woolf House' were mentioned in the original." He chuckled. "Although it's been many years since I read any Shakespeare, so I could have missed that bit."

They laughed obligingly.

"We just thought it would be nice to give you a

little introductory speech," said Hannah. "Since you're the guest of honour."

"I'm very flattered. And I feel quite the Elizabethan gentleman in this costume."

"Did Amy explain about the cue to remove it?"

"Yes. Sounds a bit unorthodox, I must say."

"Well, we wanted to do something slightly different, you know? Modernise things a little. We know you like modernisation."

"Oh, yes, I'm all in favour of modernisation. Good idea. And Amy here was saying that you want me on stage the whole way through, is that right?"

"Yes, please," said Hannah. "We're all going to be on stage the whole way through. Amy will be beside you all the time, so just follow her lead."

Suddenly, the backstage doors were flung open. A torrent of noise flooded into the corridor: yelling, chanting, clapping, whooping, stamping. The cast of *Twelfth Night* surged down the stairs and spilled into the corridor, chattering and laughing. Hannah's heart was hammering so hard she felt it might burst out of her ribcage.

As the last few Milne House actors tumbled through the backstage doors, Hannah turned to her cast and forced a smile. It felt tense and false.

"We're on," she said, and her voice didn't sound like her own. "Let's go up there and give it all we've got. And whatever happens, thank you, all of you. Thank you so much. You've been amazing."

Chapter Twenty-Five

The
Trial Begins

The noise from the hall was crazy as the Woolf House group took their places on the darkened stage. Peeping through the gap between the closed curtains, Hannah saw for the first time the four blocks of colour in the front half of the hall. Guilt flooded her as she stared at the chanting block of blue. All those people who had bothered to put on their blue PE shirts to support Woolf House's play. And she was about to betray them.

"Woolf House! Woolf House! Woolf House!"

People at the front of the Woolf House area got to their feet, raising their arms above their heads and clapping in time with the chanting. Other houses started doing the same, all trying to drown out each others' chants. The noise was deafening.

In the very centre of the front row was a trestle table, at which sat the three judges: Miss Summers, Mr Lawrence, the Head of Key Stage 3, and, in the middle, Josephine Baxter, the London theatre director. Her silver hair was swept up in a bun. She wore a grey wool jacket with bright-red buttons and a long patterned scarf, draped artistically round her neck. One day, thought Hannah, I want to look like that.

Next to the judges' table sat Mr Collins, looking distinctly uncomfortable at the rising levels of anarchy. Beside him sat Lottie's mum, elegantly dressed as always, a serene smile on her face.

Hannah thought of Miranda, at this minute sitting in a classroom waiting to speak to the director, and her stomach lurched. How long could Miranda be fobbed off with excuses before she realised something was up? And when she did realise, how would the brave souls who had volunteered to hold her in the room be able to contain her?

At the far end of the hall, Jack sat at the lighting and sound desk, looking completely in control. Hannah felt a bit better.

Then she saw her father, sitting between Sam and Jo in the back row, and her insides felt as though they had dropped down a lift shaft. How would he react to all this? Would he be completely furious? And what if she got expelled? How would he feel then?

Beside Sam sat Granny. Sam turned and said something to her and she smiled and squeezed his arm. They both looked excited.

Miss Summers left her seat and walked up the steps on to the stage. She held up her hands for silence. Gradually, the hall calmed down to a fidgety murmur, but the pent-up excitement was palpable.

"Ladies and gentlemen," said Miss Summers to the calmer back half of the hall where the parents sat, "and students," she continued, addressing the front half of the hall and the crowds of actors standing around the walls, some still in costume, many bearing traces of their performances – glittery cheeks, hair in odd unnatural styles – "we come to the final performance of the day."

Her palms damp with sweat, Hannah moved to her place upstage, at the back of the Chorus. The entire cast stood in position in their Elizabethan splendour, their backs to the audience.

Downstage centre, in pride of place, stood Nick Constable, in his purple cloak and hat.

"Without further ado," said Miss Summers, "may I introduce Woolf House's performance of *Romeo and Juliet*."

The eruption of cheering and stamping drove nails of guilt into Hannah's heart. What would the audience do when they realised? Would there be a riot? Would they all walk out?

She couldn't think about that. She had to do this. She had no choice.

Gradually, the noise subsided. Taking one last gulp of air, and feeling as though she were about to dive into a shark-infested ocean, Hannah gave the thumbs-up to Ed, the Year 9 boy in the wings who was operating the curtains. Then she stood with her back to the audience and her arms by her sides, her hands screwed into fists.

The curtains opened, the lights came up and medieval music played over the speakers. Hannah opened her hands. On cue, the entire chorus turned to face the audience. Hannah heard an appreciative murmur from the hall. That must be for Lottie's costumes, she thought, with a little glow.

On cue, the cast raised their heads to look at the audience. On cue, Nick Constable took a step forward. The audience hushed as the music faded and Nick Constable declaimed the opening speech that Hannah had written for him.

"The players of Woolf House hereby present
An entertainment for your hearts and minds.
Forgive us if we err, for our intent
Towards you is most true and most benign."

He gave a little bow and took a step back. Somebody clapped loudly (Hannah couldn't be certain, but she was pretty sure it was Lottie's mum) and other people joined in. Mr Collins applauded enthusiastically, smiling up at the stage. Sucking up to Nick Constable, clearly, thought Hannah.

Nick Constable looked delighted. With a broad flourish of his arm, he made a deep, theatrical bow. Then he stepped forward again and waited for the applause to end before beginning the Prologue to *Romeo and Juliet*.

"Two households, both alike in dignity,
In fair Verona, where we set our scene..."

Hannah could feel the audience settling back to enjoy the show. In the front row, Mr Collins smiled and nodded approvingly.

On the third line of the Prologue, the rest of the cast joined in, exactly as they had rehearsed it. Medieval music played softly and images of Verona appeared on the back wall of the stage. At least, Hannah hoped they were images of Verona, and not of Lottie's head on a dancing gnome. Judging by the audience's reaction, Jack had resisted that temptation.

When the chorus finished the final line of Shakespeare's Prologue, they bowed their heads and turned their backs to the audience as the lights faded to black. A smattering of applause broke out, but it died away as a drum began to beat in the wings. On the first beat, the lights started to fade up. This time, though, the light wasn't warm, bright and golden, but blue, eerie and dim.

On the second drumbeat, Priya turned to face the audience and began speaking Hannah's Prologue. With each slow, portentous beat of the drum, another member of the cast turned to face the audience. And as each actor turned, they joined in seamlessly with the words.

"A secret plan, long hidden in deep vaults,
For this fair village where we lay our scene,
Has surfaced at a meeting held nearby,
Where civil lies make civil hands unclean."

There was a slight movement in the hall, like a breeze blowing through a field of wheat. Hannah's heart thudded. She glanced at Nick Constable, but his expression was as self-satisfied as ever. He clearly hadn't yet realised that anything was wrong.

On the dim, blue-lit stage, a single spotlight picked out Bea, standing downstage left. As she continued to recite the Prologue in chorus, Bea reached her hands around to the back of her dress and ripped the Velcro open. She pulled the dress off her shoulders and it slid to the floor. She stepped out of it and threw it into the wings, speaking the lines the whole time. Then she faced the audience again in her black vest and leggings as though nothing had happened.

The spotlight picked out James, downstage right. He shrugged off his brocade jacket and stepped out of his Tudor breeches. He tossed them into the wings and faced the audience in black T-shirt and black jeans, speaking the lines all the while.

One by one, the actors stepped out of their costumes and resumed their positions dressed all in black, as they spoke the next four lines:

"From forth those secret vaults emerged these plans
To flood the ancient fields of Clayhill Farm:
To bury trees, streams, meadows, all the land
But reassure us it will cause no harm."

At the mention of the farm, Hannah saw Nick Constable give a slight start. He glanced around at the actors, a look of alarm on his face. Their composure seemed to reassure him, though, and, to

Hannah's enormous relief, he turned back to face the audience. The spotlight fell on him and, at an encouraging nod from Amy, standing beside him, he unfastened his cloak, plucked the ostrich-feathered cap from his head and tossed his costume into the wings. Somebody in the audience wolf-whistled and there was a ripple of laughter. Hannah saw, to her amazement, that he appeared to be flattered.

Now only Jonah, Priya and Katy, standing at the back of the stage, still wore their costumes.

Jonah, Priya and Katy walked slowly downstage, as the chorus recited the next four lines:

"The fearful passage of their gross deceit
And the increasing of indignant rage
Which, but this stealth-planned play, nought could
  defeat,
Is now the half-hour's traffic of our stage;"

Jonah, Priya and Katy turned to face the audience. At the exact same moment, they ripped open the Velcro fastening on their cloaks and let them fall to the ground in three puddles of blue, gold and scarlet.

At a nod and a smile from Amy, Nick Constable joined in with the last two lines of the Prologue:

"The which if you with patient ears attend,
What here shall miss, our toil shall strive to mend."

Nathan, Zac and Harry bent down and picked up the cloaks. They fastened them back around

Jonah, Priya and Katy's necks, only this time they were worn on the reverse side, so they all wore black cloaks with brightly coloured linings. Harry placed a judge's wig on Priya's head.

All the cast except Jonah, Priya and Katy turned and walked slowly to the sides of the stage, where they stood in two lines with their backs to the audience.

Millie and Bea brought out a small table from the wings and set it centre-stage. Grace carried on a chair and placed it behind the table, facing the audience. Owen, Nathan and Elsie brought on another table and chair, which they set up stage right, on a slight diagonal. James and Marie carried on the carved oak lectern that was occasionally used in assembly. They placed it stage left.

Hannah scrutinised Nick Constable's face as he stood in the line stage right. He didn't seem to suspect anything. The smug smile was still in place.

All the Year 7s moved downstage, stood in a row and addressed the audience in unison.

"We humbly ask you, friends and countrymen,
To play the part of jurors, sound and true.
We pray you hear our evidence today
And weigh it in your hearts once we are through."

They bowed to the audience and moved back to their lines.

Hannah felt a restless shifting in the hall, a murmuring and whispering, like leaves rustling in the wind. She saw Lottie's mum lean towards Mr Collins, presumably saying something reassuring. With the house lights down, Hannah couldn't make out the expression on Mr Collins's face.

The drum beat its slow, solemn beat again as Priya took her seat at the central table. Her hands were trembling.

Go on, Priya, Hannah thought. They haven't stopped us yet. We just might get away with this.

"Ladies and gentlemen of the jury," said Priya to the audience, and though her hands were shaking, her voice was steady, "in view of rising demand for water in this, the driest part of the country, our local water company, Aqua, has decided that a new reservoir is needed, and that Clayhill Farm, in Middleham, is possibly the best site for this reservoir."

Nick Constable jerked his head round, his forehead puckering into a frown.

"We are here today to determine two things," Priya continued. "One, whether a new reservoir is really the solution to our water needs. And two, if a reservoir is needed, whether Clayhill Farm is the best place to site it. Mr Constable, could you take your place, please?"

By the last sentence, she had to raise her voice to be heard over a rising murmur from the audience. Hannah's throat felt unbearably tight. She had to force herself to breathe.

Amy took Nick Constable's arm. His movements were stiff and his eyes cast wildly around the stage as Amy took him to the other table and drew out the chair for him.

On the white back wall of the stage, two words appeared in large black type.

MIDDLEHAM RESERVOIR

Matthew shone the spotlight on Nick Constable. Confusion, anger and embarrassment passed across his face as Katy walked towards him.

"Mr Constable," said Katy sweetly, "could you possibly tell the residents of Middleham about the exciting new leisure facility you are planning for our village?"

Amy, standing next to his table, smiled at him encouragingly. He gave a nervous laugh. His features appeared to be fighting with each other as he made a huge effort to pull himself together. He cleared his throat.

"Well," he said to the audience, "this is a bit different, eh? Not exactly the *Romeo and Juliet* you were expecting, I bet?"

There was a slight, uncertain laugh from the audience.

"What would Shakespeare say, eh? He must be spinning in his grave."

There was another little laugh. He seemed to relax slightly.

"But times change, don't they, ladies and gentlemen? And we have to change with them. We have to modernise." He paused. Then he pushed back his chair and stood up. "Which is why I'm delighted to be given this opportunity to talk about the exciting new leisure facility that we at Aqua are proposing for your village."

Dread seeped into Hannah. He was too good at this. He was taking control. What if he got the audience on his side? What if this turned into a replay of that awful meeting in Croxton?

Nick Constable walked downstage and addressed the audience confidently, as though they were old friends. He said exactly the same things he had said at the Croxton meeting, about how much the reservoir was needed and the many benefits it would bring to the local community. Katy encouraged him with nods and smiles.

Finally, when he seemed to have reached the end of his speech, Katy said, "Thank you, Mr Constable. No further questions."

With a smile, he sat back down at the table.

"Does the prosecution have any questions?" asked Priya.

At the word "prosecution", Nick Constable gave a slight start. Jonah, in his long black cloak, moved centre-stage.

"Mr Constable," said Jonah, adjusting the shoulders of his gown importantly, "you mentioned that people are using more water than they used to. But isn't it part of your job to encourage basic water-saving measures like rainwater butts in gardens, and dual-flush toilets, which use three litres of water per flush instead of nine?"

"These are measures that we actively support,"

Nick Constable said.

"So why aren't you doing anything?" asked Jonah. He turned to the audience. "Were you aware, ladies and gentlemen, that Aqua's demand forecasts are the highest of any water company in the country? Which means, Mr Constable, that you are actually doing *less* than every other water company in England to encourage people to use less water. Isn't that correct?"

Nick Constable stared at the slide that had appeared on the back wall: a graph, clearly showing that Aqua's predictions for people's water use were higher than those of every other water company in England. His eyes darted wildly around the hall as if to see where it had magically appeared from.

Great work, Jack, thought Hannah. He had done an amazing job with those statistics from Jonah's dad's councillor friend.

"Also," said Jonah, "shouldn't you be installing water meters in all the homes in your area?"

Nick Constable seemed to remember that he was performing in public and, with what looked like a considerable effort, he focused on Jonah again.

"The evidence shows," Jonah continued, "that people use an average of ten per cent less water when they are metered. We don't expect to be allowed to use as much gas and electricity as we want, so why should we expect to use as much water as we like and not pay any more for it? Why is the UK the only country in Europe that doesn't routinely meter domestic water supplies?"

Hannah had found this information in the article she had read about whether new reservoirs were necessary. She waited with interest to see how Nick Constable would answer the question.

"All new homes in our area," he told the audience, "now incorporate water-saving measures, including meters. We at Aqua take water conservation very seriously."

There was a murmur of what sounded very like disagreement from the hall.

"Most homes *aren't* new, though, are they?" said Jonah. "And if you put meters and other water-saving devices into *all* the homes you supply, maybe you wouldn't need to build a new reservoir."

Nick Constable smiled an oily smile around the hall. "Our primary duty is to our customers, to ensure that they have at all times an adequate supply of water. And, after extremely careful consideration and expert analysis, we have concluded that the best way to ensure this is to build a new reservoir."

Ben stepped out of his line and stood facing Jonah. Jonah ceremoniously removed removed his cloak and fastened it around Ben's shoulders. They bowed to each other. Jonah moved into Ben's place in the line and Ben turned to Nick Constable.

"What would you say," Ben asked him, "to the suggestion that actually we shouldn't be building more reservoirs at all? Many environmental experts say that building new reservoirs is just a relatively cheap, lazy and unimaginative solution to water shortages. The north-west part of the UK is one of the wettest areas in Europe and the south-east is one of the driest. So why don't we have a national water grid to move water from the wetter areas of the country to the drier ones? Why doesn't your company recycle water, like in London, instead of just pumping it out to sea? And why aren't you considering seawater treatment plants, like many other islands use?"

"All those options," said Nick Constable, and it sounded as though he was speaking through gritted teeth, "are extremely expensive."

"So it's all about money, then?"

A flash of temper crossed Nick Constable's face. "Of course not, but we have a responsibility to our customers to keep water bills as low as possible."

"Let's move on," said Ben. "You claim you need to build a new reservoir, which is debatable, but let's assume for the moment that you do. The next question, then, is whether Clayhill Farm in Middleham is the most suitable site for your reservoir. What would you say to that?"

Nick Constable was turning pink and his face was starting to shine in the spotlight. He gripped the edges of the table.

"This is ridiculous," he said. "This isn't..."

He stopped.

"Isn't what?" said Ben.

Hannah held her breath as she watched Nick Constable's face. They had decided that the best way to deal with any angry outburst would be to confront it head-on. If they weren't intimidated, then he would be the one looking stupid.

"You seem reluctant to answer that question," said Ben.

Nick Constable glared at him. He said nothing for a moment. But then he cleared his throat, and when he spoke again, it was as though he were reciting lines he had learned.

"We have, of course, given very careful consideration to our choice of Clayhill Farm as a potential site for our new reservoir. The owner of the farm is highly supportive of our proposals."

"Could you tell us what other sites have been considered?"

"I'm afraid we cannot reveal that information at present."

"But you have said you found a lot less wildlife at Clayhill than at other potential sites you have surveyed. Is that correct?"

"That is correct, yes."

Was it her imagination, or could Hannah detect a trace of nervousness in his voice?

Up flashed a slide of the farm in all its autumn glory. Over the image a line of text appeared.

Clayhill Farm: a poor landscape with little wildlife?

Classical music swelled, and a succession of Jack's photographs appeared on the back wall: contented cows, pigs and sheep; hedgerows bejewelled with berries; the ancient apple trees in the orchard laden with fruit. As the images appeared, the black-clad chorus positioned themselves around the stage in groups of three.

Words appeared over the photographs and each group spoke a phrase in turn to the audience. A single drumbeat separated each statement.

"Ten miles of ancient hedgerows."

"Over four hundred trees, including two hundred oaks."

"Nine ancient copses."

"Eleven ponds containing a multitude of aquatic life."

The whole cast spoke the next sentence in unison.

"This landscape has been a working farm for over seven hundred years."

As the slideshow played, Ben robed Harry in the black gown in exactly the same way as Jonah had done to him.

The music stopped. A panoramic view of the meadows appeared on the back wall. The cast stepped forward and spoke together:

"If Aqua gets its way, all this will be lost."

Chapter Twenty-Six

✿ ✿

Shocks and Surprises

The music changed to birdsong: hundreds of birds singing in a dawn chorus. On the back wall, the slideshow showed bird after bird after bird. Under each photograph was written the name of the bird and the date it was last seen at the farm. Next to some of them was written, in red, *Rare*, *Very Rare*, or *Endangered*. As those words appeared, groups of actors whispered them aloud, like a ghostly echo.

Harry walked towards Nick Constable. The chorus fell silent.

"I would be very interested to know," said Harry, "at which other of your potential sites there have been documented and verified sightings of over one hundred species of bird in the past year."

Nick Constable's face presented a perfect blank, as though he were wearing a mask.

"As I said, we cannot reveal any survey results at present."

"And would you happen to know the results of your bat surveys at Clayhill Farm?"

His face seemed to show some relief.

"I can reveal that our bat expert found five species, all of which are common in this country."

"Five species, all common," repeated Harry. "Thank you, Mr Constable." He turned to Priya. "I would like to call a witness to the stand, your honour."

Priya nodded. Nick Constable frowned.

"Sophie Gardner, please."

Heads swivelled all around the hall as, from an aisle seat halfway back, Sophie, in a smart red suit, walked on to the stage and stood behind the lectern. Priya handed her a Bible.

"Name?"

"Sophie Gardner."

"Do you swear to tell the truth, the whole truth and nothing but the truth?"

Sophie swore the oath. Harry asked her why she had chosen Clayhill for her research and Sophie explained why Clayhill was a particularly good environment for bats.

"Ms Gardner," said Harry, "seventeen species of bat breed in England. Aqua's survey found five species at Clayhill, all of them common. Do these findings tally with yours?"

"No," said Sophie. "They do not."

A slide entitled "Bat Capture Data" appeared on the screen. There was a column of Latin names and several columns of figures and Latin words. Nick Constable stared at it, frowning.

"My surveys," said Sophie, "have revealed *thirteen* of Britain's seventeen bat species at Clayhill

Farm, two of which, the barbastelle and Bechstein's –" she pointed to them on the sheet – "are critically endangered."

There were gasps from the audience. Nick Constable's face was crimson with rage.

"I have not been given access to the official bat survey," said Sophie, "although I have put in a request to see it under the Freedom of Information Act. I shall be very interested to see how thorough it was and in what conditions it was carried out. Until then, I will say one thing. Aqua may try to claim that they can provide alternative habitats for these bats. But I can tell you that, beyond a shadow of a doubt, any disturbance to the hedgerows or trees of Clayhill Farm, which has been so carefully and thoughtfully managed for hundreds of years, would have a devastating effect on the native wildlife for which it is a haven and a sanctuary."

"Thank you, Ms Gardner," said Harry. "That is all."

Priya turned to Katy. "Would you or the defendant like to say anything in response to Ms Gardner's findings?"

Katy turned to Nick Constable, scarlet-faced and tight-lipped.

"I couldn't possibly comment," he said, "until Ms Gardner's work has been properly analysed by experts."

"That's not a problem," said Sophie. "My work has been verified by the University of Linford and all my photographs, sound recordings and data will be freely available to you."

As Sophie left the stage there was a burst of applause. Heads turned and there was a swell of conversation. Hannah was filled with gratitude.

Marie moved forward and faced Harry, who robed her in the barrister's gown. Marie moved downstage centre.

"Mr Constable," she said, as the chatter in the hall died down, "have Aqua's archaeological surveys at Clayhill Farm found anything significant?"

Nick Constable's face was grim. "I cannot comment until the surveys have been analysed by experts."

"These surveys did not include South Meadow, is that right?"

"As I do not have the data to hand," he said, with a trace of impatience in his voice, "I couldn't possibly say."

Jack's photograph of South Meadow appeared on the screen.

"Sam and Jo Roberts," said Marie, "have been monitoring the archaeologists' movements on a daily basis, and can confirm that no surveys have been undertaken in South Meadow. However, Sam and Jo have conducted extensive metal-detecting surveys in this field. I would like to call to the stand Dr John Moffat, from the Archaeology Department of the University of Linford, who has analysed their finds."

A tall, balding stranger bounded up the steps on to the stage and grinned at Marie. He gave a friendly nod to Nick Constable, whose face was getting redder and redder. He sat rigid and grim-faced and did not return the man's greeting.

The archaeologist took the stand and swore the oath.

"Were you surprised, Dr Moffat," asked Marie, "to find that Aqua's archaeologists did not include South Meadow in their survey of Clayhill Farm?"

"Very surprised."

"And why was that?"

"A few years ago," said Dr Moffat, "the local archaeological society conducted an exploratory dig at the bottom of South Meadow. There is evidence to suggest that, in medieval times, when Clayhill was part of the Archbishop of Canterbury's deer park, the Archbishop's hunting lodge might well have been sited in that field. During our dig, we found pottery from the eleventh century and a piece of medieval metalwork. So we were most surprised to learn that Aqua's archaeological survey did not plan to include South Meadow, particularly as it has long been thought that an even older building might be sited there."

A close-up picture of four coins appeared on the screen.

"All these coins," said Dr Moffat, "are Roman. The earliest is from the time of Julius Caesar – " he pointed to the elephant that Hannah had admired – "and the latest from the time of Hadrian, in the first century AD. They were all discovered in South Meadow by Jo and Sam Roberts."

There was a stirring in the audience. People shifted in their seats.

"The coins are exciting enough," the archaeologist continued, "but Jo and Sam also discovered these little beauties."

On to the screen came another close-up photo, this time of the cockerel, tortoise and ram that the Beans had found.

"Aren't they in the most perfect condition?" said Dr Moffat. "You can see why the Roberts children assumed they were part of a recent set of toy farm animals. But these copper animals have a special significance. The god Mercury was very popular with the early Romano-British. People often placed statues of him in their household shrines and temples. And he was usually accompanied by statues of a ram, a cockerel and a tortoise."

A murmur swelled through the audience.

Dr Moffat smiled. "I wonder, Mr Constable, whether these finds might give your archaeologists food for thought. Perhaps it might be worth them exploring a little further, before Aqua applies for planning permission to flood South Meadow and bury its secrets forever."

"Thank you, Dr Moffat," said Marie. "No further questions."

Applause broke out as Dr Moffat left the stage.

James walked downstage and Marie robed him ceremoniously. He turned to Nick Constable, who looked as though he might explode at any moment.

"Mr Constable, at the meeting you held in Croxton Village Hall recently, you said that Clayhill is a perfect site for a reservoir because it will only affect one farm and one family. Have I quoted you correctly?"

The sweat on Nick Constable's forehead gleamed in the spotlight.

"We at Aqua realise, of course, that it is never an easy thing for anybody to have to relocate, but people need water, and reservoirs have to be sited somewhere. And it is of course correct that this proposed site does only affect one farm and one family."

Music swelled: Hannah recognised Vaughan Williams's *The Lark Ascending*, which they had listened to in music recently. On the screen appeared old photographs of the farm, beginning with the black and white pictures that Hannah's grandfather had taken when he took on Clayhill in 1945: a weed-infested, overgrown mess, with mud right up to the back door and no running water or electricity. Then Grandfather and his farm workers laying the hedges and repairing the buildings. Next, men ploughing with horses and bringing home the harvest on wagons, followed by photos of Dad at work on tractors and combine harvesters.

Over the photographs were the names of all the groups of people who regularly used the farm: walkers, cyclists, riders, birdwatchers, Scout and Guide camps, school parties: the list went on and on.

There were also figures showing the crops produced last year. The chorus groups spoke these aloud:

"350 tonnes of corn, oilseed rape and linseed."

"200 tonnes of hay and haylage."

"8 acres of wild flower meadows."

"11 acres of wild bird seed."

"With an ever-growing world population," said James, "does it really make sense to flood a productive working farm?"

The chorus lifted their heads and spoke the next line together.

"The wheat alone that was produced at Clayhill last year was enough to make one hundred and fifty thousand loaves of bread."

On the back wall appeared the video footage of Dad and Grandfather. As it played silently, the chorus groups spoke the next lines in turn.

"In 1950, there were forty farms in Middleham. Now there are three."

Photos of road names from around the village appeared.

Field Lane. Meadow Drive. Little Paddock. Farm Road. The Pasture.

"In 1950, all this was farmland," said Hannah's group.

Backstage, a door slammed.

Hannah's whole body clenched. Oh, no. Please, no.

Lottie's group spoke.

"Once our farms have all gone and our food is imported from across the world, will these road names be only faint echoes of our rural past?"

Footsteps clattered up the stairs. On to the stage, her hair pulled into tufts, her make-up smudged and her cheeks flushed, burst Miranda.

The cast froze. Hannah's heart was hammering so hard she thought she might die.

Miranda looked wild, like a crazed animal.

"You traitors! You *traitors*! Plotting and planning against me, going behind my back, after everything I've done! How dare you? How *dare* you!"

Hannah looked at Miranda, absolutely beside herself, and she felt a twinge of pity and guilt.

Miranda's wild eyes found Hannah's. She pounced on her and shook her by the shoulders. Trails of mascara ran down her cheeks. Hairpins hung adrift on clumps of hair sticking out at strange angles all over her head.

"And all for your stupid little farm!" she yelled

into Hannah's face. "Oh yes, I know what this is all about. They told me. I made them tell me. Your stupid, *stupid* little farm that *nobody* cares about!"

From somewhere in the audience, Hannah thought she heard booing. But she couldn't be sure what she was hearing, because Miranda was shaking her so hard that her teeth rattled.

"Nobody cares!" she screamed. "They wanted to see *Romeo and Juliet*, not some pathetic play about a reservoir. Nobody *cares* about the reservoir. Do you really think you can stop it with your stupid, *stupid* little play? And I had all these beautiful costumes and *everything*!"

She burst into furious tears. The crying seemed to make her shrink somehow. The actors glanced at each other uncomfortably. Nobody appeared to know what to do.

It was Priya who moved first. She walked over to Miranda, put an arm around her and started to lead her off the stage.

But Miranda gave Priya a violent shove that almost sent her flying into the audience. She wheeled around and her furious eyes lit on Hannah again.

"You wait, Hannah Roberts! You just wait! Your life won't be worth living after this. You wait and see."

Priya advanced on Miranda again, but more warily this time, like a keeper approaching an enraged beast.

"Get off me!" snarled Miranda. "Don't you dare touch me!"

Suddenly, she seemed to become aware of the

audience. She stared out into the hall. They were booing – yes, definitely booing.

Her face a mix of fury and bewilderment, Miranda gave Priya a final shove and stalked off the stage. She clattered down the backstage stairs. The door to the corridor slammed.

In the hall, there was an echoing silence. On stage, nobody moved. Had she really gone? Or was she just going to get reinforcements?

Dimly, Hannah became aware of Jack, from the back of the hall, waving madly at her. She caught his eye.

Keep going, he was mouthing. *Keep going*.

Photographs of wildlife appeared on the screen: a hedgehog, a lesser-spotted woodpecker, a great-crested newt.

The next line was Bea's. Hannah nodded at her to take her cue. Bea faced the audience and said, in a slightly shaky voice:

"More than half of British native species are in decline."

"One tenth, including those pictured here, are at risk of disappearing," said Grace.

The chorus turned to face the audience, and they all spoke together.

"All these animals thrive at Clayhill Farm."

Hannah felt weak. The worst had happened. Miranda had invaded the stage. And somehow, they had got through it and beyond it.

Unless she came back. She wouldn't come back, would she? Well, there was nothing they could do about that. All they could do was carry on.

More video footage appeared on the screen. Hannah stared. She hadn't seen this before. It was filmed at sunset and Dad's herd of dairy cows, the herd he had been forced to sell last April to pay the rent, were plodding along the back track from their field towards the milking parlour.

Hannah's eyes prickled with tears. Dad had loved his cows. Where were they now?

She blinked the tears away. She couldn't afford to get emotional. She made herself concentrate on the text on the screen instead, even though she knew it by heart. She had written it, after all.

The rich and varied landscape at Clayhill has evolved over many centuries under the stewardship of farmers.

The camera panned out to show a back view of her dad walking behind the cattle. But he wasn't alone. Beside him was a young woman, wearing a white puff-sleeved blouse and a red peasant skirt. She had thick, wavy dark-blonde hair.

"Look at those clothes," Hannah heard Lottie murmur behind her. "Classic early eighties."

The woman turned and smiled straight into the

camera. Hannah drew in her breath.

"Oh, my stars," whispered Lottie. "That's *you*."

A few of the cast stole sideways looks at Hannah. Hannah couldn't speak. She stared hungrily at the moving image on the screen. She had seen plenty of photos of her mother, but never before had she seen video footage. She hadn't known that any even existed.

Mum had turned away from the camera now and her back view was fading into the distance. Hannah wanted to rewind and look, over and over again, at that smiling face, so full of life. She wanted to absorb it, hold it close, make it part of her.

But the film faded into darkness. In the centre of the blank screen, a sentence appeared in heavy type.

If farmers disappear, so too will the English countryside as we know it.

This was Hannah's cue to start questioning Nick Constable about leisure opportunities. She knew that, and yet she couldn't speak. She couldn't get the picture of her mother's smiling face out of her head. She wanted to see it again. She had to see it again.

Lottie reached over and touched her arm.

"I'll do it," she whispered. "Go into the wings until you feel better."

Hannah still couldn't speak, but she nodded and slipped backstage into the darkened wings. She felt shell-shocked. She stared vacantly into the audience and her eye was caught for the first time by somebody standing at the side of the hall.

It was Martha. She was staring at the now-blank screen, brushing her cheeks with her hands to wipe away tears.

Chapter Twenty-Seven

The Demolition Job

"Mr Constable," said Priya, in a voice dripping with politeness, "we have heard extensively about the wildlife and the archaeological remains that would be lost if a reservoir were to be built, but of course that's only one side of the story. Could you tell us more about the leisure opportunities a reservoir would provide for our community?"

On the screen appeared a photo of a beautiful lake. Nick Constable's expression flickered between suspicion and relief. Finally it settled into its default position of smug complacency. He stood up. He seemed to relax a little as he talked about windsurfing and angling, sailing and walking, cafés and stunning views over the woods and downs.

Lottie was wearing the prosecution barrister's robes now. "Thank you, Mr Constable," she said sweetly. "That's all really interesting. There's only one problem as far as I can see."

"Problem?"

"Yes, one problem. None of these leisure activities are actually going to happen, are they?"

Nick Constable looked startled. "I beg your pardon?"

"You heard. You know perfectly well that there won't be any 'leisure opportunities' at this reservoir, don't you? Because it isn't going to have its own water supply, is it? It's not going to be a lovely lake fed by rivers and streams all year round."

She turned to the audience.

"Ladies and gentlemen, if you read the small print in Aqua's glossy brochure, you might have noticed that this reservoir is going to be what they call a 'winter storage reservoir'. You might not have thought anything of that. But we contacted a local councillor who also happens to be an engineer. He explained to us what a winter storage reservoir is. Water will be pumped into it from the river in winter when the river is high, and pumped out in the summer when stocks are low. Therefore, in the summer, the reservoir, far from being a beautiful place to relax and enjoy aquatic activities, will be a sea of mud or, in a dry season, a giant dust bowl."

There was a murmur from the audience as a slide appeared of a vast sea of mud stretching into the distance.

"Clayhill Farm is barely a valley at all," Lottie continued, "so the reservoir would be extremely shallow. So shallow, in fact, that Aqua plans to use half a million cubic metres of soil to create vast banks around the edges."

Pictures flashed up on the screen of bulldozers moving enormous heaps of earth.

271

"Not such a pretty picture now, is it?" said Lottie.

Hannah walked towards Lottie, who took off the black gown. Priya turned to Nick Constable, whose face was contorted with rage.

"Do you have anything to say in response to this, Mr Constable?"

There were angry mutterings from the audience as Nick Constable stood up. But he shot Priya a strange look as he walked downstage. It seemed to be a look of triumph.

"Let me say just one thing, ladies and gentlemen. Our job is to provide water to you. A clean, safe, steady supply of drinking water to every house in this area. That is a huge responsibility. Never mind electricity or gas: as these children said themselves, our most precious resource of all is water. Without it, we would die. Without it, millions do die, all the time, in less fortunate parts of the world. And we at Aqua manage that water. We provide you with all the water you need – no, all the water you *want* – every single day of your lives. As the children have pointed out, we don't even routinely meter water in this country. You can take as much as you want, all day, every day."

He paused and surveyed the audience. "So it strikes me as slightly strange that you're taking remotely seriously the rather hysterical arguments of a group of schoolchildren who, let's face it, have a highly vested interest in this reservoir not being built."

He gestured towards Hannah, now wearing the

lawyer's robes. "Of course Hannah Roberts doesn't want her family's farm to be flooded, despite the fact that her family has been offered a more-than-generous compensation package, which, interestingly, she forgot to mention. Of course her friends are going to support her and I'm sure we all applaud their loyalty. But we're grown-ups, ladies and gentlemen. We're not ruled by the emotions of children. We know full well that the most important thing for our health and the smooth running of our daily lives is a plentiful supply of clean drinking water. We only have to watch the news to see what devastation is wreaked when that supply is not available. But in this country we take it for granted. And why? Because the water companies do their job so well that our water supply is never threatened. And part of that job, ladies and gentlemen, is making tough decisions. Tough decisions like this one. I'm sorry about the birds and the bats, I really am. But in the end it comes down to this. Do you want the birds and the bats, or do you want your family to have water?" He paused and looked around the hall. "It seems to me, ladies and gentlemen, that sometimes we can't afford to be sentimental. Sometimes, as hard as it is, we have to take the grown-up decision."

There was a burst of applause. Hannah stood there, gaping. How had he done that? How had he turned the audience around?

But there was one thing still to be said. And it was her job to say it. She stepped downstage and stood level with him.

"You're right, Mr Constable. Your company is responsible for supplying us all with water. And we should be more grateful for what you do. This reservoir, for example. How many million litres a day will it provide, did you say?"

Nick Constable looked at her slightly warily.

"We calculate fourteen million litres a day on average."

Hannah turned to the audience. "Fourteen million litres a day! And would that solve the water shortages in the region, Mr Constable? If we had those extra fourteen million litres a day?"

His confidence seemed to be growing. "It would go a long way to providing what we need."

"Fourteen million litres a day," repeated Hannah. "Well, maybe that *is* worth flooding a farm for. If that's the only way to get that extra water. And how much will it cost to build the reservoir?"

"Well, it's hard to put an exact figure on it," he began.

"Oh, don't worry if it's too hard," said Hannah kindly. "We found the figures in your brochure. Around a hundred and fifty million pounds, is that right?"

"Somewhere in that region."

There was a murmuring in the audience.

"It sounds like a lot of money," he said, "but it's a reasonable amount for a project of this scale, and a highly worthwhile investment to ensure a steady supply of water for the future."

"Could I ask you one last question, Mr Constable,

before you go away and build your reservoir?"

"Of course."

"How much water leaks out of your company's pipes every day?"

Nick Constable looked unruffled, firmly back in charge. "An element of leakage is, of course, inevitable, but we do everything we can to fix our leaks promptly and efficiently."

There were murmurs from the audience that sounded very like disagreement.

"Can I ask you the question again, Mr Constable? How much water do you lose in leakage every day?"

"Well, of course, as you will appreciate, that is very difficult to calculate exactly."

"Oh, *really*?"

There was complete silence in the hall.

"Maybe you should try reading your own brochure. I know it looks dull beyond belief, but if you get down to the figures buried in the small print, there's some really interesting stuff there. Shall we have a look?"

A slide with two numbers on it appeared on the back wall. Nick Constable wiped sweat from his forehead as he looked at it.

"As you've just told us," said Hannah, "you expect to be able to draw an average of fourteen million litres of water a day from your proposed reservoir. That's a lot of water, isn't it? Now, here are some figures from your brochure. This," and she pointed to the top figure on the screen, "is the number of households in your region. And this – " pointing to the bottom figure – "is the amount lost in leakage per household per day. If we multiply these two figures, I wonder what we'll get?"

Another slide flashed up. One long number, in bold black type.

"That, Mr Constable, calculated using your own figures, shows the amount of water that your company loses every day through leaking pipes."

There were gasps from the audience.

"Over fifty million litres," said Hannah. "Fifty million litres. Lost, through leaking pipes. Every single day."

The noise level rose. Nick Constable, his face shiny with sweat, opened his mouth and closed it again. Emotions scudded across his face like clouds.

Hannah stood facing the audience, feeling strangely calm. People started shushing each other and the noise died down.

"Let's look at one more number, shall we?" said Hannah. "How much do Aqua calculate that it would cost to repair their leaking pipes?"

Jack flashed another slide on to the screen. There was a collective gasp and a babble of conversation from the audience.

"Three hundred million pounds, ladies and gentlemen. Could that figure possibly – *possibly?* – give us a clue as to why Aqua are choosing not to mend their leaks? Because it would be cheaper and easier for them to flood a productive working farm, home to hundreds of species of wildlife, and destroy a family's home and livelihood?"

Nick Constable suddenly let out an extraordinary noise that was somewhere between a snort and a bellow.

"This is an outrage!" he shouted. "An absolute outrage!"

"You're an outrage!" shouted someone from the audience.

Someone else called, "Hear, hear!" People clapped and laughed.

Nick Constable stared into the audience, purple in the face. Then he whipped round and stamped down the steps at the side of the stage. Someone started booing and people from all around the hall joined in. To a chorus of jeers, boos and insults, he marched down the side aisle and out of the hall. Matthew trained the spotlight on him the whole way.

On the back wall appeared a slowly moving, sweeping panorama of the farm. Birdsong played in the background. And then a hand moved across the picture and ripped a huge hole out of the middle of it.

The birdsong stopped. The image faded to black. Another slide appeared. It was a photograph of a winter storage reservoir in summer: a vast bleak desert of cracked brown mud.

At every exit, Hannah saw Jonah's security guards appear, each holding a bundle of Lottie's leaflets.

The cast moved into position on the stage, facing the audience. Marie stepped forward.

"As you leave the hall, you will receive an information leaflet. If you would like to have your say, please write to the Environment Minister at the address on the leaflet."

"Every letter counts," said Hannah. "The letters *will* be read and they *will* make a difference."

The whole cast dropped on to one knee.

> **"If good people do nothing, evil wins;**
> **If lies remain unmasked, then truth lies dead.**
> **Go hence to have more talk of all these things;**
> **Our play today and all you've heard and read.**
> **If we unite, then we can we show our strength;**
> **Together, we can make a difference."**

The lights faded to black. The curtains closed. And the applause began. Not the ripple of polite applause which was the most Hannah had dared to expect, but a roaring and shouting and stamping of feet. A raging torrent of applause.

They stared at each other, wide-eyed. Was that really for them?

The lights went up again and Ed opened the curtains.

The hall was filled with smiling faces and clapping hands. Somebody in the second row stood up. Then the person next to them stood, too. And then the people behind them. And then people started standing up all over the hall, in ones and twos and groups and waves, until every single person in the room was standing.

A standing ovation! Hannah couldn't take it in. It didn't feel real.

She looked at the front row. Surely Mr Collins and the judges weren't standing?

Her stomach lurched.

The judges and Mr Collins were walking out of the hall.

Were they leaving to discuss the prizes? Or were they walking out in disgust?

Lottie suddenly pulled her hand away from Hannah's and ran down the steps at the side of the stage. Hannah stared after her. What was she doing?

Lottie ran down the side aisle and grabbed Jack's arm. He looked so taken aback that he let her start to lead him to the front of the hall. Then he must have realised what she was up to, because he tried to pull away. But Lottie had his arm in a firm grip. She dragged him up the steps on to the stage. Jack was looking more embarrassed than Hannah had ever seen him, but, as the audience roared its approval, he gave an awkward little bow.

Wow, thought Hannah. Never, ever, ever would I have believed that Lottie would drag Jack on stage for a curtain call. It just shows, absolutely anything can happen.

They took a final bow and then, with the audience still on its feet, Hannah led the cast off the stage. So many thoughts and emotions were whirling around in her head that she felt dizzy. She needed time on her own to think about everything.

She opened the door from the backstage stairs to the corridor and came face to face with Mrs Young. The Deputy Head stood in the middle of the corridor, her arms folded and her mouth set in a thin tight line. The others, clattering down the steps behind Hannah, all talking at once, ground to a halt as they saw her.

After a long, terrible silence, Mrs Young spoke.

"Follow me, all of you. The Head wants to speak to you. In his office. Now."

Chapter Twenty-Eight

Afterwards

They were ushered through empty corridors towards the Head's office. Hannah's mood had gone from exhilaration to dread. She was definitely going to be expelled.

Mr Collins wasn't in his office. As they shuffled into the bare, grey room, Hannah's mind went back to the time she had been sent there last summer, for attacking Jack in the dining hall. She wouldn't have believed then that, this time, she and Jack would be there together, on trial for the same crime.

Mrs Young told them to stand facing the Head's desk. There was nothing on it except a computer. Mr Collins was fanatically neat.

Nobody spoke. Not even Jack, who was standing directly behind Hannah. Mrs Young didn't take her eyes off them and her expression didn't change.

Behind them, the door opened. Mr Collins walked in and sat at his desk. He had one of those office chairs with little wheels at the bottom. He placed his palms on the edge of the desk and pushed. His chair rolled backwards. From his new position, he leaned back and tilted his chin upwards, surveying the group of black-clad students from beneath lowered eyelids.

Hannah suddenly had a strong urge to giggle. She made herself think of Dad, and how he would react when she had to tell him she'd been expelled, and the urge disappeared.

The silence seemed to go on forever.

"Well," said Mr Collins eventually. "Well, well, well."

Hannah's stomach cramped in fear. She wondered how the others were feeling. She didn't dare sneak a glance at any of them. She kept her eyes fixed on the bare grey desk.

"It is difficult," said Mr Collins, after another long pause, "to know where to begin."

His eyes travelled over the group, resting on each of them in turn. Hannah knew she had to say something. It wasn't fair that they were all being treated as though they were equally responsible.

"Sir," she said, forcing herself to look Mr Collins in the eye, "it was all my idea. The others just did it to support me. Please don't punish them. They were just being incredibly loyal."

Her nose fizzed and tears prickled at the back of her eyes. She bit her cheeks and blinked them back.

"That's not quite true, actually, sir," said Jack. "It was Hannah's idea, but we were all up for it. None of us was forced into it. Isn't that right?" He looked around at the others, who all murmured agreement.

Hannah stared at the grey carpet in a whirl of confusion. Jack had stood up for her to the Head!

And he had used her first name! She had never heard him say her first name before.

"Hmm," said Mr Collins. "The idea was entirely yours, Hannah?"

"Yes," said Hannah, her insides twisting into knots.

Mr Collins cleared his throat.

"I have to say, I find your behaviour quite extraordinary," he said, holding her gaze with his watery blue eyes so that she didn't dare blink, let alone look away. "Quite extraordinary. I am almost at a loss for words."

"And yet still he manages to talk," murmured Jack.

Mr Collins snapped upright in his chair. "I beg your pardon?"

He must have the hearing of a falcon, Hannah thought. She had barely caught Jack's words herself and she was right in front of him.

"Nothing, sir," said Jack.

But Mr Collins had turned his attention back to Hannah.

"You were entrusted," he said, "with the great honour of directing your house play, and yet you abused that privilege in the most contemptible manner." He began to count on his fingers. "You have deceived your teachers, who put their trust in you. You have let down your house by flouting all the rules and thus disqualifying yourselves from the competition. You have led other members of your house into trouble, as evinced by the fact that they too are now standing in my office rather than attending the prize-giving ceremony. And, worst of all, you have thoroughly insulted and humiliated a guest of this school. Not only a guest, but the sponsor of the house play competition. Your behaviour has been outrageous."

Mr Collins rarely lost his controlled manner, but he had worked himself up over the course of this speech and now he looked truly angry. His face was almost as red and shiny as Nick Constable's had been on stage.

Hannah realised she was shaking. If she was expelled, she suddenly thought, where would she go?

And then the worst thing of all hit her like a blow to the face.

If she had to change schools, she wouldn't be with Lottie any more.

Oh, she hadn't thought this through at all, had she? Why, oh why, had she done something so completely mad?

Through the fog of misery and terror, she suddenly realised that Lottie was speaking.

"It's not like you make it sound, sir," she was saying. "Hannah didn't start by wanting to deceive anyone. We were practising *Romeo and Juliet* for ages. It was just that her farm was getting destroyed and this was the only way to make people listen."

Mr Collins cut in, and his voice was icy.

"And you thought, did you, that the house play competition was the proper forum in which to air your grievances? And not only to air your grievances, but to trick, insult and humiliate the very man whose company was sponsoring the competition, and who had agreed, out of the goodness of his heart, to appear in your play?"

"Out of the goodness of his heart?" spluttered Jack. "Didn't you hear the evidence, sir? He only agreed to be in the play because he thought he'd get popularity points. His company is trying to destroy Hannah's farm, and they're lying through their teeth about it. They're only sponsoring the plays to get the village on their side about the reservoir."

"Be quiet, Jack," snapped Mr Collins. "That is quite enough from you."

He let his eyes travel across the whole group, resting on each of them in turn as he spoke.

"Had you wished to challenge Aqua's plans, you could have done so by any number of means. But to take advantage of the trust your teachers had shown in you and hijack a school event in order to have your opinions heard is absolutely appalling."

He paused. "I shall have to consider what punishment will be appropriate in your case, Hannah. I shall see you here at 8.30 on Monday morning. And as for the rest of you, I shall be writing to your parents, and I shall have to think very carefully before any of you is allowed to participate in any house or school activity again, whether sporting, musical or dramatic, or indeed, whether any of you will be allowed to hold any position of responsibility in this school at any point in the future."

Some of the Year 7s were crying now. Hannah

desperately wanted to give them a hug. Tears were pouring down her cheeks. She had got everyone into massive trouble and all for her own selfish reasons. What had she been thinking?

Mr Collins glanced at the clock on the wall. He placed his hands on the arms of his chair and stood up.

"I think you had all better go home immediately."

There were sounds of dismay from around the group.

"But, sir," said Marie, "my sister's in the hall and I have to walk home with her."

"I live in Bletchington," said Grace, "and my mum and dad are in there and they're taking me home."

"My brother's in there and he's got my bus fare," sobbed Millie.

Other people opened their mouths to protest. Mr Collins's lips tightened. But then his expression changed. He surveyed the group with a hard little gleam in his eye.

"Very well. You will stand at the back of the hall, under the strict supervision of Mrs Young, and you will watch the other houses receive their awards. And perhaps that will help you to reflect on how you have let everybody down this afternoon: your house, your teachers, your families and, most of all, yourselves."

Chapter Twenty-Nine

The Awards Ceremony

"Sadist," muttered Jonah, as they were escorted back to the hall. "Did you see his face? He was loving the idea that we'll all be standing at the back crying while the other houses pick up their trophies."

Jack gave an exaggerated sob. "I can't believe we're not going to be allowed – " his voice wobbled – "positions of responsibility. Thanks a lot, Roberts. You have totally ruined my chances of being Head Boy."

Hannah, who had managed to wipe her tears away and get herself under control, let out a laugh that immediately felt as though it was going to turn into a sob. She clamped her mouth shut. Mrs Young, hearing the laugh, shot her a filthy look.

"I can't believe you argued back with him like that," whispered Katy to Jack. "In his own office."

Jack snorted. "Collins's office? Home from home. I spend more time in there than I do in my own living room."

"Not this term," said Marie. "You've been a bit of a reformed character this term."

"Since Danny left," said Jonah.

"Yeah, till Roberts led me astray."

They were outside the hall doors now. Mrs Young turned and glared at them.

"I said no talking," she snapped. "The prize-giving is in progress. Go into the hall in single file and in absolute silence. Stand in a line against the back wall."

"And wait for the firing squad?" muttered Lottie.

"I don't want a sound or a movement out of any of you," Mrs Young said. "You're in quite enough trouble as it is and you're very lucky to be allowed to watch the prize-giving at all."

Applause broke out in the hall and Mrs Young opened the doors. They filed in and stood along the back wall. Hannah found herself between Lottie and Jack. They had to squeeze up to fit everybody in and her arm was almost brushing Jack's. The proximity made her go hot all over.

The famous theatre director stood on stage next to Miss Summers, behind a trestle table displaying several shiny trophies. She was presenting a shield to two girls from Conan Doyle House. She shook both their hands and spoke warmly to them. Then the girls turned to face the audience and held up the shield. The Conan Doyle students cheered and whooped. Hannah wondered what the trophy was for. She glanced at the Woolf House group, sitting silently on the other side of the hall, and she was filled with guilt again. She would never be able to make it up to them, would she?

Miss Summers handed another trophy to Josephine

Baxter, who turned to the packed hall and smiled.

"The prize for Best Sound and Lighting goes to…" She paused dramatically.

"Milne House!"

Cheers and stamping came from the green-clad Milne section of the audience, as a Year 9 boy and girl ran on to the stage and collected the cup.

Miss Summers handed the next trophy to Josephine Baxter.

"And now the prize for best costume design."

Hannah felt terrible. Lottie should have won this, no question. What had she been doing, depriving her best friend of the trophy that should have been hers, just for her own selfish reasons?

"The prize for best costume design goes to … Woolf House!"

The Woolf House students exploded into celebration.

Hannah stared. She looked at Lottie, who was frowning and shaking her head.

"She must have got it wrong. She must have forgotten we're disqualified."

The judge held her palms up for silence and addressed the back of the hall. "As the Woolf House cast and crew missed my introductory talk, I just need to explain to them that, although their play has been disqualified from the competition, the superb costumes that we saw on stage in their opening sonnet were clearly made for *Romeo and Juliet*, and therefore there was no reason to disqualify them from the costume prize, which they absolutely deserve.

Could Woolf House's costume designer please come and collect the trophy?"

Lottie looked shell-shocked. Hannah gave her hand a huge squeeze. "Go on. Go and get your cup."

Lottie, looking dazed, walked up the aisle to an eruption of cheers and whoops from the delighted Woolf House students. Hannah felt the lightening of a burden, as though an enormous load had been lifted from her shoulders. Lottie had been recognised. Hannah hadn't prevented her best friend from being awarded the prize she deserved. And Lottie *so* deserved this prize.

The judge was shaking Lottie's hand, smiling and talking to her animatedly. And Lottie, always so cool and composed, was actually blushing.

She walked back down the aisle, head down, trying to hide her glowing face. Hannah gave her a huge hug as she took her place against the wall again.

"What did she say?" Hannah asked.

"Nothing," said Lottie, but she couldn't help a huge grin escaping.

The hall quietened as Miss Summers lifted the one remaining trophy, a big wooden shield with a silver plaque in the centre. She handed it to Josephine Baxter, who turned to the audience.

"Well, here it is. The one you've all been waiting for. The House Play Shield. The winning house, as well as receiving one hundred house points and all the glory and honour of being the winners, will also have a day off school at a theme park, kindly sponsored by the local water company, Aqua."

There were giggles and mutterings at this. People turned their heads to look at the disgraced group at the back of the hall and whisper to each other.

"So, without further ado," said the judge, "will the director of the winning house play please come on stage to receive the shield. The winning house is..."

She paused. It felt as if every single person in the hall was holding their breath.

Josephine Baxter gave a beaming smile. "Kipling House!"

It was as though somebody had put a match to a can of petrol. The red Kipling section of the hall exploded into noise and colour and movement, cheers and whoops and catcalls and waving of arms and stamping of feet. Hannah could see Martha and Jade jumping up and down with their hands in the air and she felt genuinely pleased for them. They deserved it. They had worked really hard and they had produced a good play. Maybe *Romeo and Juliet* could have been better. But she had made the choice, hadn't she?

Had it been the right choice? Would her play have any effect?

She would just have to wait and see.

People were reaching round to the backs of their seats for their coats. But Josephine Baxter was holding up her hand for silence again.

"There is just one more thing I want to say, and I know you've been sitting here for a long time now, but please bear with me for another couple of minutes."

She paused and the audience settled down.

"I want to say something that is probably very unorthodox and subversive, but I'm a theatre director, not a teacher, so you'll have to forgive me." She looked into the front row and smiled, presumably at Mr Collins. Hannah couldn't imagine that he was smiling back. Unorthodox and subversive was so not his style.

"The play that Woolf House presented today," she continued, and Hannah's insides did a violent somersault, "was certainly unorthodox and subversive. It was absolutely not what they were supposed to do."

Heads craned round. Hannah stared at the floor in agony, feeling hundreds of eyes on her. If only she could disappear. Why did the judge have to do this? Hadn't they had enough of a telling-off already?

"And yet," said Josephine Baxter, "their play was one of the most gripping pieces of theatre I have ever seen."

Hannah's head shot up. She stared at the judge. Had she really just said what Hannah thought she had said?

"What an amazing achievement," Josephine Baxter continued, "to create that surprise, that jolt, in an audience of over four hundred people. To begin a Shakespeare play, and then to dismantle that play, through words and through the visual symbolism of removing the costumes, on stage, in front of a packed hall. The vision was masterful. And the *daring*, the sheer courage, in bringing their villain on stage, unscripted, letting him think he was the star of the show and then gradually unmasking him, leading him into their traps, over and over again. What a fantastic idea to have a member of the cast play the part of a disgruntled actor who had wished to be in *Romeo and Juliet*, having the actor burst on stage and condemn the play and, by doing so, highlight just how right it was that the cast were doing what they were."

Hannah stared at Lottie, her mouth hanging open.

"Miranda?" she mouthed.

"And the way the play built up to its climax, with more and more damning evidence, was extraordinarily well handled. It was iconoclastic, it was compulsive viewing and it was a stunning piece of theatre."

A couple of people began to clap, but Josephine Baxter held up her hand for silence again.

"One more thing. It is the bold, the brave, the original, those who dare to be different, who use their intellects and their creativity to fight for what they believe in and to make their dreams come true, it is those people who change the world. We don't have to travel to change the world. We can do it just by standing up for those things we know are right: in our families, our schools and our communities."

Her eyes panned around the hall, taking in everybody, until finally they rested on Hannah.

"All those of you who dared to do what you

did today, you didn't win a trophy, but you might just have won something far more important." She paused. "I hope you save your farm. I hope you change the world."

She walked into the wings. And Hannah, standing with her head bowed and her heart racing, heard chairs scrape back and another standing ovation erupt around the hall.

Chapter Thirty

❀ ❀

Congratulations and Apologies

When the applause finally died away and the hall transformed from ordered rows into a swarming mass of bodies, Hannah suddenly found herself surrounded by a crowd.

"Well done," said Emily. She was holding one of Lottie's leaflets. "That was amazing. I'm definitely going to write."

"Me, too," said a couple of Year 7 girls standing next to her.

"I can't believe how they lied like that," said Vishali. "I think everyone in the village is going to write."

A group of boys from 8P walked past. "Hey, Hannah, you owe us a day at a theme park," called Thomas Campion.

"Only if *Romeo and Juliet* had won the shield," Vishali called back. "And it wouldn't have. I saw rehearsals of both, and *The Tempest* was miles better."

She turned to Hannah and winked. "Actually, I reckon yours would have won, but if you take my advice, you'll tell everyone it didn't stand a chance."

Hannah became aware of the penetrating voice of Miranda's mother, with her arm around Miranda, standing at the centre of a cluster of people several feet away.

"I know, wasn't she just *extraordinary*?"

Miranda's head was bowed and Hannah couldn't see her expression. She nudged Lottie and tilted her head in Mrs Hathaway's direction. Trying to look as if they were making their way to the refreshment table, the two girls drifted towards Miranda and her mother.

"It was *marvellous*, wasn't it?" Mrs Hathaway was saying. "So selfless, such a lack of vanity, to take on that role, to transform herself from the beauty that she is into this almost unrecognisable *creature*. I mean, that's the sort of performance that wins Oscars, isn't it? Did you *see* how she held the stage? Absolutely mesmerising."

She smiled fondly at Miranda, who continued to look at the floor.

"She's still wiped out from it, aren't you, darling?" said her mother, stroking her cheek. "Look how her make-up's smudged. Real tears she was crying. Such *incredible* passion. Such *extraordinary* talent. And do you know, she never breathed a word about it beforehand. It was a *complete* surprise to us. She's *such* a professional, aren't you, darling?"

Lottie caught Hannah's eye and grinned. Hannah could guess what Lottie was thinking. As far as the outside world was concerned, they were safe. Miranda would never be able to reject that sort of praise by confessing the truth.

But Hannah could imagine only too well how much Miranda would be hating her right now.

Miranda slipped away from her crowd of admirers, muttering something about sorting her hair out. Feeling queasy, Hannah followed her.

Lottie tugged at her arm.

"Where are you going?"

"To apologise."

Lottie gaped. "To *Miranda*? Are you mad?"

"I have to. It wasn't nice, what I did."

"*She's* not nice. She completely deserved it. And anyway, everyone's praising her for her marvellous acting. You could say we've done her a favour."

"That's not the truth, though, is it? And it doesn't matter what everyone else thinks. What we did wasn't good. It had to be done, but it still wasn't good. So I need to apologise. Don't try and stop me."

Lottie spread out her palms and took a step backwards, as though Hannah's madness might be contagious.

"Fine. I just hope you've made a will, that's all."

* * *

Hannah found Miranda in the girls' toilets, with what looked like the entire contents of an expensive beauty counter spread across the windowsill.

Miranda glanced at the door as Hannah walked in. When she saw her, she turned back to the mirror without a word.

Hannah scanned the room. They were alone.

She spoke quickly. Someone might come in at any moment.

"Miranda, I'm so sorry for what we did – what I did – to you. Deceiving you, and not letting you have your chance to be in *Romeo and Juliet*."

Miranda gave no sign of having heard. She brushed grey powder across her eyelids.

"I had to do it," said Hannah. "Aqua has been lying to everybody, and this was the only chance we would ever have for everyone in the village to hear the truth. But I know you don't care about that and there's no reason why you should. And I'm very sorry that you didn't get the chance to be in a play."

Miranda unscrewed a mascara tube and started to stroke her lashes. When she spoke, it was in a detached tone and her attention remained fixed on the mirror.

"Do you really think I care that I wasn't in your pathetic little production? To be honest, it was a relief. I was embarrassed to be associated with it. My acting was the only good thing in that play, and the judge loved my acting anyway."

Hannah held her breath. She couldn't believe it. Was she really going to get off this lightly?

Miranda screwed the mascara wand back into the tube. Then she turned and looked Hannah in the eye. Her voice was hard.

"But I will never, ever forgive you for what you did, Hannah Roberts. And I will pay you back. Remember that. You're going to wish you had never been born."

* * *

"Of course she'll never forgive us," said Lottie, when Hannah told her what had happened. "We've tricked her and humiliated her. She'll hate us forever. We're just going to have to live with that. And I think I can manage it."

Hannah's heart contracted as she saw Miss Summers weaving her way through the throng towards them.

"Uh-oh," said Lottie. "Someone else we need to apologise to."

They started on their apologies before Miss Summers had a chance to speak.

"We're so, so sorry," said Hannah, talking over Lottie. "We really were going to do *Romeo and Juliet* – well, you saw us rehearsing, didn't you? – but then it was so awful, what was happening to the farm, and we didn't know what else to do and—"

Miss Summers put a restraining hand on Hannah's shoulder.

"Thank you for apologising. But there's really no need. I thought your play was fantastic. I'm very glad the judge said what she did."

She glanced around the hall. Then she lowered her voice. "But as far as the authorities are concerned, I'm very, very disappointed in you, so don't go telling anybody anything different."

A Year 7 parent tapped Miss Summers on the arm and she turned away to speak to him. Lottie and Hannah stared at each other.

"Well…" Lottie began.

"Congratulations, darlings!" called an unmistakable voice.

Lottie's mum ploughed through the crowd as if it didn't exist, dragging Hannah's dad, who looked distinctly uncomfortable, in her wake. She swooped on Hannah and Lottie and hugged them tight.

"Congratulations, darlings. Congratulations, all of you. That was quite a coup. I'm *so* proud of you. And Arthur is, too, aren't you, Arthur?"

"I certainly am," said Dad. Hannah met his eyes. He smiled at her and there was real warmth in his smile. "What you just did up there might save the farm."

With her father standing in front of her, smelling faintly of pigs, Hannah had a moment of insight.

"No. If the farm does get saved, it will be you who saved it. That ovation – it was for the farm and the way you've looked after it all these years."

"Maybe, but it was you lot who showed everyone what's happening right under their noses. Now they'll be writing to the Environment Minister, and Aqua will have to sit up and take notice."

"It was Lottie's dad and Sophie as well," said Hannah. "And the Beans, with their Roman remains."

"Beautiful old film footage, too," said Vanessa. "It was extraordinary to see Rachel there on the screen." She turned to Hannah's dad. "I never realised how like her Hannah looks."

Dad's eyes rested on Hannah for a moment, but a part of him seemed a long way away. "Yes," he said eventually. "Hannah's very like her mother."

At that moment, Martha appeared with Granny.

"Well done, Martha," said Vanessa. "Lovely dancing."

"Yes, well done," said Hannah. "Your play was great. And your costume was definitely the best." She winked at Lottie.

"Thanks," said Martha. "I said we'd win, didn't I?"

Lottie raised her eyebrows. "Gracious as always."

Granny smiled at Lottie. "Your costumes were wonderful, Lottie. I'm so glad you won the prize. And the play ... those old films..."

Her eyes filled with tears. She lowered her head as she blinked them back. Hannah suddenly realised that Granny had probably never seen any film footage of her daughter. She walked over and put her arms around her. Granny hugged her tight and Hannah was taken aback at how small and thin she felt.

"Hi, Jack," she heard Martha say, in her most flirtatious voice.

Hannah looked up. Granny released her and they both wiped their eyes. Jack was holding something out to Dad, and Hannah was glad he wasn't looking at her. It gave her an extra few seconds to rearrange her face.

"I thought you might like this, Mr Roberts."

Dad took the little piece of plastic and stared at it. He turned it over in his hand, looking bewildered.

Hannah laughed. "It's a memory stick, Dad. It

stores the work you've done on a computer." She turned to Jack. "Sorry, Jack, he still uses a typewriter."

"Everything that was on the screen up there is stored on that," Jack explained. "All the photos and the video footage. You just plug it into a computer when you want to watch it. Hannah will show you how."

Dad was staring at the USB. "All of that is stored in this?" He shook his head. "Incredible."

"Is that film of Mummy on it?" asked Sam.

"Yes," said Jack. "It's all there."

"Can you make me a copy, too?" asked Martha.

"Sure, no problem."

Dad shook himself out of his reverie. "Thank you, Jack. That's very kind of you. It was very impressive, what you put together there. Very impressive."

Jack shook his head. "It was the least I could do. After ... you know ... everything."

"Well, I appreciate it," said Dad. "I think it might make a real difference."

Jack's eyes met Dad's. Dad held out his huge, calloused hand. And Hannah watched in amazement as her father and Jack Adamson shook hands.

Chapter Thirty-One

Christmas Eve

The sitting room sparkled like it had never sparkled before. Hannah had polished the silver candlesticks to a deep gleam and they glittered in the light from the roaring fire. Dad kept stoking the fire with dry logs, and they blazed heat into the crowded room as they crackled and shot sparks up the chimney.

Across the ceiling, Hannah had looped multi-coloured paper chains made by the Beans. The stern-faced family portraits were brightened with silver tinsel, strands of ivy and branches of holly and fir tucked behind their gilt frames. Mum's precious glass baubles hung from the picture rail and caught the light from the fire.

Best of all was the Christmas tree. They had chosen it from the plantation in the woods yesterday, riding there in the box fixed to the back of Dad's ancient tractor, holding on to the freshly cut tree on the journey home, singing carols and getting prickled by its needles as the tractor bumped over the fields. When they stood the tree in the drawing room, the top brushed the ceiling. Dad had draped it with lights and the children had decorated it with every ornament they could find.

"Oh, my word," Lottie had said. "Did you all just close your eyes and *throw* the decorations at it?"

But Hannah thought it looked beautiful. She couldn't understand Lottie's house at Christmas, with its tiny tree adorned with colour-coordinated baubles and a tasteful seasonal flower arrangement on the windowsill. If she had as much money as Lottie's parents, she would have so many Christmas decorations that you wouldn't be able to see the walls.

Hannah would happily have exchanged every one of her Christmas decorations, though, for the latest addition to the sitting-room walls. It was the front-page article from last week's *Linford Gazette*, hanging next to the fireplace in a brand-new frame.

AQUA ABANDONS RESERVOIR PLANS

Residents of Middleham were delighted to learn yesterday that water company Aqua has scrapped its controversial plan to flood a historically and ecologically important farm in order to create a new reservoir.

Following a packed public performance by Middleham Community College students last month, which highlighted concerns about the proposed reservoir, the Secretary of State for Environment, Food and Rural Affairs was deluged with letters objecting to Aqua's plans to destroy beautiful Clayhill Farm, on the outskirts of Middleham.

Aqua claimed the reservoir would be vital to provide its customers with a secure supply of water, but the company's claims were called into question when the students revealed that Aqua is losing three times as much water per day from its leaking pipes as would be provided by the reservoir.

The water company's surveys of the land they proposed to flood were also revealed to be inaccurate and incomplete, and the company was accused of failing to understand the habitat value of the landscape for a wide variety of scarce and endangered native wildlife species.

Bat specialist Sophie Gardner, 33, who gained access to Aqua's surveys under the Freedom of Information Act, said: "Their hedgerow surveys were conducted out of season and their bat surveys were undertaken in inappropriate weather conditions. Crucial surveys of butterflies, moths and molluscs were also inadequately carried out."

The play, which was researched, written and performed by Middleham Community College students, galvanised the village into bombarding the Environment Minister with hundreds of letters objecting to the reservoir scheme.

Local resident Elizabeth Flowers, 42, said: "The children did an incredible job. Aqua should be ashamed of themselves. They clearly only care about their own pay packets."

As a direct result of the letters opposing the reservoir, the Environment Minister called a meeting with Aqua bosses last week. Following the meeting, Aqua announced that it would not be continuing its programme of investigations and surveys at Clayhill Farm.

Aqua's Assets Director, Nick Constable, who masterminded the reservoir scheme, declined to comment.

However many times Hannah read that article, it never failed to give her a warm glow inside. The last sentence alone was something she would treasure for the rest of her life.

Mr Collins had assured her that the two-day suspension from school he had decreed as her punishment would remain on her records forever. It was clear that he expected her life story from this point onwards to be a tragic descent into shame and disgrace, probably ending with a long prison sentence and a painful, lonely death. Hannah had nodded seriously throughout his lecture. It was a bleak picture but, on balance, it would have been worth it.

Hannah and Lottie circulated the packed sitting room with plates of Granny's mince pies and jugs of mulled wine. They had made the mulled wine by pouring every bottle in the larder into Mum's preserving pan. Then they had tipped sachets of spice mix from Lottie's kitchen cupboards into the pan and heated it all on the Aga.

Lottie's mum took one sip, screwed her face up as though they had fed her rat poison and beckoned them out into the kitchen.

"Where's the rest of this brew?" she asked Hannah, tying an apron around her waist. "Don't worry, I'll sort it out. Just point me in the direction of the sugar, would you, sweetheart?"

Back in the sitting room, the Beans were offering round their homemade fairy cakes. Hannah and Lottie watched the faces of the guests as they stared at the lime-green icing decorated with dried kidney beans.

Hannah had warned the Beans that their efforts might not be appreciated by everyone. "Some people might not understand. I mean, they're not exactly festive, are they?"

"They're appropriate," said Jo, "and that's what matters."

The Beans offered their plate of cakes to Jack, Ben and Jonah, who were skulking in the corner with cans of Coke, making rude comments about the family portraits.

Jack frowned at the Beans in concern.

"If you two eat beans," he said, "doesn't that make you cannibals?"

"Oh, we're not going to eat them," said Jo. "We tried them. They're disgusting."

Martha, eyeing the lime-green, bean-topped cakes with horror, had pulled a recipe book from the shelf and, to everyone's amazement, produced the most delicious chocolate chip cookies. Hannah, who liked Christmas to be traditional, had made a proper Christmas cake. It crumbled into pieces as soon as it was cut, but it did taste good.

Standing in the doorway, looking around the big, brightly decorated room, Hannah swelled with happiness. This is what Christmas ought to be like, she thought, and what Christmas hadn't been like at all in the seven years since her mother had died.

The party had been Hannah's idea. "We ought to do something," she had said to Dad. "We should thank all the people who helped with the reservoir campaign, and everyone who wrote letters to the

Environment Minister to save the farm."

Amazingly, Dad had agreed. And he even seemed to be enjoying it. He still looked too tired and too thin, Hannah thought, but he was clearly enjoying the conversation he was having with Ben's dad about rare-breed pigs.

"Christmas cake?" said Hannah, offering the plate. The men scooped up a handful of crumbs each.

"I've always loved pigs," Ben's dad said. "I really fancied having one at the bottom of the garden, like people used to do, but we just haven't got the space. Those Gloucester Old Spots of yours are beautiful."

Anyone who could see the beauty of a rare-breed sow was a thoroughly good person in Dad's eyes. Those two would be friends for life now.

"Your dad seems to be having a good time," said Lottie, appearing in the doorway and following the direction of Hannah's eyes.

"So does yours."

Lottie's dad and Sophie had been chatting away since the beginning of the party, each seeming enthralled with what the other had to say.

"Birds and bats," said Lottie, shaking her head sadly.

"They're quite close to the mistletoe, aren't they?"

"Ugh, shut up. He's twice her age."

Hannah laughed. "You sounded just like Martha then."

Lottie thumped her arm. "I did not!"

Lottie's mum bustled in with a jug of mulled wine. "I've hurled about a pound of sugar into it, darlings, and I think it's just about drinkable." She handed the jug to Lottie, who plunged into the sea of guests.

Martha pushed past Hannah, carrying an empty plate.

"Guess we know whose cakes were most popular, then," she said, jerking her head at the heap of crumbled Christmas cake on the table by the window. "Mine have all gone."

"Oh, well," said Hannah, "we can't all be good at everything."

"No," said Martha, "and *some* of us can't be good at anything."

Hannah walked out into the hall, where Ben's mum, sister and brother were taking off their coats and boots. Ben's mum smiled at Hannah as she unwound her scarf and dropped it on top of the heap of coats on the hall chairs.

"We've just been looking round the farm," she said. "Joshua! Megan! Take your muddy shoes off." She turned back to Hannah. "Aren't those calves lovely? So gentle and placid. You can tell they're well cared for. Joshua, I *said* take your shoes off."

"Your farm is awesome," said Joshua, as he tugged at his shoe. "You're so lucky to live here."

Several women whom Hannah recognised from the Ecology Group tea party spilled from the sitting room into the hall, laughing and chatting.

"I'm glad to see you've framed the piece from the *Gazette*," said one of them. "Something to treasure, that."

"So I hear there's going to be an archaeological dig

here," said a woman in a green dress.

"Yes," said Hannah. "Next year, hopefully."

"How exciting. I can't wait. Will we be allowed to come and see the progress, do you think?"

"I hope so," said Hannah. "Yes, I'm sure you will."

The women went into the kitchen. The noise level from the sitting room was rising. In the corner, Granny was doubled up with laughter over something Jack was saying.

The Beans came out of the sitting room, each clutching a guinea pig to their chest.

"It's way too noisy in there for Carrots and Snowy," said Jo. "People are very thoughtless. Come on, boys, you can go back in your hutch."

Lottie wove her way through the crowd, holding an empty jug. "This mulled wine sure is popular. Your granny's on her fourth glass."

She went into the kitchen to refill the jug. Hannah wandered through the hall and paused again in the doorway of the sitting room. She looked at all the people laughing and talking. All those people who had helped to save the farm. A wave of pure joy washed over her.

Dad appeared in the doorway, carrying an empty plate. "Any more of that Christmas cake, Hannah?"

Hannah took the plate. "I'll get it. Are you enjoying the party?"

"Yes, excellent. It was a very good idea of yours."

"Mum would have enjoyed it, wouldn't she?"

Dad smiled. "She'd have loved it."

Hannah met his eyes. A question came into her head. A question she had often thought about, but never expressed before.

She took a deep breath. Somehow, now seemed the right time to ask it. Right here in the sitting room, full of laughter and colour and light, the way it used to be at Christmas when Mum was alive.

"Dad?"

"Mm?"

"Do you think … maybe … that somehow Mum knows? Do you think that … somehow … she can see us?"

"Of course she can," said Dad. "She can see us all, I'm sure of that." He paused and then he looked at her. "You've brought this place back to life, Hannah. Your mother would be very proud of you."

Acknowledgements

This story was inspired by a similar threat to the farm on which my family has lived and worked for three generations. I am grateful beyond words to the hundreds of people – family, friends, neighbours, experts and members of the community – who orchestrated and supported the campaign to save the farm from destruction.

An enormous thank you to Mum, Dad, Hazel, Mary and Mark, for so generously allowing me to misrepresent their characters and our shared history in works of fiction.

Huge thanks to my wonderful, wise and patient editor, Kirsty Stansfield, for her invaluable encouragement and guidance throughout the writing process.

Thank you to the fantastic team at Nosy Crow, and in particular to Kate Wilson, Adrian Soar and Dom Kingston. Special thanks to Nicola Theobald for the beautiful cover.

Thank you to all my fabulous friends – you know who you are – for your friendship and support, and special thanks to fellow writers Nino Cirone, Joe Friedman, Candy Gourlay, Cliff McNish and Christina Vinall, for your advice and encouragement.

Many thanks to my kind and lovely children, Freddie and Dorothea, for their enthusiasm and helpful feedback on the work-in-progress, and for being a constant source of inspiration.

And finally, thanks beyond measure to my husband, Oliver, without whose encouragement and belief I would never have started writing and whose unwavering support has allowed me to continue to write. Thank you, always, for everything.